"A heartfelt exploration of the ties [...] is an engrossing tale told across generations with the [...] history of Myanmar as its backdrop. Elizabeth Shick has written a compelling, emotionally complex novel that explores the difficulties of defining oneself amid the struggle of competing cultures. This is a timely, necessary book."

—Sabina Murray, author of *The Human Zoo* and *Valiant Gentlemen*

"Elizabeth Shick's steady, elegant prose transported me to a place I knew little about, and I found myself wanting to learn more about this turbulent period in Myanmar's history. *The Golden Land* is both a rich and intimate family portrait as well as a portal leading into another world, relevant and important to where we are in our own country today."

—Mira T. Lee, author of *Everything Here is Beautiful*

"*The Golden Land* is a gorgeous and moving novel about one young woman's journey to Myanmar, where her family's stay with their relatives, nearly 25 years ago, was cut short by political unrest. The novel immerses us in the Burma of 1988 and the Myanmar of 2011; both places are fraught with great beauty and suffering. Through the main character's journey, we learn the difference between "adapting and accepting, between carrying on and forgetting" and find hope in the paradox that love is always tangled with disappointment, democracy doesn't preclude loneliness and suffering, and yet trusting people we love is as natural and inevitable as breathing. This is a remarkable novel, at once informative and deeply felt."

—Kyoko Mori, author of *Yarn: Remembering the Way Home*

"*The Golden Land* moves back and forth in time, evoking present-day Myanmar's indeed golden past when Burma, and capturing its perilous political moment, while also uncovering a Burmese-American family's interwoven secrets, layer upon layer, one revelation leading to the next with poignant logic and a gathering momentum. Elizabeth Shick tells this story with flawless authority, giving us a rich, ever-beckoning novel that's historically sure, culturally acute, and, most of all, humanly wise as it asks how much of where we came from do we need to hold close, and how much can't we shed, however urgently we wish to."
—Douglas Bauer, author of *The Beckoning World*

"Like the Burmese puppeteer whose marionettes dance within this novel, Elizabeth Shick knows how seeming opposites are actually tied together: jiggle the past, and the future tilts; touch regret, touch loss, and set in motion love or liberation. Balancing the personal with the political, and showing romance side by side with a blood-soaked reality, this engrossing story is about the difficult necessity of revisiting trauma. *The Golden Land* radiates with cultural empathy, a glow that might light a path toward justice."
—Michael Lowenthal, author of *Charity Girl*

"The narrator of *The Golden Land* discovers a fierce bravery she didn't know she had when she returns to Myanmar to confront the past and questions of identity. Vividly drawn, intimate, and deeply healing, this important novel asks us to consider the steep price we pay when we bury family and national history."
—Hester Kaplan, author of *The Tell*

"This is the fascinating story of an American woman of part-Burmese ancestry haunted by a disturbing event experienced during a visit to her grandmother's country. Moving between Boston and Yangon, and the past and the present, the story brings two vastly different worlds to life, and explores the powerful attachment between two people of contrasting backgrounds that endures beyond distance and time. Through vivid descriptions of pre-monsoon weather, shops, food, and everyday routines in both the prosperous and less savory parts of the city, Elizabeth Shick successfully captures the essence of Yangon. With its moving depictions of political turmoil and military rule, the novel is particularly significant and relevant to the ongoing troubles faced by the Burmese people in their struggle for basic rights and freedom."

—Myanmar author (name withheld for her protection)

"Although fiction, *The Golden Land* is based on the true events Myanmar (Burma) has experienced over the years. Both engaging and mesmerizing, the novel carried me back to the heartache of those times. As I turned the pages, I was eager to discover what would come next for Aye and Shwe, Ahpwa and U Soe Htet, and Etta and Jason. Elizabeth Shick writes with so much empathy describing the emotions of her characters and attention to the nuances of Burmese culture that the characters felt like real people to me. Who would believe it's a debut novel?! A very good read, indeed!"

—Kyi Kyi May, former Head of BBC Burmese Service, London

THE
GOLDEN
LAND

A NOVEL

ELIZABETH SHICK

New Issues Poetry & Prose

Western Michigan University
Kalamazoo, Michigan 49008

First Edition, 2022.

ISBN-13: 978-1-936970-75-9
Library of Congress Cataloging-in-Publication Data:
Shick, Elizabeth.
The Golden Land/Elizabeth Shick
Library of Congress Control Number: 2022943997

Editor: Nancy Eimers
Managing Editor: Kimberly Kolbe
Art Direction: Nick Kuder
Cover Design: The Design Center
Production Manager: Paul Sizer
The Design Center, Gwen Frostic School of Art
College of Fine Arts
Western Michigan University

This book is the winner of the Association of Writers & Writing
Programs (AWP) Award for the Novel. AWP is a national, nonprofit
organization dedicated to serving American letters, writers, and
programs of writing.

Go to www.awpwriter.org for more information.

THE
GOLDEN
LAND

A NOVEL

ELIZABETH SHICK

NEW ISSUES

 WESTERN MICHIGAN UNIVERSITY

"The only real prison is fear, and the only real freedom is freedom from fear."
—Daw Aung San Suu Kyi

To the people of Myanmar.
May peace and justice prevail.

PART ONE

ONE

A thumb of ginger lies on the cutting board alongside several cloves of garlic and a pile of small, red shallots, as if any minute Ahpwa might resume chopping, grating, crushing. She was adamant about assembling her ingredients before beginning to cook, my grandmother.

Suddenly, I'm eight years old again, standing next to her with my eyes ablaze, enduring the fumes of the onion in exchange for a rare taste of intimacy. "Always prepare everything in advance, *Myi*, so the oil does not burn." We looked alike back then, or rather, I looked like her. A quarter Burmese, I had my grandmother's dark eyes and moon-shaped face, the same shiny, black hair, mine tied into an obedient braid down the center of my back, hers twisted into an elaborate knot, the impossibly long tresses coiled around a tortoiseshell haircomb at the nape of her neck before cascading, serpent-like, down the center of her back.

On closer inspection, the ginger is slightly shriveled, having sat in the open air for nearly a week now. I pick up the cutting board and tip the abandoned vegetables into the trash, then uncurl my fingers one by one and let the cutting board slide in on top of them with a thunk.

The kitchen looks much as it always did, the white jasmine hanging above the sink, an empty teacup in the drying rack. The only signs of distress are the open cupboard above the stove and an overturned chair. As I set the chair upright, a can rolls out from under the lip of the kitchen counter. I bend down to pick it up. Chaokoh 100% premium coconut milk, imported. The top of the can is crushed on one side, its label furrowed. So that's what Ahpwa'd been after when she fell.

Staring down at the mangled can in my hand, I feel a dull ache in my chest. Not sorrow, something else. A sense of wrongness, that this is not how her life was meant to end, that our family might have turned out differently. When I was little—before the family reunion in Burma, before I met Shwe and attended the protest march, before Ahpwa's breakdown and my parent's divorce and Ahpwa's declaration that we were no longer Burmese, before all that—she only ever cooked with home-pressed coconut milk obtained by grating the thick, white kernel of a mature coconut then squeezing the grated meat through a fine cloth. To think she died reaching for the canned stuff, imported from Thailand no less.

My younger sister, Parker, is the one who found her. Since quitting, or perhaps losing, the latest in a long string of jobs, Parker'd begun to spend quite a bit of time here, eating most of her meals with Ahpwa, sometimes even spending the night. Our parents died years ago, so for a while now it's just been the three of us on this side of the world. Now two. Monday evening, Parker arrived at Ahpwa's to find her sprawled out on the kitchen floor, unconscious.

As I entered the ER, Parker began to weep. "Etta," she cried, heaving the full weight of her body upon mine as if she were nine, rather than 29.

I stumbled backward, the glare of disinfectant and antiseptic lights making my head swirl. I couldn't believe Ahpwa was gone.

These last few days have been a blur of undertakers, morgue technicians and well-meaning acquaintances. Parker attends to the well-wishers. She's better with people than I am, warmer and more accessible. At least, that's what she says, and she's probably right. As the lawyer in our little family of two, I attend to the paperwork, which suits me fine. I find the banality of the forms soothing.

Parker hasn't wanted to return to the house, so I'm taking care of all the logistics here, too. Next up are the estate lawyers and real estate agents, today's visit the first step toward putting Ahpwa's house on the market, which begins with cleaning out perishables. I open the fridge: three bundles of spring onions, a posy of cilantro, one packet of thin egg noodles, and one whole chicken sitting unwrapped on a plate, its little feet tucked under its bum, skin dark and rubbery from prolonged exposure to the cold air. *Ohn no khauk swe*, that's what Ahpwa'd been preparing the day she died, noodles in a coconut chicken soup. My childhood favorite.

~

Discovering that I'm taking a rare day off work, Parker asks to meet for lunch. After the usual tussle over venue, we agree on a café not far from where we grew up. I arrive five minutes early to find her seated in a booth near the window. In the center of the table, next to the salt and pepper, sits the black and red urn I'd planned to collect from the funeral parlor later today.

"I'm taking Ahpwa back to Myanmar," Parker announces as I slide into the booth.

I unpeel my eyes from the gold-engraved urn and stare at my little sister. Seven years younger, Parker enjoyed a freer relationship with our grandmother than I did. But I can't believe this is what Ahpwa would've wanted. And what does Parker know of Burma? She'd been only six when our family visited in 1988, too young to know about the protest march, or what I'd witnessed before we so hastily left.

"Why?" I ask.

"It's what she wanted, her *dying* wish." A lock of wavy, blond hair has come loose from her ponytail, framing the right side of her freckled face with the illusion of innocence.

"I thought she was unconscious when you found her."

"Well, yeah." She places her hand at the base of the urn. "But she talked about Myanmar all the time."

"She actually said she wanted to be buried there? Rather than here, beside her own daughter?"

Parker flinches at the mention of Mother and I feel bad. Our mother had never been particularly attentive, surrendering our care to Ahpwa as she worked long hours to keep up with mortgage payments, but her death—ovarian cancer—had been hard on Parker, just 16 at the time. I was also sad, but too busy with law school to let myself wallow for long. With our father having succumbed to a heart attack years earlier, Mother's passing left Ahpwa as Parker's official guardian, and me feeling perpetually guilty for not being a more patient and understanding big sister.

"My point is that this was her home for the last sixty years," I continue, gesturing beyond the window to the formation of birch trees sheltering the sidewalk, the familiar T station across the street. "Surely she'd want to be here. With us."

The waiter approaches, scans our faces, and veers toward another table.

"Sorry, Etta, but when was the last time you talked to Ahpwa? I mean really sat down and talked with her about something *not* on your to-do list?"

Her words sting. For years, I've avoided spending any meaningful time with Ahpwa, still so resentful about everything—Burma, my parents' divorce, being forced to leave Shwe. But what irks me now is the insinuation that Parker understood her better than I did.

Parker takes a slow breath, her fingers cradling the base of the urn as if seeking strength from within. "I think she felt guilty about leaving her brother, you know? And some other guy, too. Some *long-lost love.*"

I resist the urge to roll my eyes at this latter point, the idea of Ahpwa having a long-lost love almost as absurd as her wanting to go back to Burma. But then Parker's always been a romantic. Despite what she may think, I admire this quality in her. I wish I still believed in that kind of sweeping, predestined love. But to paint Ahpwa as a romantic, too? Uncompromising, intense Ahpwa? I don't buy it. Unless. Unless Ahpwa really had changed, and I'd failed to notice.

"Fine. But can we talk about this rationally? I mean, the ashes will keep—"

"I leave Tuesday."

A shaft of sunlight hits our table, exposing tiny particles of dust drifting between us. I want to grab the urn away from her. Run out of the restaurant and far away. But there's something menacing about Parker's hand resting there, as if she's waiting to swat mine away.

"Tuesday?"

She looks at me for several seconds, weighing her words, I suppose. "Look, I'm sorry...I just didn't want you to talk me out of it, ok?" Her blue eyes are so steady, so full of conviction, I almost don't recognize her. Growing up, Parker flitted from one pursuit to the next, leaving sticker books open on the kitchen table, abandoning Barbie dolls mid costume-change, and later, swapping boyfriends like shoes. Only a year ago, I was helping her fill out job applications, lending her money when she hit a rough patch. But something's changed.

"What about your visa?" Neither of us have Burmese passports, Ahpwa having given up her citizenship when she moved to the U.S. in 1945.

"It came in the mail yesterday."

That Parker's managed to navigate the bureaucracy of the Burmese Embassy on her own astounds me.

"Vaccinations?" I ask.

"Had my last one this morning. Typhoid." She cups her hand over her upper arm as if seeking sympathy, or admiration. But I'm too stunned to respond, the depth of her concealment upending my longheld belief that she needs or wants my help.

"And no, I'm not asking for money. I got my student loans deferred. So, I can manage."

Her reasoning is maddeningly short-sighted as usual, but at least she's thinking about money—in her own, Parker kind of way. And though neither of us can bear to say it out loud, there will be money from the sale of Ahpwa's house, though perhaps not as much as Parker expects. As I meet her gaze, I realize she's waiting for my blessing. That's what this is.

"Are you sure it's safe?" I ask.

"Yeah." Her eyes soften. "It's not like before, Etta. There's a civilian government now. And Aung San Suu Kyi's been released from house arrest. Myanmar's changing."

I know all this. I must've read every *Globe* article about Burma in the last 10 years. They say the country's opening up. But I don't trust it—the memory of what I saw as a teenager, the terror I felt, more compelling than any reporter's analysis. Because once you've witnessed tyranny, you can never un-see it, never quite believe it won't lash out again. This is what Parker doesn't get. Why would she?

"You could come with me, you know," she says softly.

"Are you crazy? There's no way I can get a visa before Tuesday. You know that."

"The week after, then."

I want to believe she's sincere, that she wants me by her side on this journey. But all I feel is manipulated, Parker pulling my strings like one of Ahpwa's old marionettes.

"I have work."

"Come on. It'll be fun. We can meet up with Shwe. Don't you ever wonder about him?"

My chest tightens at the mention of our second cousin. A memory of him being pulled away by his mother. Of myself, writing letter after letter without hearing back. There've been times in my life when all I wanted was to return to Burma, to see him again and figure out what happened, why everything fell apart. Visiting Burma had been too risky back then, the military having tightened its hold over the country, and now...now, I like my life the way it is. After all those years of law school and kiss-ass entry-level positions, my career as a labor lawyer is finally starting to gel, even if I am on the employer side of the courtroom.

And then there's Jason—sweet, steady Jason. After nearly a decade living together, we've decided to marry next year. He started to ask me once before, when I hadn't been ready, and the pain from my equivocation almost broke us. I worry that following Parker on a half-baked quest to Burma will re-open that wound.

"It would mean a lot to Ahpwa," she says.

"Not fair, Parker. You want to go, then go. I have enough regrets of my own. Last thing I need is you piling more crap on top."

"Fine." She hesitates for a moment. "I just thought it might be good for you to get away. To get some perspective on...you know, everything."

My irritation flares into rage. She's referring to Jason, of course. She never did approve of him, thinks he's boring, controlling.

"Some of us have commitments, Parker. We can't just fly off to the other side of the globe at a moment's notice."

She looks away, and my fury fizzles back to uncertainty. The truth is, part of me is curious about the new Myanmar, about my cousins and aunties and uncles, about Shwe. But another part is terrified, both by the risk of renewed violence—it was only a few years ago that unarmed protestors were being gunned down in the street—and by the possibility of peace unearthing long-buried secrets, concealed by the military regime. But I can't stop Parker just because I'm afraid.

After lunch, we walk out to the sun-dappled sidewalk, Parker holding the ashes out in front of her like a Buddhist monk proffering his alms bowl.

"You need a ride to the airport?"

She shakes her head.

"Let me know when you get there." Worry catches in my throat. "And be careful, okay?"

Parker shifts Ahpwa's ashes onto her hip, and we embrace clumsily, the lip of the urn stabbing my ribs. As I watch her walk away, I wonder about her offer, whether she intended all along to invite me, or if the idea came just now—a genuine, spontaneous desire to include me in her quest. I wish we were the kind of sisters who didn't hide things from each other, who told each other when they felt joy and when they felt pain. This isn't Parker's fault.

~

Jason and I sit on our new sofa, sipping coffee and reading our respective papers—his, the online version of the *Times*, mine, the paper version of the *Globe*. He's wearing jeans and a flannel shirt, laptop balanced on his thighs, argyled heels on the coffee table, a look of concentration on his boyish face. He prefers his hair trimmed short, but today it sneaks over the temples of his glasses, longish, the way I like it. Sitting together like this on a Sunday morning is one of my favorite rituals, but right now, all I can think about is the fact that Parker left for Myanmar five days ago, and I haven't told him.

Jason doesn't like talking about emotional stuff, but he will when necessary. His mother raised him well in that respect, taking pains to ensure he wasn't governed by avoidance like the other men in her family. At least that's what she told me the first time we met, as we sat alone in their sunny, Pennsylvania kitchen, a pot of homemade chicken stock simmering on the stove. She wanted me to know what a catch her son was, what a good man I'd happened upon. I've been thinking about this exchange recently because of how solicitous he's been about Ahpwa, urging me to take more time off work, asking if I want to talk. I don't.

All this is to say that I've had ample opportunity to tell him about Parker's trip, ample time to disclose both my admiration—that she's saved money, is showing initiative, and doing something she believes in; and my concerns—that she's impulsive, irresponsible, and in a country prone to eruptions of state-sanctioned violence. Yet I've said nothing. The clumsy truth is that Parker going to Myanmar has me thinking about Shwe, about everything we went through together, and the terrible way it ended. I wonder what he's doing now, if he'd want to see me again. Why he never wrote. And these aren't thoughts I want to share with my fiancé. I know every detail of Jason's childhood, from the name of his pet rabbit to the first girl he ever kissed, but I never told him what happened on that trip to Burma, and I never told him about Shwe.

"What's up with Parker?" says Jason, looking at his watch. "Shouldn't she be pestering you about now?" She typically calls Sunday mornings, a habit going back to childhood when we spent the day with our father.

"She went to Myanmar," I say from behind my mug of coffee.

"Really? When?"

"Tuesday."

Our eyes meet, and I wonder if he's going to say something about my not telling him.

Instead, he says, "And lumped you with all the estate crap? Unbelievable. I hope you didn't lend her money again." His gaze returns to his laptop.

This is how we speak about my sister. I complain how irresponsible or needy or flighty she behaves, and he backs me up, pointing out how fortunate she is to have me to clean up her messes. I don't know how to tell him that this time is different, that she hasn't asked for my help, that I'm not the one in control.

"She took Ahpwa's ashes."

His hazel eyes flick up from the screen to search mine. Jason got along well with Ahpwa—she was always on her best behavior with him—but he knows how conflicted our relationship was. I've told him about her impossible standards and endless hours of tutoring, at least, if not about the haircut and smashed dishes.

"God, Etta. You must be furious. She's your grandmother, too."

It's nice that he's always on my side, but right now his words make me feel more isolated and alone.

"I don't know. I think maybe she needed to go there for personal reasons." I want to say more, but each detail withheld over the years seems to lead to another, creating a tangle of half-truths and omissions that I can't explain my way out of in one sitting.

"How long's she gonna to stay?"

"A week, maybe ten days?" Parker didn't give a return date, but this is what I've been telling myself. Two days to get there, three to deal with the ashes, and two to get back.

"Did she go that time, when you were growing up?"

"Yeah, we all went: Mother, Father, Parker, Ahpwa." I don't mention that this was the last family trip we ever took, nor does he seem to catch the significance of my parents being there together —they divorced within the year, Father's heart surrendering not long after.

"But she was only six." I stand up to put my mug in the dishwasher. "I doubt she remembers much."

"You didn't want to go with?" He types something on his laptop.

I stare down at his profile, day-old stubble lending a rugged, more masculine quality to his soft features. He doesn't know that I'm staying here for us.

"It's not that simple," I say.

"Sure it is. Look." He turns his laptop so I can see the display.

Suddenly there it all is, all the beautiful, terrifying images in my head reduced to a series of thumbnail photos: the magnificent Shwedagon Pagoda glittering in gold; steel-helmeted riot police marching in procession; smiling women and children, their faces smeared with *thanaka*; bloodied demonstrators lying on the ground; and the implausibly serene Aung San Suu Kyi, her trademark flower tucked firmly in her hair.

Only Shwe is missing.

I sit back down, the empty mug slippery and cold between my hands. I've seen all these images before, but never like this, good and bad side by side. How is it possible for such beauty to exist alongside such evil? This is what confounds me. Jason doesn't get it. I can see as much from the eagerness in his eyes. Like Parker, he thinks it's easy: hop on a plane and scatter some ashes. I stare at the screen, searching for something to say that won't worry Jason any more than he already is.

TWO

We left Boston on December 30, 1987, arriving on New Year's Day, 1988 in what was then called Rangoon. The plan, Ahpwa's plan, was for our family to spend one full year—January 1st to December 31st, which I calculated to be one thirteenth of my life—in Burma. Parker would miss half of kindergarten and half of first grade, I'd miss half of eighth and ninth grade, and my parents would take sabbaticals. Ahpwa insisted that the experience gained would be well worth the time away from school and work. I didn't want to go but had no say in the matter.

I couldn't understand why my parents were going along with it. I supposed Mother was doing it for Ahpwa. And Father was doing it for Mother. That was usually the way decisions were made in our household. The timing of our trip was even more of a mystery. Ahpwa hadn't been back to Burma since 1945 when she'd married my grandfather, a true-blue army captain from Western Mass, who died before I was born. I always assumed that it was too dangerous to visit. Since we never talked about Burmese politics it was hard to know what might have changed.

"Too many questions," responded Ahpwa when, fed up with my parents' evasive answers, and too intimidated to approach her myself, I sent Parker to ask.

From what I could make out, the trip had something to do with Myint Oo—the gawky boy in the photo Ahpwa kept on her bedside table. Myint Oo was Ahpwa's younger brother. Although only one year older, Ahpwa had been charged with taking care of him as a young girl. She never said why, but I gathered from the way she spoke that there was something odd about him. The photo was taken when they were eight and nine years old. Ahpwa stood slightly in front, her eyes flashing with defiance as she stared into the camera, while Myint Oo stood back, his face partially obscured.

After hours confined in rigid airplane seats, hushed and forced to eat food worse than what they served in our school cafeteria, Parker and I stumbled off the plane, our stomachs churning from the turbulent landing, only to be yanked into a restroom. As always, Mother assumed care of Parker, while I got stuck with Ahpwa.

"Hold still," she snapped as she unraveled the tousled strands of my old plait, ripping out snarls and whisking the hair back into a tight braid, which she secured with a scratchy white ribbon. "And you better not embarrass me in front of my brother. Remember to bow and treat with respect."

My eyes burned with humiliation. I was too old to wear my hair in a braid, let alone have it brushed by my grandmother. And too American to bow to anyone. As she marched me into the arrivals lounge, I considered the possibility of not doing as I was told, of acting like an American teenager for once in my life.

A village of strangers had come to the airport to greet us—aunties, uncles and cousins I'd seen only in photos, but whose features looked so like my own, I stepped back in awe. Back home, in the whitewashed suburbs of Boston, my uncommon features made me stand out, compounding the foreignness of my home life; here I seemed to disappear—an unfamiliar but not altogether unwelcome feeling.

Surveying my new extended family, I saw that all eyes were trained on an older man with fat lips and coarse, pockmarked skin standing at the center of the crowd. Dressed in military uniform, with multiple ribbons over his left pocket, he wasn't especially tall, yet seemed to tower over the others. I shuddered at the lack of light in his eyes. Could this really be the awkward, timid boy in the photo, Ahpwa's younger brother?

Ahpwa approached him solemnly, head bowed, hands straight down by her side, the coil of hair that hung from her chignon brushing the top of her *htamein*, the Burmese-style sarong she wore even in Boston. She'd spent hours teaching me the principles of Burmese etiquette, a complex hierarchy of age, gender and rank that, until now, seemed like something that only happened in myths and legends. I'd never seen my grandmother—fierce, domineering Ahpwa—bow to anyone, and the sight of it sent goosebumps up and down my arms.

After the bow, she linked her arm through his, a smile pasted on her face as she introduced us one by one to her brother, the General. Still spinning from the shock of her submissiveness, I swallowed my pride and followed Ahpwa's lead just as Mother did before me, bowing my head stiffly and quickly retreating, bewildered by my role in this strange new adaptation of our family. When it was Father's turn, Ahpwa's brother held out his right hand, placing the left one under his right elbow as the two men shook hands. I wondered vaguely if this different type of greeting was because he was a man or because he was white.

Mother pushed Parker forward, and I held my breath. As much as Parker liked attention, she rarely behaved well when put on the spot. As I feared, her face began to crumple, brow knitting inward and lower lip protruding. I ran forward and placed my arm around her shoulder, coaxing her gently forward until we reached Ahpwa's brother. For a moment, all I could hear was the sound of blood rushing into my ears. Then the General forged an exaggerated smile, and my relatives erupted in laughter and cheers, greeting each other freely at last.

All except one boy about my age, that is, who stood back

from the crowd, kicking at the floor with the same restlessness I'd witnessed among the boys at school. We exchanged a look of commiseration and began watching each other from across the room. He was taller and darker than most of the boys in my eighth-grade class, and super skinny. As our parents laughed and exclaimed, he cast me a furtive smile that started off slow and lazy, then widened gradually until a dimple appeared in the lower part of his left cheek.

Seeing that he had my attention, he began twisting his features into silly faces, and my gloom lifted. Aside from the obligatory introduction, I kept my distance from the General, and I could see from the way this boy looked at him that he feared my grandmother's brother at least as much as I feared Ahpwa.

A fleet of shiny black sedans with darkened windows and uniformed drivers waited by the curb to transport us to one of our Auntie's many houses, where our family was to stay. Back home we drove a beat-up old station wagon with clear windows all around, so the prospect of riding in one of these fancy cars intrigued me. As the herd of relatives cleaved into passenger groups, I hung back to see which car this unusual boy would choose so that I could ride with him.

"What. Is. Name?" he asked in painfully hesitant English.

"*Ja mah nah meh* Aye Tha Kyaw *ba*," My name is Aye Tha Kyaw, I replied in fluent Burmese, volunteering my Burmese name for the first time in my life. Calling myself anything other than Etta or *Myi* felt a little dishonest, but there was something exciting about the way the bold, curious sounds sprang off my tongue, as if this neglected name might offer a pathway to a whole other me. From that moment on, we spoke only Burmese.

His name was Tun Shwe, but everyone called him Shwe, which meant gold in English. And that's exactly what he seemed to me—not the shiny, polished kind of gold you find in a jewelry store, but the raw gold rocks I'd seen in my biology textbook, a little rough around the edges, but genuine and glimmery at the core. The General was Shwe's grandfather.

"He was okay when I was little," said Shwe, when I asked what the General was like, "but he's too important for kindness now."

"I know what you mean," I said. I didn't really, at least not the part about being important, but I was familiar enough with the dynamic of occasionally kind, mostly not.

As we rode, we talked about everything from MTV, which he'd never seen, to *zat pwe*, the local street performances I'd not yet experienced. He was so full of energy, as eager to explore our differences as our similarities, that despite the flutter of attraction in my chest, I felt at ease. We passed a man selling spiked, brown fruit the size of small watermelons. Shwe asked if I'd ever tasted one, and I shook my head, knowing already that I'd try anything he suggested.

"Smells like a fart, but tastes like a kiss," he said opening his eyes wide.

I shivered, and his smooth lips broke into an impish grin.

THREE

I enter Ahpwa's bedroom, armed with three Sharpie pens, a stack of unassembled cardboard boxes, and one pad each of green, yellow and hot pink sticky notes. Having succumbed to Jason's gentle but persistent persuasion, I'm taking another day off, determined to get Ahpwa's house sorted by the end of the week. Thanks to my system of sticky notes, I whizzed through the bottom floor. Green is for Goodwill, yellow for the estate sale, and pink for Parker. Leaving all the sentimental stuff for her to sort through when she returns is the key, enabling me to move freely through the house without getting emotional. I suppose it's my way of getting back at her for not including me in her plans until it was too late to change them. And for not bothering to let me know that she arrived safely in Yangon. I considered buying a fourth color of sticky notes, blue or purple for anything I might like to keep for myself, but decided against it. Packing up my childhood home alone is difficult enough; I can't afford to get pulled into all those topsy-turvy memories, and really, there's nothing I want here.

The only object downstairs that gave me pause was Ahpwa's wedding chest. Teak, inlaid with brass floral designs, the chest was one of the few items she brought with her from Burma when she married my grandfather at the end of World War II—a traditional Burmese wedding chest that had been handed down to her by her mother. I recall it sitting, padlocked, atop the credenza when I was growing up, an heirloom so intricately designed and expertly crafted that I imagined all sorts of treasure contained within. Like a forbidden jar of candy, the chest called to me, its contents all the more alluring because of that damn padlock.

When I was really little—before I knew better—I'd beg Ahpwa to open it for me, just once. But the answer was always the same: "Maybe if you're good." Seeing the chest earlier this morning, I'd had a sudden, irrational urge to smash open that padlock with one of the hammers in the Goodwill pile—to grant that little girl her wish at last. Instead, I stuck a pink sticky note on top and moved on.

As I step into Ahpwa's bedroom, I worry I might run out of pink sticky notes. When I was little, Ahpwa's bedroom seemed to me a place full of secret treasures—the four-poster bed, red silk curtains, and Persian rug lending the room a romantic, otherworldly feel. I sit down in front of her vanity and pick up the red lacquerware box where she kept her jewelry. Inside are the long, jade necklaces she wore when I was a child. Extracting a strand of white and pale orange beads, I slip the necklace over my head. Maybe I could take one, small memento? It's not as if Parker would mind, or even notice. She can be dramatic, for sure, but she's not sentimental in that way. True sentimentality demands greater restraint, the kind where you hold it all in until a crumb of toast makes you weep.

Seeing my reflection in the mirror, I startle at how much I look like Ahpwa when she was younger, all except for my hair, of course, which is shorter and less disciplined than hers was in those days.

"Why do you always wear jade, Ahpwa?" I asked when I was around ten.

"Because, *Myi,* Jade is not only beautiful, but also strong, protecting us against evil influences. Even Queen Supayalat made sure to surround herself with jade." Back then, Ahpwa was always telling me stories about Queen Supayalat—the last queen of Burma, who managed to hold her head high even while being thrown out of her royal palace on the back of a bullock cart. I loved the stories so much, I invented a game about her that Parker and I often played, and that I'd later teach Shwe.

"But how can a necklace protect someone from evil?" I persisted.

Over the course of the previous year, I'd become consumed with the link between the spiritual world and the world of science, between what I was taught at home, and what I was taught at school.

"Too many questions, *Myi*. You want to know more, go to the library."

So I did. I went to the library and looked up both the scientific and spiritual qualities of jade, becoming so enthusiastic about my clever marriage of east and west that I compiled the information into a five-page, extra-credit paper for my science teacher, Mr. Radomski.

"You're a very clear thinker," he said when he handed back the paper, "but good scientific analysis depends on fact, not folklore."

Sitting in front of Ahpwa's vanity now, the cold, dead weight of jade makes the skin on my neck shrink with loneliness. I return the necklace to the jewelry box and place a pink sticky note on top, then I tear off a second one and place it on the vanity mirror. Ahpwa instilled such strict boundaries in me that even now, at age 36, I'm apprehensive about touching her personal belongings. It was different for Parker. She grew up with an altered Ahpwa, one who was more erratic for a period but ultimately calmer and less demanding.

I spend the next several minutes darting around the room in a fury, folding, boxing and tagging the remaining items. Yellow sticky notes for the bed, rug, and dresser, green for the curtains, blankets and pillows. All that remains now is the closet. The warm, woody perfume of agarwood wraps around me as I open the door. Inside the closet, a mixture of traditional Burmese *htameins* hang side by side with Western skirts and blouses. For the first thirteen years of my life, Ahpwa only wore *htameins,* the floor-length, draped skirts of the Burmese. Back in those days, she viewed her heritage with pride, dedicating much of her spare time—and all of mine—to ensuring that I never forgot my background. After our trip to Burma, Ahpwa swung in the opposite direction like a pendulum pulled to its most extreme. She stopped wearing traditional clothes, stopped cooking Burmese dishes, stopped speaking the language, embracing her adopted country with a new, wild abandon. I called it her *America the Beautiful* phase, my mother called it *a difficult patch*, and my father—well, he tried to be supportive, but in the end, he couldn't hack it.

I flick through the hangers, glad for Ahpwa's sake that she reached a kind of compromise toward the end of her life, even if it meant using canned coconut milk. Every one of these outfits holds a memory, from the pale-yellow sheath dress she wore to my high school graduation to the royal blue *htamein* she wore the first time she met Jason. Another pink sticky note. But I can't leave everything to Parker. Scooping up the shoes from the closet floor, I dump them into a box and place a green sticky note on top. Then I stand on my tiptoes, pull down a large, cardboard box from the overhead shelf, and place it on the rug.

Kneeling on the carpet, I open the flaps of the box one by one, vaguely curious as to what Ahpwa had kept boxed up in the top of her closet. More shoes perhaps? Books? At first glance, the contents look like junk—a jumble of faded silk and sequined dowels tangled in string. Then I see a hand with painted fingernails buried within, and my heart quickens with excitement. Reaching for the hand, I no longer see plain dowels but arms and legs, gowns and caps. They are the *yoke thé*, the handmade marionettes that hung over our mantelpiece until I was thirteen, and which I'd loved dearly.

Stilled by a forgotten reverence for these old companions, I lower myself onto the carpet and begin removing parts one by one. Assembled, each marionette might be two feet tall. Picking out three heads, I unfasten the protective cushions from each face and admire the intricately detailed lines around their eyes and mouths, each eyelash a distinct brushstroke. How captivating they'd once been, so fearsome I often had nightmares after watching a show, yet still came back for more the next time. I wonder if Parker remembers them, or if she was too little at the time.

Setting aside the three, H-shaped wooden jacks used to control the strings, I begin grouping body parts by character. I can't recall the specific personalities at first. Then I spot a silken headdress embroidered with glass beads and golden thread and my heart tells me that they belong to my beloved princess, Minthamee. Sifting through disembodied arms and legs, I pick out her remaining body parts, her royal clothing now clearly discernible among the common garb of the other characters. But my excitement soon turns to dismay at her condition: not a single string connecting her limbs remains intact. How did she get this way?

The other two remain a jumble of estranged body segments— necks, upper and lower thighs, calves, feet, hands—a few still connected by a frayed piece of string, others completely severed from their correlating parts. I pick out two feet with painted toenails and set them aside with a quiver of anticipation. But I can't see how the other parts fit together. It's as if the marionettes have been deliberately stripped of their character. But why? That the puppets are among the many casualties of Ahpwa's breakdown after we returned from Burma in 1988 seems clear. But for the first time in decades, I realize that I don't know why Ahpwa acted the way she did, I don't know what prompted *America the Beautiful*.

The last time I saw these puppets on stage was a year or so before our trip to Burma. I was maybe ten or eleven, Parker three or four. The sunny side of our living room had been transformed into a makeshift stage with a waist-high, black velvet curtain strung from the window to a bookcase. We stationed ourselves in the middle of the floor under the chandelier, our long braids tied with white ribbons as always, hers blond, mine almost black. Behind us sat our parents together with some new Burmese arrivals. Ahpwa stood by the stage, whispering with a man I recognized from the wider Burmese community. I couldn't take my eyes off her.

The music started—a traditional Burmese clang of cymbals and drums that jolted us into silence. Parker crawled into my lap, and I tightened my arms around her waist. Ahpwa moved behind the waist-high curtain and began to manipulate Minthamee's strings, each limb moving so distinctly that the princess appeared to dance to the music. I watched in fascination, amazed how fluidly Ahpwa was able to move the marionette, how expressive the princess was. Two more marionettes entered the stage, and I fell into the story, forgetting all about Ahpwa and the unfamiliar man, no longer able to see the puppeteers or the strings. Afraid for the princess, lost now in the forest, I squeezed Parker closer. One of the puppets was trying to help her, the other to deceive her. One good, one evil. Why couldn't the princess see the difference?

Sitting now on Ahpwa's bedroom carpet, I'm convinced suddenly that the marionettes hold the answer. To what, I still don't know. I study the two remaining faces. Sure enough, one of the two faces has pointed, sinister eyes, while the other bears a more peaceful expression. I begin to notice other differences. One hand clutches a cane, another a dagger. Using these clues as my guide, I reexamine each piece, assigning it to one of the three characters. Then I sit back and look at the three heaps of body parts.

The marionettes seem so helpless, damaged all those years ago, then stashed away at the top of Ahpwa's closet like a dirty secret. I wish I could go back in time and save them from this fate, restore them to their original condition. But I have neither the tools nor the skill to restore broken marionettes. An idea begins to form in my mind. I run down to the kitchen and come back with three white trash bags from a box of kitchen supplies destined for the Goodwill. *Trust me, Minthamee*, I think as I scoop each pile into a bag and tie it shut. *Trust me, Ahpwa.*

With body parts safely tucked away in their separate bags, I type "Boston marionettes" into the search box on my phone, hoping to track down Ahpwa's old friend, the puppeteer. My screen fills with listings for birthday parties, school performances, fuzzy friends—no, this isn't what I want. But for all the details I remember about the show itself, I recall almost nothing of the puppeteer. That's how it should be, I know. The invisibility of the puppeteer is vital in Burmese culture. Back when Burma was a monarchy, the marionettes could say things to the king that no human would dare utter, each character believed to have its own soul. Maybe that's why Ahpwa loved them so much.

I squeeze my eyes shut, but the only image I can conjure up is the way the puppeteer's eyes twinkled when he looked at Ahpwa. Desperate now to find this man, I leave the Sharpies and sticky notes scattered across Ahpwa's bedroom carpet, and set off for YomaAllston, the closest thing Boston has to a Burmese cultural center.

FOUR

The Burma I'd learned about back in Boston was a place of formal etiquette, poetry recitals and grand, old kingdoms of yore. A place where people drank tea dressed in traditional attire, and marionettes enacted elaborate life lessons for the royal court. The Rangoon I now found myself living in was more like the inside of a teenage boy's gym locker. Mildewed buildings, rusted cars and the pong of fermented fruit gave me the impression of a city in putrid decay. With rotting teeth and haunted eyes, even some of the street kids seemed to be in a state of decomposition.

If not for Shwe, I might never have left our auntie's house, but the pull to spend time with him, to immerse myself in his essence, propelled me onward and outward, against my inclination. From that first drive home from the airport, we spent every possible minute together. He had school on weekdays, of course, but seemed to skip more often than go, and, as far as I could make out, never had any homework—a happenstance which pleased me too much to question. Before we left Boston, there'd been talk of enrolling Parker and me in the local international school, but once in Rangoon, the idea fell away with all other traces of normalness. Nor had Ahpwa resumed my daily tutoring in Burmese language and culture—whether because I was already steeped in both or because she was too busy, I wasn't sure.

The main upside to my new life was that Ahpwa and my parents were so distracted with their own agenda—whatever that was—that they left me to my own devices. Technically, Shwe and I were under the care of San San, the young nanny who looked after

31

Parker, Khaing Zar and the other cousins. But by some previously negotiated arrangement, San San let Shwe do whatever he wanted, which by extension meant that I, too, was free to roam the streets by his side.

Shwe took it upon himself to introduce me, township by township, to the city he loved. Spellbound, I let him drag me down pot-holed streets and cable-strewn back alleys, across open drainage ditches and rat-infested sewers to his favorite teashops, where we'd sit on miniature, plastic stools playing checkers with bottle caps and filling our bellies with spicy *mohinga,* the ubiquitous noodle and fish soup. He taught me to play *chinlone,* a game similar to hacky sack but played with a large, hand-woven ball of rattan, cheering me on for all sorts of saves that were really no more than dumb luck.

On one of these early outings, as we walked from our auntie's house to a nearby abandoned lot to play *chinlone,* I noticed an old woman crouched on the side of the road, her twisted mouth brimming with a red, viscous substance. I grabbed Shwe's arm and pointed in horror, worried she might soon cough up a piece of her heart.

"Her life-force," he responded with a strange, forced urgency. "It's coming out through her mouth." Then he bent over, clutching his stomach in hysterics as he laughed and laughed. "Oh, Aye. You're so American sometimes. It's only betel nut. To forget her pain. Watch, watch, she'll soon spit it out." He held up his hand as if to stop the very rotation of the earth.

The woman hawked a wad of red, gooey liquid onto the street, then looked directly up at me, revealing a dark, gaping oral cavity with small red stumps where her teeth should've been. I was too relieved, and repulsed, to be angry with Shwe for teasing me the way he had. As he gazed back at me with his syrupy brown eyes, the dimple on his left cheek like a planet drawing me into its orbit, I felt a pinch of doom. He was so beautiful, so full of life. I placed my hand on his arm again, this time more gently.

"Don't ever do it, okay?"

He flashed me another dimpled smile and bowed. "Yes, Ma Aye Tha Kyaw," he said, invoking my full Burmese name for emphasis.

I giggled, then punched him in the arm. I'd never met anyone so charming and carefree, so easy to be around. If only I could stay with him forever.

~

Not long after we arrived in Rangoon, Ahpwa's brother organized a second convoy of sleek, black sedans to ferry the extended family to the sacred Shwedagon Pagoda, an important pilgrimage site for Buddhists. The lack of warmth in the General's eyes continued to repel me, but my wariness was now tempered with curiosity. In addition to Shwe's cryptic comments about his grandfather, I'd heard my parents whispering about him earlier that same morning. Although I hadn't quite grasped the substance of their exchange, a gravity to their hushed voices told me it was worth further snooping.

Leaving our shoes under the watch of two giant *Chinthe* that guarded the entrance, we followed the General up several sets of stairs, the marble floor cold and sticky under my bare feet. Nearly all the same people who'd come to the airport joined us again, the General leading the way, stiff and imposing, while the rest of us trailed behind in clusters of two or three. Shwe and I brought up the rear, walking so close together that our shoulders grazed as we climbed. Initially, Parker clung to my side, but to my wonderment, Shwe soon cajoled her into joining San San and his little sister, Khaing Zar, up front. With a shiver of excitement, I realized that he wanted to be alone with me as much as I wanted to be alone with him.

Under normal circumstances, Ahpwa would be watching to make sure I behaved, but she and Mother were too preoccupied with our long-lost relatives to pay me any attention, let alone notice my interest in Shwe. Today, in particular, they were wholly engrossed in the General, jostling their way to the coveted spot immediately behind him. Father seemed to be the only adult paying attention to me. Keeping a few steps ahead, he glanced back at me every so often, a kind but quizzical expression in his eyes, as he forged ahead with his bumbled gait and dirty blond hair.

But I was too busy whispering and giggling with Shwe to care about Father or the General. As the family spilled out of the dark stairwell onto the main platform, I blinked at the gleaming gold stupa, its top-most vane shimmering in the sunlight. It was the diamonds—over a thousand of them—that gave it this effect, Shwe explained, with an equally dazzling smile. Surrounding the main dome were dozens of smaller shrines, each cardinal direction indicated by a smaller, golden stupa, as were the four corners of the platform, giving the impression of a city of gold. I couldn't believe how beautiful it all was, how beautiful he was.

The General halted in front of a giant bell and, like an army of ants, we formed a queue behind him, barefoot and biddable, with Shwe and me at the very end. As the General picked up a baton, a hush hurled down the column of devotees. Then he looked back at us with that same clownlike smile he'd put on for Parker and me at the airport and struck the bell. There was something mechanical about the way he moved, as if everything he did was choreographed. I couldn't believe this stiff, fearsome figure was the same awkward but sensitive brother that Ahpwa'd spoken so tenderly about over the years. I tried to gauge Ahpwa's reaction, but her expression was inscrutable, a kind of half-smile, neither openly skeptical nor especially pleased, as if she was still trying to decide what she thought.

As we waited for the others to take their turns, Shwe explained the legend that visitors who ring this bell were destined to return to Burma. Then he leaned in close, putting his mouth next to my ear, and in a breathy whisper that made the hair on my neck stand to attention, added, "I hope you ring it, too."

A shiver shot down the back of my neck, and I forgot all about Ahpwa and the General.

By the time Shwe and I reached the bell, everyone but my father had moved ahead. A goofy smile on his face, he shuffled toward the bell with his hand on the top of his *longyi* to prevent it from falling down. The *longyi* had been a gift from Mother, the cloth the same bright blue as his eyes. Her way of thanking him for making the trip, I supposed. Learning to tie the *longyi* properly had taken him almost 45 minutes that morning, but he'd been determined to wear it the traditional Burmese way, knotted in front for men. I took this as a good sign at first, an indication that he and mother were moving closer together rather than further apart, but the longer I watched him struggle with that knot, the more desperate his eyes grew, as if that loop of blue *longyi* fabric was not a beginning but an end.

Standing by Shwe's side, I watched carefully as Father placed his right hand at the end of the baton and his left hand in the middle, then hit the bell front and center, emitting a loud, clear *gong*. He passed the baton to Shwe, who grinned back at him with a smile that seemed to me half little boy and half man. Shwe wore a longyi, too—his, a dark green checked with black—but unlike Father, Shwe moved fluidly when he walked, his carriage easy-going, confident. As he lifted the baton, the veins in his forearms bulged slightly, and I sucked in my breath. Then he drove it forward and hit the bell, its timbre like a live current resonating from the top of my head through the tips of my toes.

"Nice one," said Father, giving Shwe a high five. And in that moment, I saw not only that Father approved of my new friendship with Shwe, but that my lack of close friends back home, my isolation, had been a source of concern for him.

Shwe beamed and passed the baton to me. Wrapping both hands around its base, I looked first at Shwe then Father, my palms slick with perspiration. Then I heaved the baton backward and swung hard like a baseball bat. Too hard. The weight of the baton shifted, my hands lost their grip, and the rod slipped out of my grasp, tapping the bottom lip of the bell with a mortifying *plink*. The brigade of relatives had moved out of sight, leaving the three of us standing alone under the glow of the great golden dome. Under different circumstances I might have felt more embarrassed, but my breath was steady, my head clear.

"Let's give it another try," said Father, breaking the silence.

Thankful for the second chance, and for a father, who understood me better than I understood myself, I wiped my hands on my *htamein*. He positioned himself behind me, arms framing mine as if teaching me to play pool rather than baseball. After a few practice thrusts—the trick was a combination of restraint and precision, I now saw—he stepped back. I drove the baton forward slowly but deliberately, producing a clear, melodic *dong*, not quite as glorious as Shwe's, but loud enough to restore my dignity.

~

Another day, toward the end of January, Shwe and I took the four-hour circle train around Rangoon, nibbling on boiled peanuts as we circumnavigated the city alongside several market women, a trio of saffron-robed monks with freshly shaven heads, and a single, white hen, dashing around the car in distress. As the train clacked and jerked, we hurdled from the concrete landscape of the city center into people's backyards, where frayed underwear hung on makeshift laundry lines strung between outhouses, and from there past remote rice paddies, where whole families bent over, cultivating the land under the hot, Burmese sun.

Shwe was teaching me something important about Rangoon, and about our family. My cousins lived quite comfortably. They might have lacked the appliances we had back home, no dishwasher or microwave or washing machine, but they had enough maids and cooks to make sure they never had to think about laundry or meal prep or my personal peeve, the dreaded loading and unloading of a dishwasher. He made sure I saw the contrast between the way we lived and the conditions of those less fortunate—the toil of the rice farmer, the desperation of the chicken vendor, the haunted look in the eyes of the woman chewing betel nut.

What I couldn't quite grasp back then was how much the country had deteriorated since Ahpwa left Rangoon at the end of World War II. Burma had gone from the world's single largest exporter of rice in 1948 to being classified by the United Nations as a least developed nation in the late 1980s. Chairman Ne Win's 1987 decision to issue new bank notes in multiples of his lucky number, nine, had only made matters worse, obliterating people's savings overnight, all on the prophecy of a fortuneteller. My grandmother must've known some of this, but she could not've known the extent of suffering and strong-arm tactics that prevailed, or we'd never have come.

FIVE

The friendly proprietor of Yoma remembers the old puppeteer right away. U Soe Htet, she calls him, U being an honorary term used when speaking or referring to an older man. Yes, that's him, I think. U Soe Htet. I woke up this morning not remembering this man at all. Now I can think of nothing more urgent than finding him. She says he moved to an assisted-living facility about a year ago. She doesn't know which one but shares with me a list of homes from their bulletin board. I order a tamarind juice and dial the first number on the list.

"No, he's not a resident here," says the receptionist at the first facility.

"Sorry, I can't help you," says the next one.

Six, seven, eight calls. Still no luck. What if he's moved out of state, or worse? In the span of one morning, I've come to believe that this man, this puppeteer, holds some hidden piece of the puzzle when it comes to Ahpwa, some secret knowledge as to why she behaved the way she did, both before and after *America the Beautiful*, before and after 1988. I think of Parker now in Yangon. Is this what she's after too? An explanation for what happened to our family? Longing and regret knot under my breastbone, a fog of apprehension distorted by time and distance. How I wish she'd get in touch, let me know she's safe.

After about a dozen calls, I speak to a nurse who confirms that U Soe Htet is a resident at their facility in Westwood. I hug the wide-eyed waitress and drive straight there.

Waiting in the sun-filled lobby, three trash bags full of wooden body parts tucked under the chair, I worry suddenly that U Soe Htet won't remember our family. In the giddiness of finding the marionettes, I convinced myself that he was the remedy to my discontent, but the longer I sit here, watching goldfish swim hopelessly back and forth in the lobby fish tank, the more far-fetched my mission seems.

Twenty-five years is a long time. What if my pre-teen-self conjured up that twinkle in his eye when he looked at Ahpwa, his only connection to my family that he was once hired to put on a puppet show? How insolent of me to arrive at this man's home with three bags of marionette pieces, as if he's still under obligation to our family, still under our employ. I should leave. But as I reach down to collect the marionettes, something stops me, the idea of relegating them back to that cardboard box, back into the shadowy corners of my memory too difficult to bear.

As soon as he sees me, he begins chattering away in Burmese—so enthused by my presence I'm convinced he's mistaken me for someone else. Slightly stooped, with crinkly eyes and a full head of thick, white hair, he speaks so rapidly that I strain to follow his words. Luckily my Burmese quickly returns.

"So you've come at last." His face lights up. "I knew this day was to be an auspicious one, but I never expected it would be you, my dearest."

I look around the lobby, wondering if I've misunderstood, until it dawns on me that he thinks I'm Ahpwa.

"Oh. Oh, no," I begin to stammer. The idea of posing as Ahpwa, however unintentionally, a thousand times more inappropriate, more disrespectful, than trying on her necklaces or going through her personal belongings. Worse still is the realization that if U Soe Htet thinks I'm Ahpwa, he doesn't know she died. In my haste to find him, I forgot that I might have to be the one to tell him the sad news, a responsibility that, until now, I'd entrusted to Parker.

As he leads me to his room, I tell him that I'm not Ahpwa, that I am her granddaughter, her *Myi*. But he just chatters on about the astrological charts he consulted that morning.

"Hello, Soe!" says a cheerful-looking resident with bright orange hair and pink lipstick.

"Oh hello, Hope," he responds with a wave.

"Soe sure seems happy to see you," she says to me. "I don't think I've ever seen him quite so chipper."

He does seem happy, almost dancing his walker down the corridor. I, on the other hand, am shriveling in discomfort. But maybe it's better this way. At least I don't have to tell him she's dead.

He slips off his shoes and leaves the walker by the door. I place my shoes next to his and follow him inside. His unit is small but well-appointed with a single bed, dresser, two armchairs and a small table. On the walls are a series of amateurish paintings, all with a Burmese motif—saffron-robed monks walking in procession, trees with cylindrical clusters of bright yellow flowers, a small golden pagoda—along with a framed certificate of appreciation from the Mass Cultural Council. In one corner is a small kitchenette, on the other side, his bathroom.

"*T'ain-ba, Myi*," he says, with a chuckle that tells me he's already realized his mistake. Sit, granddaughter.

As relieved as I am that he no longer thinks I'm Ahpwa, I can't help feeling a little deflated. Once I got past the squirm of impropriety, there was something exhilarating about the idea of *being* Ahpwa, experiencing my inscrutable, domineering grandmother from the inside out, seeing how this intriguing man responded to her as a woman. Plus, now I really do have to tell him that she's gone.

"You look as if you could use some tea," he adds, using the phrase *lah phet yay*, a special Burmese-style tea, made by brewing tea leaves together with generous amounts of sweetened, condensed milk.

He ambles over to the kitchenette and begins spooning loose tea leaves into a ceramic teapot, leaving me alone with the ghost of my grandmother. Speaking Burmese again has made me yearn for the rhythm of my childhood, when Ahpwa gave me daily language lessons, and tea and etiquette shaped our hours together. As much as I feared and resented her back then, I see now that those daily Burmese lessons made me feel important, connecting me, however reluctantly, to something larger than home or school or even family. Parker missed out on all that, I realize with a flash of clarity. Maybe that's why she was so eager to go back to Burma. Guilt tugs at my conscience—for not trying harder to understand, for not being a better sister. How I wish she'd come home so I didn't have to do this alone. And so I could stop worrying.

As the tea steeps, U Soe Htet thrusts a small, postcard-sized photo album into my hands, then returns to the kitchenette. I'm guessing it holds 24 photos, or 48 back to front. There's a pink rose on the front and the word *Memories* written in cursive along the top. I leaf through them one by one. U Soe Htet standing in the yellow robes of a novice monk. U Soe Htet dressed in a black and gold graduation gown in front of a University of Rangoon banner. U Soe Htet standing behind the lectern of a large lecture hall. U Soe Htet posing next to an American flag, his right hand in the air. U Soe Htet sitting together with a beautiful, moon-faced woman, her long, black hair spilling over her shoulders like molasses.

I almost don't recognize Ahpwa, her hair so black and free, an unfamiliar softness to her expression. When I was little, she only ever wore her hair in a traditional knot at the back of her head, her satiny locks wound around a tortoiseshell comb before flowing down the center of her back. I thought it the most elegant hairstyle in the world, so artfully arranged, so shiny and smooth, not a single hair straying from place. I longed for the day when I, too, would wear my hair this way, when I could finally escape the unsophisticated braid with a ribbon tied at the end.

Other times, most notably during my daily Burmese lesson, my grandmother's hairstyle fueled a growing sense of unfairness and resentment. "I am not Apwa. I am Ahpwa," she'd say, using the officious tone she always adopted when teaching. "You must aspirate, dear. Watch." As I sat erect, wishing I could be outside in the sun with Parker, she'd pull the coil of hair out from behind her back, positioning it upside down in front of her lips. "Ah HHHHpwa," she'd say, blowing the loose lock of hair as she spoke. The ragged split-ends of my own braid were a poor vehicle for this trick, hardly registering whether or not I'd expelled enough air. On a good day, she might let me use hers, but Ahpwa was a very strict teacher. We didn't have many good days.

The woman with the long flowing hair in U Soe Htet's album is Ahpwa alright. The curve of her face and vividness in her eyes are unmistakable. I study the photograph, trying to make sense of what I'm seeing, how close she and U Soe Htet are sitting, how happy they both look, his arm around her waist.

"She was very beautiful, wasn't she?" says the old man, seated now in the other chair, the tea service laid out on the table. How long has he been watching me?

I nod, too overcome to speak.

"I know, *Myi*." He hands me a cup of thick, sugary tea. "I miss her, too."

So, he does know. I should be relieved. Instead tears flood my vision, and for the first time since Ahpwa's death, I begin to cry. I do miss her. I miss her old-world advice and fiery cooking, the stories she recounted while braiding my hair—of Queen Supayalat

43

and King Thibaw, of meeting my grandfather in the Burmese jungle during World War II, of her childhood days, growing up with her little brother, Myint Oo. I even miss schoolmarm Ahpwa, the strict, impossible-to-please teacher, who made me copy row after row of loopy Burmese script and recite reams of Burmese poetry. I may have suffered during those lessons, but I retained every detail. U Soe Htet hands me a tissue, and we sit silently drinking our *lah phet yay*.

When I bring out the marionettes, U Soe Htet clasps his hands together in delight. He surveys each bag then chooses the one containing the long brown robes and peaceful face. "Yatheik," he pronounces, placing the pieces on the carpet next to his chair. "The hermit who inhabits the forest, guiding those who have lost their way."

With a few deft moves, he untangles the strings and arranges Yatheik's body parts into a cohesive, albeit unconnected, whole. Then he tends to the next marionette, identifying him as Nat Pyet, an evil spirit who lives in the forest and eats raw meat.

"I'll need a young coconut and two bunches of bananas, preferably green." He inspects an arm segment. "Ribbons to wrap the joints—one hundred percent silk, please—and some very strong string. *Thanaka* and tamarind paste for the faces. Oh, and a piece of hard wood and a chisel."

"Yes, of course." I take a notebook and pen out of my purse and start scribbling down his instructions.

I leave him squatting on the carpet, laughing and talking to his old friends, the marionettes.

~

I spend the rest of the afternoon on a quest for marionette

supplies. The ribbons and bananas are easy, and the woman from Yoma can help with the tamarind and green coconut. But *thanaka* is another question. A cosmetic paste made from the bark of native trees, it is ubiquitous in Burma, worn as a cure-all sunscreen, acne medication and skin moisturizer. Putting *thanaka* on her face before bed was the one tradition Ahpwa never let go of, even after exorcising Burma from our lives.

I decide to try Chinatown. When I was little, Ahpwa occasionally let me tag along on her weekly expedition to find some of the scarcer ingredients of Burmese cuisine, things like sun-dried shrimp powder and fermented bamboo shoots, snake gourd and chayote. I liked how distinct Chinatown felt from my everyday, suburban life, the vibrant colors and endless decorations, merchandise displayed in open piles, from therapeutic herbs and medicinal candies to live fish—to say nothing of all the associated smells, which I pretended to hate but secretly savored. Mostly I cherished those outings because Ahpwa was invariably in a good mood on the days we visited Chinatown.

Recalling a long-ago quest for *thanaka* with Ahpwa, I pass under the Chinatown gate, and head southwest for several minutes. Left, right, left, left...or straight? Everything looks familiar but different, the same old storefronts but modern new signs, or remodeled storefronts with the same old signs. The streets bustle with end of the workday shoppers and early diners, jostling me to and fro. I let myself melt into the crowd, savoring the anonymity that Chinatown affords at this hour. After a few minutes, I duck into a gift shop teaming with oversized teddy bears and bric-a-brac to ask for directions.

At last, I find the place I'm looking for, a basement shop owned by a Chinese-Burmese couple now in their seventies. I slip off my shoes before entering. The woman doesn't remember Ahpwa or U Soe Htet specifically but is pleased to know there are still people in the suburbs carrying on the tradition of *thanaka*. As she scoops the creamy, fragrant paste into a container, I try to calculate when the last time I visited Chinatown was. It must have been before 1988, before *America the Beautiful*. Ahpwa stopped going, so I did, too. Then came college, law school, and finally my life with Jason.

It's just after 5:00 when I leave the shop. I take out my phone only to realize that the two people who might share my excitement about the day's events are both gone, Parker because she's in Myanmar, and Ahpwa because she's dead. I get back on the turnpike, rush-hour traffic at its peak. U Soe Htet will not be expecting me back so soon, but I want to see the expression on his face when I present the supplies he asked for. I imagine him clasping his hands together as he did before, exclaiming how quickly I was able to find everything, praising my efficiency.

That's one characteristic of mine that Ahpwa never criticized. *You always know how to get things done, Myi.* But is that good or bad? I wonder, as I head west. Parker seems to think I'm *too* efficient, especially where Ahpwa was concerned. But the distance between Ahpwa and me was more complicated than that.

The car in front of me brakes without warning. As I swerve into another lane to avoid collision, the green coconut I bought for U Soe Htet rolls from the passenger seat onto the floor. I lean down to pick it up, and with sudden, stinging clarity, remember the can of coconut milk on Ahpwa's kitchen floor. The car behind me honks. I swallow my grief and press my foot on the gas.

SIX

Rangoon, Burma
1988

With Shwe by my side, I began to see another, more endearing side of Rangoon, learning to appreciate the very same sights and smells that had initially repulsed me. He took me to his favorite markets and teahouses, chatting and joking with the vendors while making sure I tasted a carefully selected assortment of street eats, from coconut flavored glutinous rice cakes to pickled tea leaves to fried chickpea tofu. Ravenous, I devoured it all.

The vendors didn't know what to make of me at first—although I looked and dressed like a local, my Burmese was unusually formal and heavily accented. They only accepted me because I was with Shwe. Everyone loved Shwe. He was what Father called a people person, genuinely curious about the people he met regardless of their background or status. Yet, he was always making up stories about who he was and where he lived, never completely open about himself. Initially, I thought this a kind of game he liked to play—seeing how far he could take a tale, how much people were willing to believe—but as the weeks passed, I began to suspect a deeper significance to his taletelling, even if I could not quite pinpoint what that might be.

One morning in early February, as we sat at our favorite teahouse, playing checkers with bottle caps—mine Blue Mountain Cola, his Max+ Orange—I asked why he always pretended to be someone else.

"So they don't treat me differently," he said without looking up, as if this were the most obvious thing in the world.

I followed his gaze to the checkerboard that someone had

painstakingly painted onto the plywood tabletop. I was tired of not understanding, tired of curbing my questions.

"Come on. Your turn." His right knee jiggled up and down with impatience.

I slid one of my cola caps diagonally to the right, away from home base. It was a risky move. "Why would they treat you differently?"

He launched his piece over mine, capturing my cap and kinging his own. "Sometimes you're really stupid, Aye."

My eyes stung. He'd never spoken to me like that before.

He must've felt bad, maybe remembered that I wasn't from Rangoon, because after a second, he touched my hand. "Grandfather, that's why."

I stared into his eyes and nodded solemnly, too relieved that he'd confided in me to admit that I still didn't understand. I knew his grandfather was in the military. I could see that the people on the streets were suffering while our family had more than enough to eat, that the lights in our house still worked when the rest of the neighborhood fell into a darkness so complete, we couldn't see beyond the front stoop. But I could not quite make the leap to what Shwe might mean. I couldn't understand what role the General played in that suffering, or what that meant for Shwe and our family more broadly. What I did know was that he would tell me when he was ready, not a moment sooner.

Of all the places he introduced me to that winter, my favorite was the lovely Inya Lake, an oasis of green established by the British in the 1880s. This was where we went when we wanted to be alone, a near constant desire from my perspective. Part of the appeal, at least for me, were the many couples who frequented the grounds, stealing a moment of intimacy in a society that discouraged public displays of affection. Nearly every time we visited the lake, we came across two or three such couples sitting behind propped-up umbrellas to shield them from view.

One time, around mid-February, I suggested we spy on one of these unsuspecting couples. Breathless with anticipation, we clambered behind a clump of bushes that offered an uninhibited view of the lovers. The couple was several years older than us, probably in their mid-twenties, the man very handsome with broad cheeks and a square jaw. I couldn't see the woman's face but liked the way her flowing, black hair glinted in the sunlight. The man stroked her cheek, drew her toward him with tender urgency. As their lips met, I sucked in my breath, conscious of Shwe's body crouched next to mine, of the prickly hush unfurling between us. What would it be like to touch his face, to press my body close to his just as the young woman did with her lover?

Then Shwe shifted, bush and lake and sky tumbling back into focus. In the glare of the sunlight, I began to feel embarassed, wary of Ahpwa's disapproval. But what really scared me was the possibility that acting on those urges would destroy the special bond Shwe and I shared. Because what if he didn't feel the same?

Afterwards, as we walked along the water's edge, Shwe told funny stories and I laughed a little too loud, still jittering over what I'd felt when the couple kissed.

"I like your laugh," he said, stopping abruptly to study my face. "And the way you listen with your eyes. I feel stronger when I'm with you, like I can stand up to Grandfather."

Any lingering awkwardness I'd felt a moment before evaporated into the shimmering lake. Beyond the initial rush of excitement, Shwe's praise filled me with a newfound sense of confidence, recognition that I, too, might one day sever the strings that bound me to my family, expand my range of movement beyond the purview of Ahpwa. Perhaps not immediately, but soon. For now, I'd stop wearing my hair in a braid, let it sweep over my neck and shoulders like the young woman we'd spied upon.

Other times, we sat by the lakeshore throwing stones into the water, our thighs clamped together as we shared our most intimate secrets. I told him about my life back home, about Ahpwa's impossible expectations and the carefulness between my parents, about the way I remolded myself at home and at school, never quite belonging in either, about my alternating impulses to protect Parker from it all one the one hand and throw her into the fire on the other.

Little by little, Shwe began to open up to me as well, describing what it was like to have the General as a grandfather— the unwelcome fawning of teachers at school, the corrosive standoffishness of the other children—and I started to see that there was something more sinister about his grandfather than Ahpwa, that the General's presence went beyond the confines of Shwe's family, into his school and the market and the streets. Could this be what the grown-ups were always whispering about? I considered asking him but was afraid he'd clam up again.

For the first time in my life, I found myself wishing that Ahpwa'd taught me more about Burma—not the mythical, magical Burma in her heart, but the dark, gritty Burma of everyday life, the smoldering political landscape that had so far evaded my comprehension. I wanted to be closer to Shwe, and this was the one side of him that I couldn't seem to reach.

Aside from this small obstacle, Shwe was perfect for me. Unlike the boys at school, he had none of the usual teenage hang-ups. He wasn't afraid to be silly or sensitive, or to partake in activities kids back home might consider juvenile. Father had insisted on bringing a whole suitcase full of board games from Boston. Rather than sneering at the idea of playing with our younger cousins, Shwe dove in with abandon, shouting and laughing when he lost all his money in *Monopoly,* or when Parker sent his pawn back home in *Sorry!* This came as a huge relief. Since turning thirteen, I'd struggled with how to present myself in the world. I still loved dolls and playing make believe as much as six-year-old Parker but knew this wasn't considered cool among my peers at school.

By far my favorite game was our made-up adaptation of a story Ahpwa had told us time and again—the tale of King Thibaw and Queen Supayalat. Thibaw was the last king of Burma, Supayalat, the younger sister of King Thibaw's intended bride. During the wedding ceremony, she pushed in next to her sister to be anointed queen at the same time. Enamored with Supayalat, King Thibaw never consummated the marriage with the older sister, and Supayalat became supreme queen.

Fearful of anyone who might usurp the throne, Supayalat orchestrated a massacre of 100 immediate blood relatives, including siblings and first cousins. Their royal status secured, the couple lived a life of luxury and isolation inside their gilded palace in Mandalay. Those who wished to address the king and queen were required to perform the *shiko*, approaching the throne by walking on their knees. Anything less was to risk having a gold-encrusted slipper hurled at them with painful accuracy. I imagined servants going about all their duties on their knees, sometimes fully prostrating themselves so that the queen could walk on their hair.

In 1885, when the royal family was exiled to India by British colonial troops, Thibaw crumbled, but not Supayalat. As they were transported on the back of a bullock cart out the servant's gate of the palace, she pressed back her shoulders, placed a hand-rolled cheroot in her mouth, and instructed one of the British soldiers to light it for her. I never knew if this was an exaggeration on Ahpwa's part. Nor could I make out her opinion on the matter. Half the time she portrayed the queen as a power-hungry Jezebel, but other times she took the queen's side. In either case, the rise and fall of Queen Supayalat made for a fantastic adaptation of the childhood game of playing house, and Parker and I engaged in regular reenactments, me assuming the role of queen, while Parker played the various servants. Unable to pronounce Supayalat, Parker dubbed the game "Super Yacht," and the name stuck.

Shwe and the other cousins took to the game right away. I continued to play the queen, naturally, while the little ones joined Parker as my devoted servants, and Shwe assumed the until-now vacant role of King Thibaw. Instead of the sickly, ineffectual ruler that Ahpwa portrayed in her stories, Shwe's Thibaw was strong, commanding and incredibly dreamy. Sometimes I added a scene in which King Thibaw took Queen Supayalat's hand in his, just to feel that delicious tingle travel down my spine.

The last time we played Super Yacht was at the very end of February. Whatever was distracting the grown-ups had intensified. They'd leave early in the morning with big purple circles under their eyes and return late in the evening, the skin pulled tight across their faces. No one bothered to explain what was going on, not even Father. I could understand concealing the details from six-year-old Parker, but I was thirteen, and Shwe several months older than me. Perhaps they thought our innocence would protect us, or maybe they didn't think at all.

Shwe knew more than I did. I could tell by the way he tuned his ear toward the grown-ups when they entered the house, hushing anyone who made too much noise—including me. I wanted to ask him what it was all about, what the grown-ups were up to and why he, too, was acting so secretive all of a sudden. But I figured he could only answer in two possible ways: either he'd blow me off again, which would make me sad and drive us apart; or he'd take me into his confidence, and whatever it was would consume us. As long as I remained in the dark, we could go on pretending that everything was fine.

On this particular day, San San had gone to the market to buy candles and other supplies for the weekend, leaving us older kids in charge. She didn't do this often, but life was so different in Burma, the grown-ups acting so mysterious and unpredictable, that I didn't question it. We decided to act out the occasion soon after Queen Supayalat's wedding when she had her and Thibaw's closest blood relatives bludgeoned to death in velvet body bags, then trampled by elephants. As usual, Shwe and I played king and queen, while the younger cousins acted as our servants. He seemed a little antsy, his right leg jiggling up and down incessantly, but I didn't think much of it.

First, we line all our younger cousins in a row, making them prostrate themselves on the ground so we could walk on their hair, a practice that always gave me a certain, guilty pleasure when it came to Parker. But we'd done all this before; the little ones were still in the spirit of the game. Then we changed roles. Shwe and I became the royal assassins while the younger cousins acted the parts of the relatives to be killed. We began this new enactment by rolling each cousin in *longyi* like giant burritos. Initially, they seemed to find being wound up in cloth great fun.

Ever ticklish, Parker began to giggle, and Khaing Zar soon followed suit.

"Silence," bellowed Shwe, whacking his pretend club—really a fold-up umbrella—slowly and rhythmically on his open palm.

I looked at him in surprise, then recognition. Taking his cue, I yanked the *longyi* up over the children's heads so they couldn't see, surrendering to the raw thrill of domination. Someone whimpered, either Khaing Zar or Phyu Phyu, I couldn't distinguish the voice. Then Parker joined in, whining my name in that distinctly high-pitched voice she invariably used to get her way, and something inside me cracked, six years of putting her needs above mine transforming into a blinding, reckless rage.

I swung back my foot to kick her when I felt Shwe's hand on my arm. The alarm in his steady brown eyes highlighting what I'd almost done.

"Don't be a cry baby, Parker. You'll ruin the game," I snapped. But inside I was shaking. Seeing her all wrapped up like a package—a nameless, faceless wad of cloth—I understood how those executioners had hardened themselves to their assignment, ceasing to recognize their subjects as human. For a terrifying moment, I'd forgotten that this was my little sister.

Thandar disentangled herself and stood up, crossing her arms over her chest. "It's not fair," she said. "I want to be the killer."

"Who cares? It's a stupid game anyway," Shwe answered, yanking the blankets off the little ones.

"Yeah, game over," I said.

SEVEN

Boston, Massachusetts
2011

Jason's sitting at the dining table when I return from the assisted-living facility. He's changed out of his work clothes into jeans and a teal-colored sweater that brings out the flecks of green in his eyes. His laptop is open, loose papers scattered around the table.

Still buzzing from the day's events, I bend down to give him a quick kiss before launching into the highlights, from the thrill of finding the marionettes to my suspicions about Ahpwa and U Soe Htet and the unexpected tenderness I feel toward the curious old man.

"Ahpwa had a lover? No way!" says Jason. Then, almost as an afterthought: "Wait, what about your grandfather?"

My skin prickles with irritation. Of everything I've just described, *this* is what he chooses to focus on? Shrugging off my jacket, I return to the entryway closet. I can hardly blame him for not understanding the significance of finding U Soe Htet and the marionettes. I don't fully get it myself, and unlike Jason, I know the background. If only Parker were here to share my excitement. She'd get it.

"Oh no, it wasn't like that. My grandfather died ages ago, before I was born." I stuff the jacket into the overfull closet, more annoyed with myself than with Jason. The truth is I've only ever told him a sanitized version of my family's 1988 trip to Burma. Growing up, I had no one to share it with; Parker was too young, my parents too preoccupied with Ahpwa. By the time Jason entered my life, I'd kept the real story inside for so long, I was afraid to crack open the lid even a little, lest all that anguish come spilling out again.

We met during my third year of law school, his second and final year of business school. I was in the main computer lab finalizing an article for the law review, entitled "Rule of Law and the One-Party State: A Look at Asia." It was my first submission to the review. As I was formatting the final draft of the document, the computer crashed. I froze, my eyes pasted to the screen in disbelief, until an attentive lab assistant appeared by my side, reassuring me with his soothing voice and relaxed manner, an eagerness to his expression that made him seem innocent and wholesome.

"Don't worry. Happens all the time." He smelled like a combination of Ivory soap and freshly cut grass. "I'm Jason, by the way."

Sure enough, he ejected the disk, rebooted the computer, and retrieved the file before my disbelief had crystallized into panic. The document restored, he asked what I'd been working on, and we began to talk. He was a self-confessed computer geek, working in the lab as part of his financial aid package. The next day we talked again, and the day after that he asked casually if I wanted to "get some dinner sometime." I kept to myself in those days, but he made me feel so at ease that I agreed.

Months later, he confessed that he'd been attracted to me long before that first encounter in the computer lab, that he'd deliberately arranged his work schedule to correspond to those times when I frequented the lab.

"You never even knew I existed," he teased.

"Of course, I knew you existed," I protested. That wasn't technically true, but it felt true—Jason having so quickly become a defining part of my life that I no longer remembered a time without his calming presence.

He stands up from the table and stretches. "Tell me later?

We need to get moving."

I'd forgotten we'd had dinner plans with his college friends. I used to look forward to these dinners, but lately all the talk revolves around babies, either those in the making, or those sitting at the table rendering meaningful conversation impossible.

"Can I check my email real quick?" I ask. Parker's been gone over a week now and I still haven't heard from her. I've tried not to worry. Anticipating my concerns isn't her forte, and the telecommunications network in Myanmar is prehistoric. But with every day that passes, my restlessness grows. I feel as if I've been holding my breath since she left, suffocating from a new, crushing emptiness. How I long to share with her what I've learned about Ahpwa, for us to build our new, post-Ahpwa normal together. I wonder, too, about Shwe. What he's like now, whether he'd want to reconnect after all this time.

Jason looks at his watch, a pinched expression on his face. He hates being late, I know, and I don't like putting him out. But I have a hunch that Parker's written, and I can't wait a minute longer.

"I'll be quick, I promise."

He nods.

I sit down across from him and open my laptop, giddy with relief at the sight of my sister's name at the top of my inbox. Maybe this is it, I allow myself to hope, maybe she's writiten to tell me she's found whatever it is she was looking for, that she's coming home. I no longer care whether or not she brings Ahpwa's ashes back, not really. I still believe Ahpwa belongs here in Boston, with us, but more than anything, I just want Parker to come home so we can put an end to the whole ordeal, so we can forget about Burma and move on with our lives.

The message is classic Parker. No salutation, no explanation, just a string of incomplete sentences punctuated by X's and O's.

Sorry, Internet access difficult. Myanmar amazing—<u>you should come</u>! Found job teaching English. Moving to apartment soon. Will send number when phone hooked up. XXXOOO, Parker

P.S Shwe says hi.

"Are you ok?" says Jason, tapping his stack of papers into alignment.

"She got a job." I can't believe it.

"Who—Parker? Really? She's gonna stay in Myanmar?"

I don't like how upbeat he sounds. "Teaching English," I add.

"That's great!" He looks at me for a second, then adds, "I mean, isn't that what you always wanted? Parker to show some initiative without you having to arrange everything for her?"

Not like this, I think. And not there. I've been telling myself that I'm worried for her safety, and that's partly true, but as I stare at her maddeningly carefree email, a far less noble motivation emerges: I don't want Parker to take Burma from me.

Or Shwe.

"I'm worried about her," I say instead.

"She'll be fine." He waves his hand dismissively. "Come on. We're gonna be late."

I don't move.

"Etta, she's 29. She can take care of herself."

"So I should just leave her there?" Images of steel-helmeted riot police cloud my vision. Of Shwe leaning in close for a kiss.

"What other choice is there?" says Jason. "Come on. We have to go."

~

I leave a note on the coffeemaker the following morning, telling Jason that I've left early in order to visit U Soe Htet before work, and apologizing for the night before. The dinner flopped. I was too distracted by Parker's email to make conversation with his friends, and too annoyed with Jason to care. His crime? That's what I'm trying to figure out as I head west on the turnpike. I suppose I blame him for not showing enough concern about Parker or enough enthusiasm about U Soe Htet. But is that fair, considering I've kept him in the dark about my past?

So, who am I angry with? I ask myself as I pull into the parking lot of U Soe Htet's facility. Parker's the logical culprit. For running off to Burma so quickly. For leaving me to sort through the consequences of Ahpwa's death alone. But Parker's Parker. I love her no matter what. So Ahpwa then. Maybe I'm mad at her for climbing up on that stool and falling, before we had a chance to put things straight. Or maybe I'm just mad at myself.

I find the old man sitting on the carpet in his room, wrapping the princess' joints in the silk ribbon I dropped off last night. Yatheik and Nat Pyet perch on his dresser, no longer a jumble of body parts, but two fully formed marionettes as vivid and expressive as I remember. In front of them is a ceramic bowl, with the two bunches of bananas I bought for him arranged like hands around the young coconut. Next to the bowl stands a small posy of flowers I recognize from the lobby. An image of U Soe Htet sneaking down to steal flowers in the wee hours of the morning fills me with affection.

"An offering to the *nats*, so they don't grow envious of the marionettes," he explains with a chuckle as he stands to greet me. "*Lah phet yay?*"

59

While he prepares the tea, I sit down on the carpet to examine the improvements he's made to Minthamee. In addition to new ribbons, her face has been touched up and her strings replaced. He's even managed to reaffix some of the loose sequins on her gown.

We move to the armchairs, where U Soe Htet gives me a lesson on the distinctive qualities of Burmese marionettes. I learn that each character may be made of a different type of wood according to the status of the marionette, and that the faces of the marionettes are painted with specially prepared dyes made from a combination of soapstone, *thanaka* and tamarind.

"You know the male marionettes have 20 strings while the female ones have only 19?" he asks with a glint in his eye.

I love seeing how the marionettes transform the old man, as if allowing him to escape the walls of the retirement home and travel back to a happier time. It's this magic that I haven't been able to explain to Jason, this connection to the marionettes that I share with U Soe Htet, taking me back to a time before everything was broken, when Parker could still sit in my lap, the princess was safe, and the forces of good and evil were equalized. If the marionettes can be restored, maybe there's hope for Parker and me, too.

U Soe Htet's delight is infectious. I can't get enough of his stories, so many of which revolve around Ahpwa, beginning with the first day he laid eyes on her.

"I was the immature side of twelve, still very much a boy, when she appeared like a mirage in front of our year-nine class, the loveliest, most elegant 17-year-old I'd ever seen. The Japanese occupied Rangoon. Your Ahpwa had come to talk to us about our responsibilities, about the possibility of volunteering for our country. I was taken not only by her beauty but by her eloquence, her comportment and her dedication to the cause of independence." His Burmese is very formal, but I'm able to follow easily. Ahpwa taught me well.

"Sounds like you were smitten," I say.

"I was smitten." He chuckles again, shoulders shaking gently, eyes disappearing into a web of wrinkles. "When I saw her in Boston some twenty years later, I tumbled again, charmed as much by her beauty as by her way of browbeating the Burmese community into doing things her way."

Sounds like Ahpwa, all right. He admired the very same qualities that I resented—her strength, her pride, and that unwavering conviction that she knew best. The wistfulness of U Soe Htet's tone confirms what I already suspected, that he'd loved Ahpwa, a revelation that both bewilders and intrigues me. Our grandfather died before I was born, so she was single for as long as I knew her. But to imagine Ahpwa loving and being loved by a living, breathing man?

Suddenly, I want to know all the details: how they met, how many years they'd known each other, whether she'd loved him back. The longing in his voice tells me that she was the one to break things off in the end, but he doesn't let on why, or perhaps doesn't know himself.

That's when it hits me: The person I am most angry with is not Parker or Ahpwa, but Shwe—for never answering my letters, making me wonder and weep as I began to doubt whether our connection had been real. I've been thinking more and more about him these last few days. Not because I still harbor romantic feelings for him 23 years later, but because he reminds me of the intensity of that time, back when I still believed in the idea of all-consuming love.

EIGHT

Rangoon, Burma
1988

By mid-March of our extended family reunion in Burma, I'd come to the momentous, if slightly premature, conclusion that 1988 was to be the best year of my life. Shwe felt the same. I could tell by the way he squeezed my hand at the end of each day, a promise that the following one would be just as magical, if not more so. I'd lie in bed at night reenacting every aspect of that gentle, intimate squeeze—and more and more frequently, imagining his hand on my leg or around my waist instead.

He'd begun to talk about our future together as a given, as if we were destined by some cosmic scheme to spend our lives as one. How and where we'd live, and under what conditions, were trivialities that didn't seem to concern him. I could think of nothing better than spending a lifetime with my beautiful second cousin, but whether by nature or experience, I was more pragmatic. My newfound freedom from Ahpwa was only temporary, I knew. Eventually my family would return to America, and I would go with them, life reverting to a familiar pattern of control and submission.

I tried to explain this to Shwe, warn him that it was too good to last, but he didn't seem to hear me. One evening, as we lay side by side on our auntie's living room floor, his fingers grazing mine, he sat up abruptly.

"I've got it," he said, his eyes shining with excitement. "We'll go see a fortuneteller. She can tell us...you know." He gave me one of his intense, trying-to-seem-mature looks.

The suggestion behind his unsaid words sent a flutter of excitement through my chest, but I was uneasy about visiting a fortuneteller. I knew they were consulted regularly in Burma, especially when determining the viability of a love match. Ahpwa'd taught me all about the Burmese tradition of *ma ha bote,* a combination of astrological, numerological and tarot card readings that went back centuries, and which many believed could predict—and potentially alter—the outcome of events. But I always considered it more of an entertaining pastime than a legitimate means for making life decisions.

"Even Chairman Ne Win asks advice from fortunetellers," continued Shwe, drowning me in his impassioned gaze.

I didn't care what the president did or didn't do with fortunetellers, but I liked the idea of spending the day alone with Shwe.

"How about tomorrow?" I responded. Because who knew? Maybe they really could predict a successful love match.

The next morning, as I waited for Shwe to arrive, Ahpwa appeared in the doorway of the bedroom I shared with Parker, shooing her away. Part of me was touched—my grandmother hadn't sought me out since we left the airport bathroom two and a half months earlier—but I couldn't shake a sense of impending doom, as if her abrupt reemergence in my life signaled an end of something else.

"Shall I braid your hair, *Myi*?" She plucked the hairbrush from the table and sat down on the bed behind me.

"Ok," I answered, uncertainly. Ahpwa was always doing that—disguising her directives as questions. One day, I planned to respond with a polite "no, thank you" just to see her reaction.

As she brushed and separated my hair, I tried to figure out what she was up to, discern her true motive in coming to my room this particular morning. Was this her way of warning me not to wear my hair loose? I didn't think she'd been paying attention to me or my hair of late, but maybe I was wrong. Maybe she saw more than I supposed, in which case, I was screwed.

"Keep still, *Myi*. Stop squirming," she commanded.

When the final segment of the braid was plaited and ribboned, Ahpwa stood up and straightened her *htamein*. "You are not to go out today. Do you understand?"

"What? Why?" After that last game of Super Yacht, the last thing I wanted was to spend another day in the house with Parker and the younger cousins. Unless…could this have something to do with whatever it was that the grown-ups were always whispering about? I'd been looking forward to the day out with Shwe, but if there was a reason to stay home, if Ahpwa would only explain why, maybe I could convince him to put the fortuneteller off another day.

"Don't ask questions, *Myi*. Just do as I say." The severity of her tone stirred my growing rebelliousness.

Before Burma, I often fantasized about going against Ahpwa's orders, but never once acted on that desire. This was about to change; I was too wound up, too tightly coiled with frustration and desire to stay at home today. I needed to be out in the city where I could release some of that energy. I needed to be alone with Shwe. Surely, if there were any real danger, Ahpwa would've taken the time to explain it to me.

When Shwe arrived shortly after, I decided not to mention Ahpwa's warning. We played cards until the grown-ups left, then slipped out while San San was busy with the younger ones. Although she usually let us do as we please, I didn't want anything to get in the way of our outing.

I tore out the braid as soon as we hit the street. As we ran to the bus, I ignored the pinch of guilt in my side, focusing instead on the excitement of being alone with Shwe. The people at the bus stop gazed at me a little longer than normal, but that was nothing new. They were just trying to figure out what was different about me.

The first bus was packed. I suggested we wait for the next one, but Shwe just laughed and pulled me on, steering me into the center of the bus where we stared solemnly into each other's eyes. At the next stop, more people got on, thrusting us closer still. As we swayed back and forth, our bodies pressed together, my nipples began to stiffen, and I soon forgot all about Ahpwa's warning.

Twenty minutes later, the bus ejected us onto the shoulder of a busy traffic circle downtown. In the center of the roundabout stood the gilded Sule Pagoda, an important Buddhist temple whose lower levels served as a hub for the city's thriving fortuneteller industry. I slipped my hand into Shwe's, and we ran across the street to the looming pagoda where dozens of people waited for the chance to know their future.

"How about that one?" said Shwe, pointing his chin toward a cross-eyed old man with an almost wild look on his face.

I shivered. Now that we were finally here, I felt uneasy. All I'd really wanted was to spend some time alone with Shwe.

"Okay, then her." He gestured toward a small Burmese woman with sharp eyes and gray-streaked hair, a purple silk shawl draped over her shoulders.

I gave him an uncertain smile, which he took as agreement.

We waited to the side until the fortuneteller finished with the preceding client, a clean-shaven Burmese man dressed in a Western-style suit. Shwe approached, handing her a wad of sweaty-looking bills he'd been clutching since home. She nodded and pointed to two plastic stools in front of her card table. Sagging from the weight of previous fortune-seekers, the cracked, red stools were so low to the ground they seemed made for toddlers.

With mosquitoes circling my ankles, I lowered myself onto the stool, caught between the childishness I'd left in America and the pull of this new relationship we'd come to have appraised.

As her gaze settled on me, the lines in her face formed an owlish pattern around her eyes. The air seemed to grow thinner, tiny particles of electricity hovering just above my skin as she inspected my features, my hair, my clothing. I tensed. Could she tell that I wasn't fully Burmese? The more she stared, the more vulnerable I felt, as if she could see every bad decision I'd ever made or would ever come to make. Perhaps this hadn't been such a good idea. Perhaps I should've listened to Ahpwa.

I scanned the wall behind the soothsayer, my eyes settling on the astrological wheel over her head: tiger, lion, guinea pig, mythical bird, rat, dragon, tusked elephant and non-tusked elephant. I knew from Ahpwa that these were the eight astrological signs of the Burmese zodiac, each corresponding to one of eight cardinal directions and seven days of the week—Wednesday being divided in two. My gaze lingered on the dragon, its blazing eyes and fiery breath capturing my imagination.

"Stop daydreaming about dragons," she hissed in a high-pitched whisper.

A tremor of fear shot down my spine. How did she know? And what else might she be able to discern? Could she sense the leftover shards of resentment I'd felt toward Ahpwa since the morning or how my whole being had ached with longing when pressed up against Shwe on the overfull bus? The prospect of having my fortune read swung suddenly from a concession I was making for Shwe to something far more intrusive.

"It is an auspicious time for the new generation." The soothsayer seemed to focus on a spot several inches above our heads. "Although its significance may take time to reveal itself."

I snuck a glance at Shwe, and saw that he was transfixed,

his head tilted backward, his smooth, wide lips parted as he stared at the woman in awe.

She peered at the two of us on the edge of our stools and demanded to know the time and day of the week on which each of us was born. Shwe's voice cracked, as did mine, and I wondered what, specifically, made him nervous in that moment. Was he really so mesmerized by *ma ha bote*, or was he, like me, thinking about what she might say about us? He told her he was born on a Saturday at 7:34 am. I tried to recall which mythical animal was associated with Saturday but could only remember my own sign, Garuda, and that of Ahpwa, the Lion.

The fortuneteller nodded and began consulting her many charts of numbers, geographic designs and other mystical symbols. As she worked, my misgivings merged into one, all-consuming concern: What if she told us we were a bad match? Even if I chose to ignore such a warning, Shwe would not be able to do the same—of this I was certain.

She addressed Shwe first. "Ahhh, the dragon." I flinched, surprised and embarrassed that it was Shwe's own sign I'd fixated on earlier.

"You are passionate and philosophical by nature." She spoke in monotone. "You will face great betrayal in your life."

I found the directness of her manner alarming. Was it normal for fortunetellers to be so blunt? As I listened to her predictions, I oscillated between complete incredulity and a gnawing fear that I might somehow contribute to the betrayal that Shwe would face. Yet he showed neither alarm nor disbelief. On the contrary, he seemed to accept her word as destiny.

"I see an awakening on the precipice of your manhood," she continued, "followed by a difficult choice. Remember, not everything is as it seems."

The fortuneteller turned to me and hesitated. I stared back

at her, concentrating on the rasp of her breath as I tried to suppress my growing panic. The longer she remained silent, the more nervous I became. What if she really could read my mind, see the evil thoughts that sometimes seized me, how close my foot had come to crushing my little sister's ribcage when we played Super Yacht?

"The sign of Garuda is never easy, never straightforward," she began. "You are generous to a fault, but too independent, reluctant to let others know the inner workings of your mind. Your mother, she is alive?"

I started, unprepared for such a question, then nodded.

She shook her head. "You are ambitious, that's for certain. But stubborn when crossed."

Shwe laughed, only to be silenced by the fortuneteller's glare.

"You will experience a long period of solitude in which you will wrestle with your inner self. Don't forget those who are closest to you."

She was beginning to lose me again. Didn't everyone go through periods of solitude and introspection? Couldn't her words apply to anyone?

"You will take a great voyage, forever changing the course of your life."

Now I knew she was a fraud. Given my accent which, despite Ahpwa's best efforts, was not that of a native speaker, virtually anyone could tell that I was already on a voyage. The dragon comment must have been a lucky guess.

I was about to get up when Shwe waved his hand between us. "Wait. What about this?"

I shot him a look of desperation. Hadn't the woman insulted us enough? The last thing I wanted was for this doomsayer to extinguish the magic I'd experienced these last two months. But when I looked into his syrupy brown eyes and saw how much he wanted this, I relented.

The fortuneteller sighed. "I'm afraid I cannot say much, children, only that the tenderness of your feelings will be tested in many ways. If you wish for a positive outcome, you must visit your respective shrines at the Shwedagon. Take with you an offering of flowers and incense, and go quickly."

NINE

Boston, Massachusetts
2011

The estate lawyer asks me to stop by her office for a quick meet. We have to wait for probate, but with Parker and me as the only heirs, and no debt to speak of, she expects a straightforward execution of the will. She could've told me this over the phone.

"The real reason I asked you to come in is to give you this." She slides a white, legal envelope across her desk, my name written across the front in Ahpwa's distinctive script. After a lifetime of silence, I'm as stunned as I am hopeful. While part of me can't imagine her sitting down to write me a letter—knows how out of character that would be—I want so badly for line after line of her flawless handwriting to fill up the pages contained within that I squirrel the letter into my bag, dreaming of the many secrets to be revealed: A confession of love for U Soe Htet. The real reason our family left Burma in the middle of the night 23 years ago. An explanation for why she was so hard on me. An apology.

I wait until the safety of the car to open the envelope, holding my breath as I remove the single sheet of yellow legal paper, folded in thirds then half again. I note the ragged edge where Ahpwa—or perhaps the estate lawyer—tore the sheet from a legal pad. No pen marks show through the folded layers. Maybe she wrote in pencil?

I unfold the paper and stare at the empty blue lines. A flash of confusion gives way to the same old fog of resentment and hurt. There is no explanation or apology, of course. No words whatsoever. Just a small key taped to the center of the paper. I peel off the key and hold it up to the sunlight, trying to guess what it might unlock. Then suddenly, I'm giddy with disbelief.

An hour later, I'm back in my childhood home, sitting cross-legged in front of Ahpwa's old wedding chest, which I've moved from the credenza to the living room floor, the pink sticky note from the other day still stuck to its lid. As I slide the key into the padlock, silence opens up around me. I feel as if I am a little girl again, vulnerable and unprepared for what I might find within.

The contents are a disappointment—newspaper clippings, old photographs, a few postcards, some crafts Parker and I made in elementary school. Nothing to warrant such secrecy on Ahpwa's part. I shouldn't be surprised. This was her way: By forbidding me to see inside the chest, she was teaching me to respect boundaries, to accept my place. So why leave this key to me now, after her death?

Brushing away the cascade of sparkles that have come loose from the crafts, I sort the various mementos into piles on the carpet. Most of the newspaper clippings are in Burmese, the curling, ring-shaped letters strung together like links of a necklace. I scan an obituary of my great-uncle, General Myint Oo, who died in 2008. Apparently, he'd become quite a devout Buddhist in his later years, building shrines and donating to schools and orphanages across the country. He died from a massive stroke while helping clear fallen trees during Cyclone Nargis, the devastating storm that killed over 100,000 people and left millions of others homeless.

I open a manila folder to find a stack of more recent articles from the Irrawaddy and Mizzima websites printed out on plain paper, though Ahpwa did not own a computer. As I flick through the articles, my finger catches on the underside of one of the staples, leaving a smudge of blood on the top corner of the paper. I worry for a second that Ahpwa will be annoyed. Then I look up at the chandelier, a fixture in so many of my childhood memories, and remember that's she's gone, that she'll never be angry with me again. Pinching my thumb and pointer finger together to stop the blood, I return to the articles.

A few are written in Burmese script, but the majority are in English, all either by or about Moe Pwint, a Burmese journalist who won the PEN *Freedom to Write* award while incarcerated at the notorious Insein prison. I skim an essay about political prisoners kept in dog cages and shudder. Throughout my childhood, Ahpwa pointedly avoided teaching me about politics, preferring to leave such matters to "men and the media" as she liked to say. Why did she have these articles, let alone keep them stashed away?

The photos are worn around the edges. Ahpwa's parents. Ahpwa's wedding day. Me as a baby. Parker as a baby. My law school graduation. Nothing surprising until I come across a snapshot of a middle-aged Burmese man holding a Yatheik marionette. A wave of joy washes over me as I recognize the man's twinkling eyes. Was this why Ahpwa kept the chest locked, to keep her love affair with U Soe Htet secret? Slipping the picture into my purse, I return to the stack of photos. The next photograph is of a much younger Burmese man—early twenties at most—whom I don't recognize at all. I slip this into my purse as well. Maybe U Soe Htet will know who he is. Last is the photo of Ahpwa and her brother that I remember from my childhood, the one that sat on her bedside table until *America the Beautiful*, its edges tattered from the frame it once sat in.

Just one item remains now—a bright orange, children's shoebox with the signature white Nike swoosh along each side. I place the box in my lap and open the lid, surprised to see the gaudy, purple and fuchsia scarf I'd knitted for Ahpwa when I was ten. Brushing my hand over the soft surface, I cringe at the unsightly nubs and twisted yarns. As touched as I am that she kept it, I can't ignore the lump of disappointment in my gut. I shouldn't have let myself get so excited about the key. This was just another of Ahpwa's irritating life lessons on restraint.

I'm about to put the lid back on when I glimpse a flash of white through the folds of the scarf. More photos, I assume. I scoop out the bundle and unwind the scarf. Inside is a stack of yellowed airmail envelopes. I close my eyes, dizzy with longing. Here are my letters, the ones I wrote to Shwe after we returned from Burma in 1988. But I don't understand. Why would Shwe have sent my letters back to Ahpwa? I flip through them quickly, checking each envelope, then go back and check them again, unable to believe what I'm seeing. The envelopes are still sealed, every last one of them unstamped and without a postmark. Ahpwa never mailed them.

My stomach hardens with the weight of Ahpwa's betrayal. I remember so clearly her offer to mail that first letter. "It's no hassle, *Myi*. I pass the post-office on the way to the grocery store." I'd been touched by the gesture, allowing myself to hope that our lives might soon revert to something resembling normal. Because trusting the people you love is like breathing, you do it without thinking. But I should've known better. She was never that sweet.

I throw the bundle of letters across the room in a blaze of fury. Why did she offer to mail them if she was just going to stash them away? I could understand if she was trying to protect our relatives in Burma. Although I didn't know it at the time, any association with the West was cause for suspicion in those days. But if that were her reason, why not say so? Why go through the charade of mailing my letters, watching me run to the mailbox every day after school, when she knew very well there could be no reply to a letter never received? The only thing I can think is that she didn't trust me to understand, an insight that stings more than I care to admit.

I pick up one of the letters now strewn across the carpet. Penciled in the top right corner of the envelope where the stamp should be is the date: May 7th, 1988—almost two months after we returned to the United States. I turn the envelope over. Scattered over the back is a pageant of mismatched hearts, each one a different size, color and slant. The glue crackles with age as I run my fingers over the seal.

All these years, I thought Shwe'd been the one to break off communication. I imagined him reading my letters every week and choosing not to respond. The more time passed without hearing from him, the more I tormented myself with possible explanations—that he blamed me for making us go to Inya Lake, that he resented me for leaving, that he simply didn't care. None of this makes sense now, but to the lovelorn thirteen-year-old I once was, the sting of rejection trumped logic. To think now that he never heard from me either. A new, crushing image of Shwe takes shape in my mind—not angry or bitter, but broken.

Part of me wants to tear open the envelope, curl up on Ahpwa's old sofa and read every last letter. But to open them now, 23 years later, feels wrong somehow, like an invasion of privacy. Even if I was once that girl, we're no longer the same person. I'm not ready to confront the evidence of my own heartbreak, to be reminded how much that little girl suffered. Standing up wearily, I collect the remaining letters from around the room and arrange them into chronological order, from March 1988 to March 1989, then wrap the scarf tenderly around them and place the bundle back in the Nike box on the floor of the wedding chest.

With the letters out of sight, I repack the various mementos into the chest and shut the lid, staring for several seconds at the pink sticky note on top. None of this is Parker's fault. Nor is it her business. This is between Ahpwa and me. And Shwe and me. No one else need know, not Parker, not Jason. Maybe that's selfish, but I can't help feeling there's something sacred about those letters, something delicate and vulnerable—that in order to protect the girl who wrote them, I need to contain the fear and longing within. I dig the bundle of letters out of the Nike box and tuck it into my bag.

~

Jason suggests Chinese for dinner. I set the table as he calls in the usual order: spring rolls, chicken with cashew nuts, stir-fried broccoli. He opens a bottle of shiraz while we wait. I sit across from him at the dining table, the expanse of solid oak heavier and more vast than I recall. He asks about my meeting with the estate lawyer, and I tell him what she said about the will, everything to be split between Parker and me. I don't mention the key, or the letters.

Selecting which details about my childhood to share with him and which to keep to myself comes naturally—after all, I've been doing it for years. Still, it weighs on me, the accumulation of half-truths like a tower of blocks, threatening to topple over at any moment. Even if he doesn't feel it, I can't ignore the void that stretches out between us. I drink the wine too fast. He refills my glass. Is this what I want for us, a relationship marked by omissions and half-truths?

I talk about selling Ahpwa's house, describing each step in elaborate detail from sorting to staging to final sale. It's an old house, but the location is a plus. It will sell quickly.

"Take your time, Etta." He speaks in a hushed, measured tone as if I'm a delicate flower whose petals will wilt if he speaks too quickly or too loudly. "There's no rush." And for a second, I wonder if he's referring to the wine or the sale of the house.

The food arrives. We talk about his work, the Obamas, some friends who've just had a baby. I push the broccoli around my plate with my chopsticks, trying to stay focused on here and now, the food and the wine and the patient, loving man who will soon be my husband. But I can't stop thinking about Burma. About Shwe wandering alone through the streets of Rangoon after we left in 1988. About Ahpwa loving U Soe Htet, then leaving him without explanation. About Parker in Yangon now, climbing the stairs to the Shwedagon when it should be me.

"Are you okay?"

"I have to go to Myanmar," I say, realizing only as I speak the words that they are true, that this is what I've decided.

Jason scans the table as if to find an explanation among the cartons of leftover Chinese food. I can see him evaluating my words like pieces of fine crystal, carefully weighing each one then turning it over to see where it came from, how it was made. He doesn't know how not to be in charge. That's what it is. By deciding to go to Myanmar—a decision that has nothing to do with him or us—I've altered how we relate to each other. His gaze slowly refocuses, then zeroes back on me.

"Sure. Of course. You should've gone with Parker. She should've waited for you," he says at last. "She's your grandmother too, for crying out loud."

Ahpwa's ashes. If only it were that simple.

"Yeah, I don't know what she was thinking."

"Ok, then. Let's get you to Myanmar." He pushes back his chair, grabs his laptop from the side table, and just like that, begins searching for flights.

I remain still, awed by the rush of relief that my decision has brought, knowing that this is what I should've done all along. Then I take out my own laptop and send Parker a quick email, telling her that I'll be there as soon as I can sort out work and a visa and tickets.

She responds the next day:

About time!
Please bring crisp 100-dollar bills (no creases) and as much extra chunky peanut butter as you can carry.
XXXOOO Parker

TEN

Shwe wanted to go directly to the Shwedagon to fulfill the fortuneteller's prescription, but I needed time. I was still trying to reconcile the two sides of my identity, still teetering back and forth between dumbstruck acceptance of *ma ha bote* and a deep, smoldering distrust of it all. It was Shwe who'd really shaken me, his blind faith in the fortuneteller telling me one of two things: Either *ma ha bote* was real, which scared me more than I cared to admit, or Shwe and I were less alike than I wanted to believe. To go from the fortuneteller to the holiest Buddhist shrine in the country was a little too intense for me, a little too transcendental, especially with Shwe by my side. I'd wanted to be close to him today but not like this. Couldn't we go first to Inya Lake? I pleaded. It was Shwe's turn to relent.

The lakefront was quiet. Not a single leaf stirred in the treetops. The water, too, was completely still, as if nature was holding its breath. We settled under a palm tree, shielding behind a large, red umbrella someone had discarded. He leaned close to brush a lock of hair from my cheek, sending goosebumps up and down my arms. Something had changed between us. It was as if the fortuneteller's predictions had unshackled us, clearing the path for a new, more openly physical way of being together.

With a gentle pull, he drew me close. Our lips knocked awkwardly against each other. Then we kissed again, his mouth impossibly soft and warm, and the air around us seemed to melt away, eliminating the remaining distance between us. I fell into a trance, daydreaming about staying in Burma after my family returned to Boston, enrolling in Shwe's school so that I could spend every waking moment by his side.

Not until Shwe stood did I hear the chanting and singing coming from the road. Dozens, no hundreds, of people marching toward us. Many wore white, others had white bands wrapped around their arms or foreheads. Some carried knapsacks. Students. I'd never seen so many Burmese congregated in one place. The people I'd encountered in Rangoon were so calm and quiet. To hear them now raising their voices unnerved me.

Shwe pumped his fist in the air in solidarity and my pulse quickened. I could see from the way his eyes shone that he wanted to join in, be part of whatever this was, but was it safe? I stood up. Most of the protestors were men, but there were women, too. Many were holding hands, faces turned up to the sun. They were friendly, I reassured myself.

As the students swarmed closer, a young woman dressed in red beckoned to us. Her hair was pulled back, with two perfect moons of pale yellow *thanaka* on her flushed cheeks. Shwe pulled me into the crowd, and we linked arms with the woman and her friends. Someone started to sing the national anthem. I joined in, grateful for once to Ahpwa for having taught it to me. No one here seemed to notice or care if my mannerisms were not quite right, or my accent sounded foreign.

I didn't know what we were protesting but felt so bound to the people around me that I couldn't imagine disagreeing with their cause. I let myself be carried by the crowd, walking, singing, talking, chanting—seized by something bigger than myself, being accepted, being Burmese. It felt as if we were invincible, as if I was invincible. The same glow of belonging reflected in Shwe's eyes.

The next minute we were at a standstill, students staring at each other in confusion. No one seemed to move for several seconds, then a whisper of apprehension swept over and around us. My stomach hardened. Something was wrong. And though I still didn't understand what that might be, I realized with sudden clarity that it was connected to what the grown-ups had been whispering about for months. With a shudder of fear, I pressed closer to Shwe.

All at once, everyone began shouting.

"Watch out!"

"They're here!"

"Run!"

"*Thwa*," screamed the woman in red. Go!

But there was nowhere to go, everyone pushing into each other, the flesh of strangers rammed up against me. As the crowd heaved, I glimpsed a grey mass creeping towards us: riot police, hundreds of them, their steel helmets glinting in the sun. Shwe's face turned grey. The soldiers had blocked our access to the road. We were trapped. He squeezed my hand, crushing my knuckles together.

The words 'military crackdown,' overheard one day in the kitchen, came into my head, and I realized that I did know what this was, and that I shouldn't be here. I pictured myself lying on the ground, mangled and bloodied, arms and legs bent in the wrong direction, Ahpwa shaking her head in displeasure. My mouth filled with bilious rage. She'd known about this. That's why she'd come to me this morning, all guileless and sincere. She'd told me not to leave the house but hadn't trusted me enough to explain why.

Shwe yanked my arm, dragging me sideways to an old tamarind tree, and from there to our clump of bushes, where we crouched, out of sight. My throat grew dry, choking on the thuds of the Billy clubs as students scrambled up the embankment to escape the riot police. I watched a young man trip over a bed of flowers, dodging one blow after another, only to be bludgeoned by a third, his blood spilling onto the flowers.

A woman in red plunged into the lake, two riot police lunging after her. Was it our friend, the one with two perfect moons of *thanaka* on her cheeks? My body went rigid as she swung wildly at the two men. One grabbed her arms, while the other forced her head under water. She kicked and thrashed, her limbs cutting in and out of the lake in a frenzy of splashing and resilience. I willed her to keep kicking, keep resisting.

The splashing slowed, then stopped altogether. I scoured the surface of the lake, still believing she might escape the hands of the riot police, break free under water only to reemerge, triumphant, in another part of the lake.

A swath of red fabric floated to the surface. The riot police flicked the water from their gray green uniforms and strode back to shore. Shwe rubbed my back as I retched and retched.

Next thing I knew, Shwe and I were alone, the lake as still as when we'd arrived. A fire engine appeared, then another. Through the branches of the bush, we watched the firemen unwind their long, canvas hoses and wash away the blood from the flowers and grass.

Shwe pulled me up, and we picked our way out of our hiding place, creeping through back streets, now eerily empty and quiet. As we scurried home, I looked over my shoulder again and again, terrified that someone was tracking us. But Shwe just kept going, moving with the same steady determination, neither walking nor running, and never once looking back.

As we entered the familiar streets of our auntie's neighborhood, I began to shake, quiet, breathless tremors that racked my whole torso. On top of the shock of what we'd witnessed, I was sick with guilt. That Shwe and I had been there, that I'd put us in danger, first by disregarding Ahpwa's orders, then by cajoling Shwe into going to the lake instead of the pagoda, all because I ached to be alone with him.

"It's my fault," I said between gasps of air. "She told me to stay home."

"Who told you? Your Ahpwa?"

I nodded and he put his arm around my shoulder. "No, Aye. This isn't your fault. Shh."

"What if she finds out? What do I say?"

He stopped walking, put one hand on each of my shoulders, and looked me in the eye. "Aye, they didn't notice. Trust me. Just act normal. It will be okay."

He wrapped his arms around me, and I began to feel safe again, the intoxication I'd experienced earlier that afternoon having transformed into a deeper, more primal connection, the horror of what we'd experienced sealing us together for eternity.

Parker, Khaing Zar, Thandar and Phyu Phyu sat on the living room carpet with San San, playing *Candyland*. I wanted to run to Parker and squeeze her tight, but Shwe held me back, guiding me toward the bathroom instead. I'd just finished washing my face and re-braiding my hair when I heard the grown-ups at the front door.

I hurried to the living room to find Shwe sitting on the sofa. He placed his hand on the seat next to him. In his other hand, he held the deck of cards we'd played with that same morning. I sat where he indicated, astonished by how well he was coping. I could barely put one foot in front of the other, but he seemed to know what to do, to be guided by some inner restraint I lacked. It occurred to me that he understood something about the protest that I'd not yet grasped. I wished I could ask him, but that would have to wait until we were alone again.

"Act normal," he mouthed. "We'll play Rummy." He shuffled the cards, counting out seven each as I'd taught him just two months before.

In the next room, the grown-ups spoke in quick, hushed tones. But here in the living room, everything seemed to be moving in slow motion—Shwe, the cousins on the rug, even my own breath. At the lake, I could think of nothing but getting through that moment, keeping hidden from the riot police, staying alive. Here, now, all sorts of new concerns arose. What the grown-ups knew and didn't know already this morning. Whether my being at the lake could be traced back to my family, putting them in danger. Why we'd come to Burma in the first place. What Shwe wasn't telling me.

"You go first," he said. Then, more quietly, "Pick a card, Aye. That's right. Now put one down."

He picked up the next card and laid down four eights in the shape of a fan. Eight of hearts. Eight of diamonds. Eight of spades. Eight of clubs.

I drew another and set it down again, without looking at the cards in my hand.

He nodded approval.

Shwe won that game and dealt another. Looking down at my cards, I was confused to see the same four eights now in my hand. What were the odds? That's when I realized that he hadn't shuffled—whether because he'd forgotten or didn't care, I wasn't sure. When I looked back at him to gauge which it was, his eyes had turned cold and hard, as if steeling himself for something still to come.

Footsteps echoed down the hallway, each one closer than the last. My heart pounded in my ears. I didn't know what to expect, only that it couldn't be good. Nothing could be good on this day, maybe ever again. The door swung open and Shwe's mother appeared like an apparition, framed by the light in the hallway. A moment of relief gave way to a new apprehension. Something wasn't right.

She surveyed the room, her eyes locking with Shwe's, lips like razor wire. A flicker of recognition passed between them, followed by a look of warning.

"Time to go."

I watched in disbelief as Shwe stood and extended his hand to Khaing Zar, his exit adding to a growing swell of indignation in my gut. At the way the grown-ups spoke to us, the way they demanded compliance, pulling us apart now without explanation. Ahpwa had known about the protest, I felt sure. If only she'd told me. If only she trusted me.

ELEVEN

I'm standing in front of the bedroom mirror getting ready for my last visit to U Soe Htet. I leave for Yangon later today. The old man couldn't have been happier when I told him earlier this week that I was returning to Myanmar. "Yes, *Myi*. It's time." He seems to intuit the purpose of my trip better than I do. Although we've never spoken about what happened in 1988, I sense that the answers I seek are not unrelated to his own: What happened in Burma that made Ahpwa reject her country, her heritage, and even her lover?

Now that I'm about to get on that plane, the idea of leaving him gnaws at my conscience. U Soe Htet has changed in the short time I've been visiting him, becoming more like the man I imagine him once to have been, the suitor who charmed Ahpwa with his enthusiasm and his puppetry. With no one visiting him, even if only for a short time, I worry that he will become more isolated, sleeping all day and waking at night, focusing all his energy on his marionettes, and his ghosts.

Jason sits on the bed watching me brush my hair, a wistfulness in his eyes that unsettles me. I can't remember the last time he watched me this way. Ever since I decided to go to Myanmar, he's gone out of his way to help, scouring the web to find the best flights, and taking time off work to drive me down to DC for my visa. He even ran to Whole Foods last night to buy Parker's peanut butter.

In bed, too, he's been especially attentive, lingering over my face, my inner thigh, the nape of my neck, as if committing my body to memory. I keep telling him not to worry, that my return flight is only two weeks away, and most likely I'll come back even earlier. But I, too, feel a kind of looming emptiness that makes me hungrier for sex, wanting to hold him as close as I can for as long as possible.

"I suppose you're going to ask me to visit him while you're gone," says Jason, leaning back on his hands. It's half question, half accusation, but with an earnestness to his tone that tells me he's given considerable thought to the possibility.

"You'd do that?" Asking Jason to visit U Soe Htet never occurred to me. They are two distinct parts of my life.

"I'd do anything for you. Don't you know that?"

I stop brushing my hair. Though it's early for a Saturday, he's already showered and shaved, his jaw shiny and smooth, with a gleam of vulnerability. Jason doesn't want to be segregated from my past, has never wanted to. For years he's been trying to nudge his way in, suggesting brunch with Ahpwa or dinner with Parker, attempting to pull us all closer together. I'm the one who's resisted, too afraid to let in the light lest he see the real me and decide I'm not the person he thought I was.

"Come with me today?" I ask, uncertainly.

He stands up, and I realize that this was his plan all along.

~

U Soe Htet ushers us to the two armchairs, then quickly shuffles off to make some tea. Jason surveys the little kitchenette, single bed, and marionettes propped up on the dresser, then turns his gaze to me. Refusing our entreaties to take one of the armchairs, U Soe Htet climbs onto a wooden barstool where he launches into a lengthy discourse on the latest Red Sox statistics, as if this is a topic he and Jason have debated at length. I wonder if he's mistaken Jason with someone else, as he did initially with me, or if Jason simply reminds him of a type he once knew. Despite the close bond I've formed with U Soe Htet, I know little beyond a few basic facts about his experience in this country. Jason, on the other hand, focuses straight away on the American portion of the old man's life.

"So, what brought you to the US?" Jason asks, sipping the thick, sugary tea.

"Excellent question," says U Soe Htet from his perch on the stool. "It was thanks to a colleague of mine from Boston University, Dr. Jonathan Wizen. He'd come to Rangoon as a visiting professor back in 1961 and was so hopelessly confused about our culture, I felt compelled to teach him a few essentials."

"Like what?" asks Jason, the expression in his eyes open, inquisitive. I'm reminded of those first, heady days when we fell in love, Jason asking question after question about my family, and about Burma, questions I answered dutifully, if not completely. When did he stop asking?

"Oh, you know, teahouse etiquette, how to haggle at the market, which direction to walk around the Shwedagon. We would often talk well into the night, striking up a fast friendship. I hated to see him go, but he needed to get back to his family. Two months later, I received a letter from the Asian Studies Department at BU, inviting me to serve as visiting lecturer for the spring semester. So I thought, why not?" He throws his hands in the air with abandon.

Not only is U Soe Htet perfectly lucid, his English, which I assumed must be lacking, given his insistence on speaking Burmese with me, proves excellent. Like Ahpwa, he speaks with a slight British inflection, hinting at his younger days as a student in the colonial education system.

"I arrived in Boston in the beginning of January, so you can imagine how cold and miserable I was. In Rangoon, the average daily temperature was almost 90. Now here I was enduring subfreezing temperatures for days on end. The university organized secondhand coats and other warm clothes for me, but still I shivered, longing for my Golden Land. February was the worst. Snow, sleet, rain, slush. Well, you know what it's like." He laughs, and his eyes disappear into the creases of his face.

Jason sits with his long legs crossed, leaning slightly forward as he listens intently to the old man's words. I see now that I haven't given Jason enough credit when it to comes to my family, that I've mistaken his choosing not to pressure me for indifference. Part of me is sorry to be leaving on this trip just now when I'm finally beginning to unravel these knots in our relationship.

"In the beginning of March, I received some news that would change my life forever," continues U Soe Htet. "Tell me, young man, do you know what happened in our country in March of 1962?"

"No, I'm sorry."

U Soe Htet shoots me a stern look from his stool. "I see you haven't bothered to teach your friend our history."

This isn't stuff Ahpwa taught me either, but I've done some self-educating in the years since. "Was 1962 when the military took over?" I venture.

"Yes, *Myi*. That's right. A military coup d'état. We'd only been independent for 15 years, but those army thugs wanted more power for themselves. The coup confirmed what I'd already come to fear, that our beloved country was in trouble. As desperately as I wanted to feel the Burmese sun on my face once again, I was fearful. The military does not care for academics."

Ahpwa would've been in her thirties in 1962. Though she'd already lived in the US for many years, her parents were still alive back in Rangoon, her brother still in the military. I shift in my chair, uneasy at the thought of Ahpwa's brother, General Myint Oo. And of his grandson, Shwe.

"My answer came in July," continues U Soe Htet. "Just as I was preparing to leave Boston, the military opened fire on students participating in a nonviolent demonstration. Troops were instructed to shoot for three minutes, rest for two minutes, shoot again for three minutes." U Soe Htet pauses, and his silence presses down on me. "Over a hundred students were killed, including many from my department. The next morning, the government blew up the student union building, and the day after that they closed the universities indefinitely. I'd be arrested on the spot if I returned."

U Soe Htet's story hits me hard, my own memories of conflict as raw today as they were 20 years ago. I look away quickly only to be caught by the penetrating gaze of Nat Pyet, the evil spirit who inhabits the forest, his sharp, menacing eyes uncannily lifelike in their renewal.

"So B.U. kept you on?" asks Jason, his face ashen with disbelief. I wish, suddenly, that I hadn't brought him here, that I could prevent him from knowing the shape of oppression in Burma, or at least stop him from associating it with me.

"I was lucky," U Soe Htet continues. "BU offered me a full-time teaching position and facilitated the paperwork for me to stay in America." He looks out the window as he sips his tea. "Lucky, but also unlucky. Because not a day has gone by that I have not yearned to return home. My only consolation that I left no wife or children behind."

U Soe Htet's longing rouses something in me that I haven't felt for years, a mingling of compassion and indignation that is at once familiar and fresh. I feel breathless and bold, a shaky, new resolve forming in my gut: To stop all this heartache once and for all. To bring peace to U Soe Htet, especially. I want this for him even more than for myself.

"You could come with me," I blurt out, buoyed by the idea of a joint mission, knowing the joy returning to Burma would bring him, not to mention the comfort his presence would provide me, how much stronger I could be with U Soe Htet by my side.

"No, *Myi*. My time has passed. It's up to you now. Go find your Burma. Your possibilities."

I suppose I knew he couldn't come, knew this was something I had to do alone. But the conviction in his tone makes me uneasy. I worry he's misunderstood my motivation for going, thinks my intentions more ambitious than they are.

Jason squeezes my hand, and I wonder what it means. Does he want to be invited? Or is it a gesture of support, telling me he believes in me, too?

"And now, a gift for you," says U Soe Htet, ambling over to his dresser, where he takes out a small object wrapped in newsprint. My eyes well with gratitude, not so much for the gift but for the opportunity to know this gentle and fascinating man, who loved my grandmother despite her obstinacy and severity, or maybe even because of those qualities. I will be forever indebted to him for turning me back around to see the sun.

Jason places his hand on my back as I unwrap the parcel. Inside is a hand-carved wooden statue of a *nat*, one of many local spirits worshipped in Burma alongside the Buddhist faith. Turning the statue over in my hand, I realize that it's a miniature version of one of the marionettes I brought to U Soe Htet. Yatheik, the spirit who inhabits the forest, guiding those who have lost their way.

After one final round of *lah phet yay*, it's time to say goodbye.

Jason turns to U Soe Htet. "How'd you like to go to a Red Sox game? I can get tickets through my work." I'm amazed that Jason is going to take the old man out of the facility, a possibility that hadn't occurred to me.

U Soe Htet rocks from side to side singing *Take me out to the ballgame*, and I close my eyes and smile, the visit proving fuller than I expected. I feel a twinge of sadness to be leaving both men behind, but I can see now that they'll be okay, that they don't need me to enjoy each other's company.

On the drive back from the retirement home, I think about the trip ahead—seeing Parker's freckle-splashed face, sitting on a plastic teahouse stool eating *mohinga*, finally putting things right with Shwe—and my sadness at leaving Jason and U Soe Htet is soon swept away by excitement.

Back at the apartment, I wrap the Yatheik statue in tissue paper and place it into my carry-on beside the bundle of unopened letters, still wrapped in the pink and purple scarf. Maybe Myanmar will be the place to read them, maybe not. As I tuck my passport and tickets into my purse, I find the photos I meant to give to U Soe Htet, one of him holding the Yatheik marionette, the other of a young man I don't recognize. I turn to Jason, uncertain at first, and then with growing confidence. Would he mind? Of course not.

"Promise me you'll call once a week," says Jason as we walk from the car park to the terminal. "I don't care how much it costs, ok? I need to hear your voice at least once a week."

"I won't even be gone that long," I protest.

"Just promise." A hint of desperation in his voice makes me stop and look at him.

Suddenly I'm scared too, Jason's plea unleashing what I've been trying not to admit, a nagging feeling that once I board this flight, my life will never again be the same.

TWELVE

No one spoke, the scrape of Parker's spoon against her plate the only sound. Mother, Father and Ahpwa sat stone-faced, not even looking at each other. Dinner was one of my favorites, pork curry and a salad of sliced yellow tofu with spicy bean paste, but no matter how much chili I added, my tastebuds refused to respond. I kept my head down, chewing each mouthful slowly and deliberately as I braced myself for Ahpwa's fury.

I didn't know how Ahpwa found out where we went but had no doubt that she knew every detail, from the fortuneteller to the kiss to the protest march. The only question in my mind was when my punishment would be announced, and what form it would take. Unlike Shwe's mother, who hid her displeasure with tight-lipped restraint, Ahpwa was not one to rein in her anger. She'd spell out all the ways I'd disappointed her, rebuke me not only for the danger I'd put myself in, but for what could've happened to Shwe, the trauma I would've caused the family if either of us had been killed. My foolishness. My self-obsession. My lack of respect.

She waited until we finished eating to make her pronouncement, her voice unusually tepid. "Have a bath now, then pack your belongings. We leave at midnight."

So this was my punishment. To leave the only place I've ever felt free. To part with the boy who quite possibly saved my life just hours ago. To disappear into the night without so much as a goodbye.

"But why?" said Parker, braver in her innocence than I could ever be.

Silence.

"Etta?" She singled me out as the one person who might tell her the truth.

I shook my head. Poor Parker. She hadn't wanted to come to Burma either, but, like me, she'd adapted to the rhythm of life in Rangoon, to San San's kindness and the companionship of Khaing Zar, Phyu Phyu and Thandar. How could I tell her that it was my fault, that I was the reason we had to leave?

I couldn't find the courage to speak, but her question made me curious enough to look around the table. Neither Ahpwa nor Mother met my eyes. Even Father, normally so easy-going, seemed to have withdrawn into himself, a haunted look on his face. Their silence chafed against my skin. The terrible not knowing. The absence of explanation. I thought back to this morning, when she told me to stay home without bothering to explain why, treating me like six-year-old Parker rather than entrusting me with the truth. If only Ahpwa would scream and shout, spell out my misdeeds like she usually did. Put a name to my crime.

"Is it because of me?" My voice cracked.

Ahpwa turned to face me, her eyes dull and glazed at first, then gradually narrowing as I seemed to come into her range of focus.

"Because of where I went? Because I disobeyed your orders?"

My parents' expressions remained blank.

Ahpwa continued to stare at me, the crazed look in her eyes telling me everything I needed to know.

I ran to the bathroom and tore off my clothes, noticing only as they fell to the floor the patches of dirt on the seat of my *htamein*. No wonder Ahpwa had looked at me that way. I peeled off my bra and underwear in disgust. In the few months we'd been in Rangoon, my body had betrayed me, a mass of dark hair creeping over my pubic area, breasts swollen and tender to the touch. Worse still were the fantasies that unfolded in my mind, urges I knew were wrong but was unable, or unwilling, to control. I couldn't imagine how I would bear Ahpwa's punishment but had no doubt that I deserved it.

Three quiet knocks.

I wrapped a towel around myself and cracked open the door. San San. In her hands, a white, enamel basin of water. "I heated some water for you," she said. "To ease the pain inside." A softness to her tone told me that she was on my side, that she understood how miserable I was to leave Rangoon—even if she couldn't know the contour of my guilt. I stepped back from the door, and she slipped in, placing the basin of hot water in the bathtub.

I hadn't paid much attention to San San these last few months, but saw now how pretty she was, her bright eyes and delicate features in perfect harmony with her smooth, clear skin. She had a way of making herself invisible, being in a room without attracting attention to her presence. It struck me that she'd witnessed my relationship with Shwe from the beginning, quite possibly the only one to perceive the depth of our attachment, Father's attention having long since turned elsewhere.

How I ached for Shwe. Not the fairytale infatuation of the last several weeks, something stronger and more profound, the memory of our kiss dwarfed by my need to understand. What we'd seen. What it meant. And to let him know that it wasn't my choice to leave.

"Please, San San," I whispered, increasingly lost in my own despair, "will you say good-bye to Shwe for me? Tell him…" My words dissolved into quiet sobs as I realized how powerless I was to promise him anything, knowing that from now on, every move I made would require Ahpwa's permission.

"Don't worry, Miss Etta. I will look after Shwe for you," said San San as she slipped out the bathroom door.

After my bath, I wrapped the towel around my chest and crept back to the bedroom I shared with Parker, shrinking against the wall to avoid Ahpwa's notice. San San had packed Parker's suitcase, her clothes for the plane laid out on the bed.

Parker sat on the floor, putting together a small, wooden jigsaw. "It hasn't been a year, has it? You said we were staying a whole year." She looked up at me with big, blue eyes.

"No, Bird, it hasn't been a year. We're leaving early," I managed to say.

"Why?"

Such a small word. I looked up at the ceiling, afraid I might cry again if I met her eyes. I hated lying to Parker. But how could I tell her what I'd seen? She was only six years old.

San San took Parker for her bath, leaving me alone to dress and pack. As I gathered my belongings from around the room, I pitched my ears to the grown-ups down the hall. There was so much I needed to understand—not only what they knew but how they knew it. More importantly, I needed to understand what I'd witnessed, how the riot police could've done what they did, killing all those innocent people, and whether it might happen again.

I tossed my pajamas into the bag along with two handfuls of underwear, careful not to make any noise. At the sound of Mother's voice, I froze, a pair of slippers clutched mid-air. I couldn't make out her words, but there was no mistaking her tone, smooth and consoling.

Then a low and steady wailing rose into an unrestrained howl. "So young, so full of potential. How can this be?" It took me a second to believe this could be Ahpwa. I'd never heard her so emotional, so undisciplined.

Mother's voice again, quiet, soothing, reassuring.

Then Ahpwa: "I am so ashamed."

I sat down on the bed and closed my eyes, slippers still clenched in my hand as remorse descended over me like a thick, grey cloud. To think I'd shamed Ahpwa.

"How can I tell him that it's me who's responsible? That I might've stopped it," Ahpwa continued.

Tell who? Stop what?

Father's voice, firm, steady: "There's nothing you could've done. This is bigger than all of us."

I looked down at the slippers I'd worn every day for two and half months, the soles just beginning to crack. Bigger than all of us? What was he talking about? It struck me then that I might not be the only reason we were leaving, that they had secrets too. That's why no one was confronting me. I should have been relieved; instead I was scared, Ahpwa's wail summoning back the screams of students, the thuds of the billy clubs. My stomach heaved, and I wished suddenly that I'd been caught. At least then I could shed this secret, tell someone what I'd seen.

Parker and San San came back into the bedroom, and I held out my arms. She climbed onto my lap, smelling like coconut and jasmine. Then San San sat down next to me and put her arms around us both.

"Tell Shwe that I'll write to him," I said.

"Yes, Miss Etta. I will tell him, and I will take care of him. Don't worry."

PART TWO

ONE

I follow the stream of passengers down the escalator to immigration, separated from the arrival's hall by a two-story glass wall. I spot Parker right away, her blond hair setting her apart from the crowd of people waiting for loved ones. Dressed in a traditional baby blue *htamein* that reaches her ankles, she looks lovelier than ever. With a rush of affection, I realize how much I've missed her. No matter what happens with Shwe or Ahpwa's ashes, I'm glad I came.

I'm about to wave when she turns to speak to the man next to her. Dressed in a plain grey tee shirt and jeans, he has long, dark hair gathered into a ponytail and thick, muscular arms. I can't make out the features of his face from here, but something about the way he stands, hands stuffed in his pockets, tells me it's Shwe. Fighting a sudden compulsion to flee, I duck into the ladies' room before they see me.

I spent much of the flight imagining what it might be like to see Shwe again, checking again and again that the letters were still there as I ran through various scenarios in my mind, knowing that he probably dismissed me years ago, yet still hoping otherwise, that despite the distance and lack of contact, the connection would still be there. But in none of these scenarios did I expect to see him right now. I'd counted on Parker coming to the airport alone, the two of us sitting side by side in the back of a taxi, restoring our bond as we brought each other up to date on the last few weeks and decided together what to do about Ahpwa's ashes.

"*Mingalaba*," says a young woman leaning on a mop in the corner of the bathroom. Auspiciousness to you.

"*Mingalaba*," I answer, startled.

Barely old enough to be working, the young woman is dressed in a pale-blue uniform, a stroke of *thanaka* painted down the length of her nose and across her cheeks. She pushes her mop around the floor, while I smooth out my shirt and splash my face with water. The circles under my eyes are a deep purple, my hair staticky and snarled. I dig around the bundle of letters in my carry-on in search of a brush and some concealer. Nothing. In the distraction of saying goodbye to Jason, of trying to ease his angst about my departure, I must have packed them in my checked bag. I zip up the carry-on and begin combing through my hair with my fingers.

"*Hla deh*," says the woman in the mirror. You are beautiful.

The reflection of her face, so open and welcoming, fills me with excitement—not because she's told me I'm beautiful, but because, until this moment, until this woman spoke to me, I didn't really believe I was coming back.

"*Jezu tin badeh*," I answer with a slight genuflection the way Ahpwa taught me. Thank you.

She covers her mouth to suppress a giggle.

And then I laugh, too. I've always had trouble with Burmese notions of hierarchy. The young woman might bow to me, but given the difference in our age and class, I need not bow to her.

She stands off to the side as I wash my hands, then passes me a rolled-up wad of toilet tissue to dry them.

"How long have you been away?" she asks, and I realize with a tickle of satisfaction that she thinks I'm fully Burmese, one of the many exiles who've returned to Burma since the country began to open up last year. Growing up in the whitewashed suburbs of Boston, I was quick to correct anyone who suggested I wasn't American. But as I stand here now in this airport bathroom mistaken for fully Burmese, my lungs swell with pride.

"Too long." I dab my hands carefully with the toilet paper so that it doesn't stick to my skin.

"*Pyet asin pyin khana.*" She quotes an old Burmese proverb I remember from Ahpwa's lessons. An error may go on forever but can be set right in an instant.

"Thank you." I bow again, flouting convention on purpose this time. Then I head back into the arrivals lounge and wave to Parker and Shwe before I lose my nerve.

Parker points at me and begins jumping up and down. Shwe looks up and nods. His brow and jawline are more pronounced, more masculine, and he's much taller and broader, of course, but he's every bit as captivating as I remember. He says something to Parker that makes her laugh, and I feel a pinch of insecurity. If only I could hear his words, gauge the pitch and intensity of his tone.

As I wait in the immigration queue, the barrier between us obscured now by frosted glass, I consider possible ways to greet him—hug? kiss on both cheeks? shake hands?—then eliminate each one as too American, too pretentious, too formal. The immigration officer stamps my passport with a loud thwack, and I startle.

Collecting my suitcase, I take an uneasy breath and plunge into the crowd of people. Parker runs forward and jumps on me, nearly knocking me over. I smile and hug her back, the warmth of her embrace tempering my apprehension about Shwe, for a moment, at least.

"I didn't think you'd really come." She squeezes the air out of my lungs.

Why not? I want to ask but let it go, hugging her once more before turning to Shwe.

"Hi." My voice catches.

"Hey, Etta." Hands still in pockets.

I wince. Shwe never called me Etta. Not once. From that

very first car ride until the day we left the country two and a half months later, I'd only ever been Aye.

We don't embrace or kiss or shake hands. Instead we stand silently looking at each other. I search his face for how much he remembers. I want to tell him how often I've thought of him, how much he still means to me, but a remoteness in his eyes strangles my words. Seeing Parker watch us, I look away.

"I'll take that." He reaches for my suitcase. A long, angry scar runs from his elbow down to his wrist.

"What happened?" I touch the scar without thinking.

"Nothing. It was a long time ago." He takes his arm back but there's no trace in his tone or manner of the inner turmoil I feel. Either he doesn't share the same memories, or he's long since made peace with them.

As we head toward the airport exit, Shwe walks several paces in front. On the back of his neck, the greenish-black head of a reptilian creature stares back at me, its horns and fangs sharp and curved like daggers, the rest of its body disappearing under the collar of his tee-shirt. A dragon, the zodiac sign for those born on a Saturday.

I recall the fortuneteller with a rush of tenderness and regret, but does he even remember? Part of me wants to pull out my letters right here in the middle of the airport and wave them in the air for him to see. Show him that I did write. For a whole year. Long, sappy love letters describing my every fear and desire. But what would that prove? The truth is that I did give up on him. Ahpwa might've prevented me from contacting him initially, but I've had countless opportunities to seek him out in the intervening two decades. Why did I wait so long to come back?

"What was that about?" Parker grabs my arm as she pulls me out of Shwe's earshot.

"What?" I say, the thrill of seeing my little sister already clouded with irritation.

106

"You guys didn't even hug."

"Burmese people don't hug, Parker."

"Really? Well I hugged everyone when I arrived."

I look away, stung by my own arrogance.

"And we are Myanmar, Etta, not Burmese." She runs ahead to catch up with Shwe.

Watching the two of them in front of me—Shwe gliding along with an air of indestructibility, as if nothing can touch him, Parker hovering next to him like a hummingbird, chatting and gesticulating without pause—I wish suddenly that Jason had come with me. But is that right? Do I want Jason because he's Jason, or because I don't want to be alone?

~

As we emerge into the sun-drenched parking lot, the humidity almost knocks me over. I follow Parker and Shwe to an old taxi parked in the splintered shade of a palm tree. The car is an unfamiliar model, boxlike with sharp angles reminiscent of the 1980s. Shwe opens the trunk and places my suitcase next to a crate of tools on the unfinished floor panel. I lift my hand to block the glare of the sun. Shwe drives a taxi?

"It's yours?" I ask.

He places his hand on the roof of the car. "Yep, my one and only possession. Don't know what I'd do without her."

I'm baffled by the way he speaks about the car, so carefree and easygoing, as if driving a taxi is the best job in the world. Perhaps it's snobbish, but I can't help thinking it beneath him. He was so inquisitive as a teenager, so determined, I imagined him in a more intellectual profession. Or at least a more high-profile one, given how prominent his family was.

Parker takes the front seat as if by right. Under different

circumstances, I might challenge her, but it's better this way. Sitting in the back gives me time to collect myself, make a plan.

The taxi looks even older on the inside, the once-stylish, leather seats worn bare, with holes in the floor where rust has run riot. I can't see a seatbelt, but Parker doesn't seem bothered, so I let it go. The last thing I want is to call attention to how vulnerable and out of place I feel right now. The steering wheel's on the right side, as in the UK, so when Shwe pulls out of the lot, I expect him to merge into the left lane. Instead he keeps to the right, so close to the side of the road he could reach out and touch the passersby. I grip the threadbare seat as he navigates the first disconcerting intersection, making the wide left turn from the wrong side of the car. That's when I remember: they drive on the right here, with the steering wheel on the right, too.

The air conditioning doesn't seem to work. Or works but doesn't reach the backseat. That must be it because Parker and Shwe seem perfectly comfortable while I am sweltering. The more I think about the heat, the more stifled I feel.

"How do you open the window?" I touch a naked rivet where the window handle should be.

Shwe reaches over Parker's lap, opens the glove compartment and pulls out the disembodied window handle, which he passes back to me.

Parker grins. "Isn't it charming? Like being on the set of an old movie."

Here is the fundamental difference between the two of us. Parker's a perpetual optimist, always making the most out of any situation, while I tend to be more pragmatic, and maybe a little too serious. I study the handle, carefully fastening it on to the rivet before rolling down the window. The air is thick and moist but a relief from the suffocating atmosphere inside the taxi.

We pass an old colonial mansion marbled with black

mildew, followed by a large construction site, where barefoot workers balance precariously on bamboo scaffolding three stories high. I look at Shwe's profile—the ponytail, the bulge of his Adam's apple, a sinister dragon talon clawing the side of his neck. How many more tattoos lie beneath his tee shirt? How many more scars? Once upon a time, we were so close we shared the same thoughts. Now I barely recognize him.

You don't know how lucky you are, Ahpwa said so often after we returned from Burma in 1988 that it became a kind of game to complete the phrase in my head before she did. But I didn't feel lucky, and she didn't elaborate. It wasn't until my early twenties, when I began to quietly educate myself, that I learned about the continued brutality, widespread arrests, and university closures. By that time, my memory of Shwe had fossilized into something precious but unreachable, buried under layers of sadness and guilt. I couldn't imagine him among the jarring images of teargas and Merck rifles I saw in the video footage because, in my mind, he remained the beautiful, sensitive teenaged boy I'd once known.

A cloud moves across the sun, casting a shadow over the road. Shwe switches on the radio and the plaintive notes of a familiar Adele song fill the car. The singer has a lovely voice, but I know it's not Adele because she's singing in Burmese. I look out the window, humming along to the song as I try to make out the words. There's something familiar about the wide, open boulevard, but no, it can't be; there aren't enough trees. We stop at a large intersection, where men in straw hats weave among the cars selling small packets of betel nut wrapped in green leaves. A woman with a club hand approaches Shwe's window and he hands her a few *kyat*.

Soon we're driving alongside a body of water, its banks landscaped with clusters of low-lying purple shrubs shaped into

Myanmar script, spelling "Welcome." I sit upright, craning my neck for a better look. A white brick pathway runs along the edge of the lake. Walkers and joggers compete for space with umbrella-capped carts selling assorted refreshments and what looks like bubble-making machines. Young couples huddle behind umbrellas in a wooded area off to the side, just as Shwe and I once did.

I concentrate on my breath. In, out. In, out.

The grounds are more elegantly landscaped now, but I can still pick out the tree under which I had my first kiss, the patch of bushes from where I watched riot police force a young woman's head under water until the surface grew quiet and still. Today, as then, the lake seems implausibly serene.

I look in the rearview mirror and see that Shwe is watching me, a trace of the old softness in his eyes.

TWO

Parker and I drifted through the cold, dark rooms opening heating ducts and drawing back curtains. The furnace clicked and hissed, as if protesting the sudden commotion, rejecting our premature reentry. I stopped in front of my bedroom window, struck by the bleak reality of a Boston winter, the leafless trees like skeletons against an anemic sky. After 36 hours of traveling, we were home.

Downstairs, Mother cooed and coaxed in that same, cloying tone she'd used with Ahpwa in Rangoon—the one she'd never used with me, or even Parker. Then Father joined in, and her pleas were replaced by thumping and shuffling as they shepherded Ahpwa up the stairs. I peeked out my bedroom door just as they reached the landing, Ahpwa suspended between my parents like an unstrung marionette. My grandmother looked as if she'd aged a decade, her cheeks pale and hollow, her beautiful black hair streaked with ribbons of grey I'd never noticed before.

"She's tired from the trip," said Mother, as if that explained anything.

"She just needs a little time," added Father, his voice weak and unconvincing, like crumpled up newspaper.

Ahpwa swung her head in my direction, a wildness in her eyes that sent a chill down my spine.

~

One day bled into the next, a blur of hushed meals and long, dark nights, of jetlag and loss. No matter how high we turned the thermostat, I couldn't stop shivering. No one knew that we'd returned, so we stayed home from work and school that week, taking "a little time to recover from the journey," as Mother declared over and over. Ahpwa remained in her bedroom, my parents taking turns carrying up trays of tea and soup. Parker and I were under strict orders not to disturb her.

One morning, while Mother was out grocery shopping, I entered the kitchen to find Father assembling Ahpwa's breakfast tray: one small bowl of sticky rice, a glass of prune juice, and a pot of freshly brewed *lah phet yay*. He looked up from the tray and searched my eyes as if considering how best to answer a question I hadn't voiced.

"How'd you like to bring Ahpwa her tray today?" He made a halfhearted attempt at his old conspiratorial wink.

I looked at him in confusion. Mother said not to bother Ahpwa. I didn't want to get in trouble, or worse, get Father in trouble, the tension between them mounting by the day. But the prospect of seeing Ahpwa touched a soft spot, revealing an emptiness I hadn't known was there. The truth was that I missed my grandmother; I missed her exacting lessons and constant upbraiding, the way she pursed her lips when she called me *Myi*, disappointment and love all tangled together in a tone reserved only for me. In Burma, I'd been too preoccupied by the twin mysteries of Shwe and the city of Rangoon to feel anything beyond relief at her lack of attentiveness. Now that we were back in this cold house, I saw that our family didn't function without Ahpwa; she was the spindle around which our household rotated, the central defining force upon which we all relied in one way or another.

I squared my shoulders and took the tray from Father. Navigating the stairs while holding the tray was harder than it looked. I didn't anticipate not being able to see my feet. As I stepped onto the second-floor landing, my foot caught on the lip of carpet at the top of the final stair. I lurched forward, jutting out my arms to protect the tray. I didn't fall, but when I looked down at the tray, prune juice had sloshed over the rim of the glass, saturating the napkin. Ahpwa would be furious. I considered turning back, retreating to the kitchen to sponge down the tray and get a new napkin, but a blaze of defiance propelled me forward. A scolding would be a relief.

Ahpwa lay in bed, head propped up on a stack of pillows, staring at me with an intensity that stole my breath. Her hair was wild, a halo of grey tangles that made her look almost childlike.

"Good morning, Ahpwa," I said with a slight genuflection. "I brought you some breakfast."

She remained silent, but I sensed her eyes on me as I set the tray on the bedside table. Could feel them on me still as I walked over to the window to open the red, silk curtains.

"Is there anything else I can get for you, Ahpwa?" I stood in front of her bed with my hands down at my sides, my heart drumming in my ears.

The same, unsettling stare, inquisitive but detached, like a spectator watching a performance, a bystander in her own house. What did she see when she looked at me? Had my transgression really caused this illness, this collapse, or was there something more, something bigger than us, as Father had said back in Rangoon?

I picked her hairbrush off the vanity and held it out with a trembling hand. "Would you like me to brush your hair, Ahpwa?"

Still no response. I imagined taking a step forward, sitting down next to her on the side of the bed. Picking up a lock of that long, beautiful hair, still shiny and strong despite the new streaks of gray. Pulling the brush through the snarls until her hair ran smooth and glossy. But my feet remained stuck to the ground. If only she'd stop staring at me, if only she'd speak, shout even. That's what I wanted above all—for Ahpwa to shout at me again.

"Okay, I guess I'll go now then." I backed slowly out of the room, thankful to have escaped her wrath for now but fearful of what lay ahead. Though I did not yet know its shape, this was the beginning of *America the Beautiful*, a period in which everything I believed about my family would be turned on its head.

THREE

"You look like hell," says Parker as we enter her too-bright apartment. "Maybe you should take a nap or a shower or something."

"Gee, thanks." I feign offense, but after the stiffness of the car ride, her ribbing comes as a relief.

Shwe dropped us off a few minutes ago with little more than a grunt, though Parker did make him promise to pick us up later for dinner. Apparently, she's organized a get-together with all of our cousins. There's so much I need to talk to Parker about—how long she intends to stay, what she has or hasn't done with Ahpwa's ashes, what she knows about Shwe's life—but she's right: I'm so tired, my body feels like a pile of bricks.

"Sheila's gone back to Melbourne for a few weeks," says Parker. Sheila's her roommate, an Australian woman who works at a social enterprise for former prostitutes. "So, luckily for both of us, we don't have to share a room."

I feel a prick of rejection that Parker doesn't want to room with me; we always shared a room growing up. But mostly I'm relieved. I don't think I could cope with her watching my every move. Especially here in Yangon. Besides, Parker's a slob.

"Wake me up before dinner?"

After a quick hug, I drag my bags into Sheila's room and heave them onto the bed. Aside from a crooked Burma Railway poster hanging above the headboard, the walls are bare. Two grated windows look out over a crowded market, where flashes of color peek through clouds of dust and smoke. I can already feel the pull of the market, the smell of burning charcoal and chatter of vendors swirling together to make my heart beat just a little faster. Tomorrow....

An old-fashioned teak dresser with corroded brass handles and a broken foot stands against the opposite wall. On top of the dresser, like an exposed artery, sits the red and black urn from the funeral parlor. I draw back in surprise. The last time I saw the urn was when Parker and I argued in the café. She didn't seem to want me near it then, guarding our grandmother's ashes with a possessiveness that shook my confidence.

Leaving the urn in the room I am to sleep in means one of two things: either she's done it, she's scattered Ahpwa's remains somewhere in Yangon, or she wants my help, and understanding. An image of Parker sitting on the plane with the urn in her lap hits me in the gut. It can't have been easy, doing all this alone. I'm still not convinced that this is where Ahpwa belongs, and I sure wish she'd consulted me before making such a big decision, but I can't help admiring her bravery in coming all this way on her own.

I approach the urn with a mix of grief and curiosity. I can't quite believe Ahpwa's gone, that she's not about to walk in right now to admonish me for not putting a towel under the suitcase or some other wrongdoing that no one else in the world would notice. Placing both hands around the urn's base, I lift it just enough to gauge its weight.

Relief washes over me; the urn is still full. The idea of Parker bringing Ahpwa here had made me more uneasy than I'd been willing to admit. Not for the reasons Jason thinks, not because I'm jealous or resentful of Parker suddenly taking charge, but because I can't shake the feeling that there was something more to Ahpwa's narrative, that her love for U Soe Htet wasn't the only thing she was hiding. And until we know more, I don't see how we can decide on her final resting place.

Whirling back to the bed, I dig around my carry-on until I find the small statue of Yatheik that U Soe Htet carved for me. I place the statue on the dresser next to Ahpwa. At least now, they can be together. Tomorrow, I'll run down to the market to buy flowers for any jealous *nat* spirits lingering nearby. Then Parker and I can begin the task of figuring out what to do with the ashes.

I leave the three jars of extra chunky peanut butter on the bed, as far away from the urn as possible. Ahpwa hated peanut butter. Even at the height of *America the Beautiful*, she considered it an unfortunate defect of an otherwise perfect nation. Growing up, we must have been the only family in our entire neighborhood that didn't have a jar in our house. I still can't eat so much as a peanut butter cookie without feeling disrespectful, but it doesn't seem to bother Parker.

Finally, I take out the letters, still wrapped in the purple scarf, and lie down between the empty suitcase and the peanut butter. Before I left Boston, I thought Myanmar would be the right place to open the letters, but now that I'm here, I'm not so sure. Writing a love letter is like tying a bit of your soul to a balloon and letting it go. Once the envelope is sealed, the words cease to belong to you. I close my eyes and imagine my adolescent words and doodles floating over the Bay of Bengal.

~

Parker's sitting on the edge of the bed eating peanut butter out of the jar with a spoon when I open my eyes.

"Wha's thah?" She points to the purple scarf, her words muffled by a mouthful of peanut butter.

"Please don't eat on my bed," I say.

"It's not your bed, it's Sheila's." She thinks for a minute, then adds, "Actually it's the landlord's."

I glare at her. "Okay, please don't eat on this bed, which is owned by the landlord, rented by Sheila, and currently occupied by me."

"Geesh, you don't have to get all lawyer-ey." She takes one final lick of peanut butter and puts the used spoon back into the jar. If I didn't know better, I'd think she was trying to gross me out on purpose. But Parker is never deliberately malicious; her specialty is annoying me without trying. She walks over to the dresser and places the open jar of peanut butter between Ahpwa's urn and the Yatheik statue, which she doesn't acknowledge.

I swallow my frustration. "So what's the plan, Parker?"

"Shwe's coming back at 6:00 and then all the cousins are going out to dinner."

"I meant with the ashes."

"Oh, that." She looks back at the urn and frowns. "I thought it would be clear once I got here, but all my leads just kind of fizzled." Her eyes widen with a hopeful expression. "I thought maybe, now that you're here…"

"Seriously?"

She offers me an apologetic smile and lies down next to me. I don't know whether to throttle her or cuddle up next to her. I choose the latter.

~

I slip on the traditional red silk outfit that Parker's given me as a welcome gift with the proviso that I wear it to dinner tonight. Buttoned on the side, the *yinbon* is perfectly fitted to my torso, its matching *htamein* gently hugging my hips before descending into a mass of hand-embroidered Burmese designs. If only Ahpwa could see me now.

I enter the living room at twilight just as Shwe reappears.

"Oh good, you're here." Parker sweeps through the room to greet him with a familiar kiss on the cheek. "Just hopping in the shower. Make yourself at home." Then she disappears into the bathroom, taking all the air with her.

I look at Shwe from across the room, wishing I could feel as free with him as Parker seems to, and as I once did. He, too, has changed for the evening. Instead of a tee shirt and jeans, he wears a white *leh gadone* with a black and red *longyi*, knotted in front as is customary for men. The effect is surprisingly masculine, the flow of fabric accentuating his perfectly proportioned muscles and limbs. He raises his eyebrows, and my cheeks flame. How long have I been staring at him?

"Want some?" He holds up a bottle of Mandalay Rum he's produced out of nowhere.

"Sure," I say, uncertainly. I'm not much of a drinker, especially of rum.

Sitting down in the middle of the sofa, he pours us each a glass, then leans back with a familiarity that tells me he's been here more than once. I take the chair opposite the sofa.

"Nice *htamein*," he says. It's more observation than compliment, but at least he's talking.

"Thanks. I like your *longyi*. Did Parker make you dress up too?"

His lips form the beginnings of a smile.

"I feel a bit like my grandmother, dressed like this." I take a sip of rum and grimace.

"She was very beautiful, your grandmother."

A quickening under my ribs, like a small child opening her eyes after a long sleep.

For a second neither of us speaks.

"I hear you're a lawyer," he says.

The directness of his manner unsettles me, but the rum

loosens my lips. "It's funny, Ahpwa always wanted me to become a lawyer, and for most of my life I resisted the idea—mainly because it was hers, not mine. She didn't care what I liked or didn't like, just made me study all the time, insisting I had to be better than everyone else. It's hard to explain how much I resented it, how much I resented her."

He nods, and I wonder whether it means that he remembers this about me, or simply that he's listening.

"But when I started college, with the freedom to study whatever I wanted, I found myself drawn to courses in social justice and human rights, and before I knew it, I was enrolled in law school and, well, that was that." I pause, alarmed as much by what I've left out as by what I've said. Being a lawyer in a large employment law firm bears little relation to human rights.

"And you like it?" he asks. He doesn't say it the way Parker would; I detect no judgment or condescension in his tone. But when I look into his deep brown eyes, I see the truth.

"How about you? Is there something else you do besides drive a taxi?" I take another sip of rum.

He studies me for a few seconds. "You're a bit of a snob, aren't you?"

"Oh, I didn't... I mean, it's a perfectly noble...Shit." I cover my mouth with my hand.

Then he laughs for the first time all day, and the room seems suddenly lighter, more spacious.

"Fact is, I love driving a taxi. I get to spend the whole day exploring a city I can't get enough of, meeting all kinds of people I might not otherwise meet. Government employees. Foreigners. Drug dealers." He laughs again, and I'm ready to put a thousand more feet in my mouth to see more of this side of him.

"But yeah, there is something else I do besides *drive a taxi*." He draws out the last three words. "I'm a writer, a journalist to be specific. I usually write under a pseudonym, but I've just started a blog in my own name. As a kind of experiment. You should check it out."

I nod, still kicking myself for my earlier blunder but reassured by the fact that my instinct was correct, that I still know him. Shwe being a journalist fits. As a teenager, he noticed everything—a new stain on his mother's blouse, the smell of burning rubber on the street, the absence of the lady who sold mangos on the corner. He was always watching and listening to the grown-ups, always wanting to know why, even if that meant sneaking around to find the truth. As I look at him now, splayed out on the sofa, it occurs to me that maybe that was the whole point—he liked sneaking around. This insatiable curiosity of his left me a little breathless in those days, sparking my own desire for knowledge, my own tentative, liberation from Ahpwa. But there's a recklessness about him now, a flash of defiance in his eyes, that scares me.

"Shwe is Moe Pwint," says Parker, breezing into the room in a royal blue *htamein*.

Moe Pwint. Where do I know that name? A nagging sense of familiarity pricks under my skin as I run through the various publications where I might have seen it—*The Globe*? *The Economist*? *Newsweek*? Then I remember: The printouts in Ahpwa's wedding chest. The journalist who won a PEN award for a series of essays smuggled out of Insein prison. Ruminations on morality and immorality, torture and resistance. Dog cages. I look back at Shwe in desperation, hoping that I'm wrong, that he's not the same person who wrote those essays, who experienced those horrors. He doesn't return my gaze, but a faraway look on his face tells me that it's true, his life has been far worse than I let myself imagine.

"He's super famous. Right, Shwe?" adds Parker. "You guys ready to go?"

I force myself to stand, take a step forward, act normal. But inside, I'm spinning backwards, chiding myself for not knowing, for going about my small, insignificant life while he crouched behind bars in a cage half his height. Alone and afraid. I know on a certain level how illogical I'm being. I was only thirteen years old, after all, not to mention halfway across the world. Knowing wouldn't have changed anything. Yet I can't shake the conviction that it's my fault, that his life might've turned out differently, if only I hadn't left so abruptly back in 1988.

I follow Parker and Shwe down the narrow stairwell, stepping cautiously so as not to lose my balance. On the street, a clamor of color and noise make my head whirl, honking cars and hungry vendors filling the air with unchecked enthusiasm. Not until I sink into the back of Shwe's battered taxi does it hit me: Ahpwa knew that Shwe was Moe Pwint. That's why she kept the stories. What I can't understand is why she didn't tell me, why she hid them away in her chest of secrets. It's nearly dark now, pedestrians like shadows in the fading light, yet few of the cars have their headlights on, as if the drivers are waiting for a truer part of the night to begin.

FOUR

Boston, Massachusetts
1988

The peal of the doorbell resounded through the quiet house like a monk's gong. Ahpwa was still cloistered away in her bedroom. Aside from a few trips to the grocery store, no one had come or gone since we landed back in Boston one week before.

Parker flew down the stairs but I beat her to the door, swinging it open to find the older Thai woman who usually trims our hair. As I stood staring at the woman in confusion, Ahpwa glided down the staircase dressed in a white sweater and grey woolen skirt.

"Go fetch an old sheet from the linen closet," said Mother, coming up behind me in the front hall. "Ahpwa's organized for us to have our hair cut."

I shrunk back at the high-pitched falsity in Mother's voice but was too stunned to see Ahpwa out of bed and dressed in Western clothes to make a fuss. The house buzzed with expectancy as we took turns washing our hair in the kitchen sink. Ahpwa, who as far as I knew had not spoken in a week, now chatted with the hairdresser while Mother and Father moved the sofa against the wall and covered the rug with the old bedsheet. Mother, Father, Parker and I squeezed next to each other on the sofa, an audience of four.

Ahpwa seated herself majestically in the middle of the room, her long, wet hair hanging loose over the top of the stool. I couldn't take my eyes off of her. I didn't know what to expect—a new hairstyle perhaps, or a short trim to clean up loose ends. For as long as I could remember, Ahpwa and Mother had worn their hair in the same traditional knot at the nape of their necks while Parker and I wore ours in a single, ribboned braid down the center of our backs. The hairdresser fastened the white, vinyl cape around Ahpwa's neck, combing through the cascade of hair before separating it into segments, which she fastened to Ahpwa's head with sharp metal, dragon clips.

With a sudden blaze of purpose, the hairdresser sliced through the bottom layer of hair from the nape of Ahpwa's neck all the way around to her chin.

I watched in disbelief as locks of Ahpwa's beautiful, thick hair fell to the floor like shiny black snakes.

"Whoa!" said Parker, the only one in the room who still had a voice.

The hairdresser continued to shore through the remaining tresses until Ahpwa's entire neck was exposed. Disbelief crystallized into panic as I realized that this would soon be my fate too. I held my breath as she stood up and unfastened the cape. *Not me, please. Not my hair*. Father put his hand on my knee, but I could tell by the force of his grip that he was as alarmed as I was.

Mother stood and took the cape from Ahpwa. I exhaled.

Her fine, brown hair had never been as thick and beautiful as Ahpwa's, but seeing Mother submit to the hairdresser's scissors was nearly as unsettling as watching Ahpwa. Why didn't Mother stand up to Ahpwa? What was it about Ahpwa that made us all so powerless? I thought of Shwe and steeled myself to be stronger and more independent, the way I'd started to be in Burma. I'd start again now, setting a new precedent for all of us.

Mother tossed her head with a shrill laugh, then gave the cape an offhand shake and held it out to me.

I looked uncertainly at Father, my resolve quickly fading.

He shook his head slowly, as if to say, *Sorry, I don't know either*.

"Come, granddaughter. We mustn't keep the hairdresser waiting," said my new, short-haired grandmother, her shiny, wet hair curling under her jawbone like the tail of a scorpion. It was the first time she'd spoken to me since our return.

Staring at that white cape, now covered in sticky wet hair, I saw that Burma had not made me stronger, but weaker, the events of the last ten days draining whatever courage I might've once had. I accepted the cape and climbed onto the stool, resigned to my fate. I deserved this punishment, after all. Even if my crime had gone unnamed, I knew what I'd done. What I'd risked.

As the hairdresser combed through my hair, I felt as if my scalp were enveloped in a cushion of mist. I heard a distant snip of scissors, then a sharp intake of air from Father. Parker whimpering. The hairdresser removed the cape and handed me the mirror. I smarted at the bluntness of the style, an unsophisticated bob that made my cheeks and forehead look excessively wide. In the span of ten minutes, I no longer recognized the person I'd been in Burma, the blossoming young woman Shwe'd wanted to impress having been transformed into a puppet, a spineless, passionless collection of wooden parts.

On Parker, the hairdresser's cape reached all the way to the floor, as if she were wearing a wizard costume. A small blond wizard. Under different circumstances, it might've been funny. A better, stronger big sister might've tried to distract her with a joke, but I couldn't summon the energy. I was about to rejoin the others on the sofa, when she erupted.

"NOOOOO! I DON'T WANNA LOOK LIKE A BOYYYYYY!" she screamed, whipping the cheap, polyester cape off her neck and hurling it across the living room.

I stepped back in alarm. Didn't she know better than to embarrass Ahpwa in front of the hairdresser? Had I not taught her that, at least? This was bad. Very bad.

No one moved. Parker put her hands on her hips and looked around the room with an air of startled victory, as if this was not the outcome she expected, but she was nevertheless pleased. Then she turned and darted up the stairs.

The hairdresser stared down at her kit, fiddling with the flawless lineup of scissors and combs.

Ahpwa pursed her lips—whether in disapproval or confusion, I could no longer tell.

"I'll get her," said Mother, getting up wearily.

"Let her be," said Father, placing his hand on Mother's arm. "This has gone too far."

For one, viscous moment, I worried that he was referring to me, that I'd somehow messed up again. But wasn't the pile of black hair on the floor proof of my obedience? I understood then that "this" did not mean me, but Ahpwa—how irrational she'd become since leaving Burma.

Everyone except the hairdresser turned to look at my grandmother. The old Ahpwa would have taken this opportunity to lecture us on family mores, that particular set of customs and conventions that defined who we were and how we behaved. Even if I didn't always understand Ahpwa's actions, I took comfort in their predictability, in the constancy of her beliefs. This was Ahpwa's power—an unwavering certitude about what was right for our family.

But my grandmother's response was not addressed to any of us. Instead, she turned to the hairdresser, and said in her most formal English, "Thank you for your services. That will be all for today."

As she escorted the hairdresser to the door, Father put his face in his hands, while Mother closed her eyes and laid her newly coiffed head against the back of the sofa. I didn't know which bothered me more—Ahpwa's unpredictability or the fact that Parker was getting away with this, that I'd had to cut off my beautiful, long hair, and Parker hadn't. Even harder to swallow was the recognition that Parker had stood up to Ahpwa, while I, the older sister, the one who was supposed to be stronger, braver and more mature, had chickened out. So this was how things were going to be now. In addition to having no hair, I would have no voice.

I stared at the tangled mess of hair clippings strewn across the bedsheet and wondered how we'd ever get it clean again, all that sticky hair clinging to the sheet like a bad dream. The easiest solution would be to bundle the whole sorry incident into a ball and throw it in the trash with the broken egg shells and misplaced dreams.

"Don't worry, Sweetheart," said Father. "It'll grow back."

I gave him a hopeful smile, but I already knew that I wouldn't wear my hair long again.

FIVE

Parker's reserved a table at Taing Yin Thar, an upscale Myanmar restaurant that recently opened in north Yangon. Joining us are some of the cousins I remember as little girls: Thandar, Phyu Phyu, and Shwe's little sister Khaing Zar.

We meet Khaing Zar in front of the restaurant, chitchatting and swatting at mosquitoes as we wait for the others in the thick night air. She has the same brown hair and dark eyes as Shwe but is more petite, with a slender frame and a warm smile. I find her easy to talk with, the questions she asks simple but sincere: *How was my trip? What do I think of Yangon? How does it feel to be back?* As we talk, she slips her arm around her brother's waist, like a mother quietly reassuring her son, and I'm glad to see that he has someone, that he hasn't been alone all these years.

I learn that Khaing Zar is a program officer at the United Nations World Food Programme. I'm about to ask more about her work when a sleek, black SUV pulls up in front of us. Shwe and Khaing Zar stiffen as the driver jumps out to open the back door. Dressed in a glittery, silver *htamein,* an elaborately made-up woman unfolds herself from the back seat, taking a moment to straighten her dress. In the meantime, a second, equally bedazzled woman emerges from the other side, and they both turn to face us. Our cousins, Thandar and Phyu Phyu. Not only rich, but flashy, pretentious, a type I'd normally dismiss as misguided and shallow. Why so different from Shwe and Khaing Zar? I'm instantly on alert, wanting to know at what point exactly their lives diverged. After a round of awkward hugs, more air than flesh, we head inside.

I seat myself between Shwe and Khaing Zar, while Parker sits on the other side of Shwe, Phyu Phyu on the other side of Khaing Zar, and Thandar at the head of the table. Khaing Zar orders the food as the rest of us catch up on each other's lives. Phyu Phyu is married with two kids and works in the hotel industry. Thandar is also married but without children. She owns a chain of jewelry stores in Yangon and Mandalay and is thinking about opening one in the new capital, Naypyitaw. Parker listens intently, asking lots of questions of our newly reacquainted cousins. But I can tell that she's also watching me, monitoring my actions for any indiscretions. Shwe keeps to himself, quietly nursing another glass of rum, as though the only way to get through this dinner is to numb his senses, to pretend he's elsewhere.

As we wait for the food, Thandar expounds on the politics of beauty contests in Yangon, her officious tone prickling under my skin like nettles. My eyes wander from her unnaturally thick eyelashes to the diamond and sapphire necklace around her throat. I remind myself that she owns a jewelry store, that this is her profession, her livelihood, but it's no good: I find the glitz excessive, unnecessary. Aside from my engagement ring and some gold earrings Jason gave me a few years back, I wear almost no jewelry. I look at Shwe to gauge his reaction, but he's withdrawn into himself, a faraway look on his face. I resist an urge to touch his arm. Khaing Zar gives me a knowing look.

"The Miss Butterfly Beauty Contest is this weekend. I can arrange tickets for you if you're interested," says Thandar, her hawk-like eyes converging on Parker and me.

"I'd love that!" says Parker.

I smile in agreement, but in my head, I'm already scheming how to get out of the invitation. I'm being snobby again, I know, but beauty contests aren't my thing, and I can't imagine spending any more time than necessary with Thandar. Parker's less judgmental in that way. She gives everyone a chance. Other than Jason, that is.

Shwe signals to the waiter to bring another glass of rum. How many is that now—three, four? Aside from his sister, no one else seems to notice how much he's drinking. Or maybe they do notice, and just don't care.

The salads begin to arrive—fresh pennywort leaves mixed with green chili, sour lime and roasted chickpea flour; succulent river prawns combined with fleshy pomelo then tossed with crispy fried onions, crunchy roasted peanuts, and fresh green coriander; pickled tea leaves mixed with hard green tomatoes, crunchy fried peas and tiny dried shrimp. Sharp, spicy, crunchy, salty, sour— every bite is an explosion of flavors, revving my taste buds into high alert. I've always loved spicy cuisine. The hotter, the better. When Ahpwa stopped cooking Burmese food during *America the Beautiful*, I lost so much weight, my father took me to the doctor. I still keep a jar of homemade chili paste in our fridge, adding the fiery mixture to just about everything I eat. To Jason's disbelief, I sometimes spread it on my toast, savoring the moment when the spicy chili ignites with a sip of hot coffee.

Thandar clears her throat. "You know we used to spy on the two of you?" She looks back and forth between Shwe and me.

I stop chewing in alarm. What does she mean? What did they see? A rush of tender, private memories ricochet through my mind. The enchantment in Shwe's eyes as we lie inches apart on the living room floor. Sitting on the sofa with our legs pressed furtively together. His impossibly soft lips the day we kissed. Memories I'm not ready to have paraded out for Thandar's enjoyment. Especially before Shwe and I have had a chance to talk about that time— what it meant then and what it means now.

"Of course, our spy missions were rather limited, thanks to old San San, but we had fun trying."

Beside me, Shwe's energy begins to sharpen and shift. I steal a glance, but his expression remains dark, unreadable.

"What ever happened to San San?" I ask in an attempt to steer the conversation in a different direction. And because I want to know.

Khaing Zar looks at her brother for a minute, as if to obtain his permission. "She lives out in northern Yangon with her two children."

"How is she? What–"

"The only time we ever managed to escape her control was the *Tabaung* festival. Remember *that*?" Thandar flashes her eyes at Parker and Phyu Phyu. "We followed them to the fairgrounds, hiding behind the other merrymakers every time they looked back."

Shwe shakes his head, his first contribution to the conversation all night. "They left before *Tabaung*." His voice is deep and smooth, not at all agitated.

I sneak another look at him, touched that he remembers so clearly the timing of our visit, that these details remain important to him, as they are to me. How I wish we could talk privately, rather than having our relationship dismembered limb by limb in front of the others.

Thandar waves her hand dismissively. "Then it must have been *Tabodwe*. That's right. I remember eating sticky rice while watching the two of you on the Ferris wheel, hoping to witness a kiss."

My cheeks flush as I remember the Ferris wheel. We watched the men build it that same afternoon, a whirl of beams and shouts and sweat that made me dizzy with fear. Once assembled, the contraption seduced me with its height and speed, a chance to see the world from a new perspective. Shwe gave me one of his intense, soul-strangling looks, and I clambered on next to him.

Unlike the Ferris wheels I'd seen back home, this one was fueled by manpower alone. A team of sinewy young men pulled the carts forward one by one until ours dangled at the very top, tipping back and forth like a rogue rocking horse. With the cars filled, the barefoot attendants scrambled up the spokes of the giant wheel, using their weight and the force of gravity to make it spin. Our cart plummeted downward, reaching the bottom within seconds, then dipping upward, ascending back to the top only to enter freefall once again. Giddy with fear and desire, I clutched onto Shwe. I, too, hoped for a kiss that day.

"So, Parker, how's your new job?" asks Khaing Zar.

I shoot her a grateful look, relieved not to have to discuss this private memory in front of the others. I remain quiet as Parker talks about how much she loves her job, how enthusiastic the kids are, how dedicated the other teachers.

"I hope they're paying you more than a local salary," says Thandar. "I don't know how anyone can survive on so little."

"A bit more," says Parker with a nervous laugh.

I make a mental note to ask her about this later.

As the others pepper Parker with questions, Shwe looks at my ring and says, "I see you're engaged."

His tone is curious but cool. There's no suggestion that he cares one way or another about my marital status. Why should he? Yet, all I can think about are the promises we made as teenagers— silly pledges about loving one another always, not marrying without the other's blessing, and never, ever becoming like our parents or grandparents.

"Yeah." I nod. "How about you? Did you ever marry?" Part of me hopes he has someone special in his life, someone like Jason to love him and keep him steady. As if this will somehow make us even. But another part feels like a child clinging to a toy I've long since outgrown but am unwilling to let go to another.

"Nah." He looks down at his drink.

Parker leans in. "Turns out Shwe's quite the lady's man. He especially likes Western girls. Isn't that right, Shwe?" I flinch, unaware that she was listening to our conversation.

He shrugs, takes another sip of rum.

I search his expression for a sign that she's wrong, that Shwe's not so irreverent or inconstant in love. That the silly, sensitive boy who taught me to skip rocks and play chinlone, and who always knew how to make me laugh, still exists. When he won't meet my eyes, I realize that it's true, a betrayal more painful than if he'd been married to the same woman for years. Because if Shwe's a lady's man, what does that say about the tenderness we once shared?

SIX

In the days and weeks that followed the haircut, I withdrew further into myself, convinced that the only person who could understand me was 10,000 miles away. At night, I scribbled long, heartfelt missives to Shwe, letters in which I confessed everything I'd felt for him in Burma and continued to feel for him still in Boston. In page after page of translucent, onion-skin paper, I told him about *America the Beautiful* and the strange, new tension between my parents, the nightmares that kept me up at night—visions of being chased through a maze of firehoses as I struggled to catch up with Shwe.

At the end of the week, I slipped my pages into the red and blue bordered airmail envelope that Ahpwa gave me, decorating the back with elaborate, colorful designs I thought he'd like. Then I painstakingly wrote out my aunty's address in both English and Burmese script and handed it back to Ahpwa, trusting the letter to make its way across the ocean to Shwe.

Life post-Burma had assumed a haze of detachment, as if I were watching myself perform in a silent movie, a motion picture that left me feeling numb and listless. After the haircuts, Ahpwa resumed her previous position at the center of our household, with one, mind-bending caveat: we were no longer Burmese. No more sweet, milky tea or spicy coconut noodles, no more reciting Burmese poetry or sitting through endless tutoring sessions; we were American now.

At school, I kept to myself, too thunderstruck to care about the nuances of schoolyard gossip. While other girls gushed about first kisses and slow dances, I remained quiet, my feelings for Shwe too tender to expose. The boys I watched through a prism of loneliness. They wore IZOD shirts and chinos, had feathered hair and played video games. Or they wore jeans and leather jackets, had flattop haircuts and played in a rock band. Before Burma, they appealed to me, in that fleeting but intense, middle school kind of way. Now I watched these same boys and girls from a distance, wondering if they noticed the way the starlings flocked together at the end of the day, or how the light changed just before dusk. After school, I'd rush straight home to check the mailbox.

Weeks passed. No return letter from Shwe.

"Sending a letter to America is too much risk," my grandmother told me one day in May as I stood next to the mailbox wiping my eyes with the back of my hand. "Things are very bad there now. The censors, they go through everything."

Ahpwa spoke so rarely about Burma, let alone Burmese politics, that this caught my attention. Could the Burmese government really prevent Shwe from writing to me? Until now, the only way to make sense of what Shwe and I witnessed that day, the only way to keep him safe in my mind, had been to view the massacre as an anomaly, something that never should've happened and could never happen again. The alternative was too much to bear—even if that meant the decision not to respond to me had been his and his alone.

A few weeks later, my eighth grade Social Studies teacher, Mrs. Clark, introduced a unit on the U.S. Constitution. As she went on about government for the people and by the people, the importance of individual rights and separation of power, I looked out at the puffy, white clouds moving slowly across the frame of my classroom window. How different life in Rangoon had been from this safe, boring classroom where we only ever talked about life in the abstract. How vivid and alive it had felt, unnerving, as if any minute the ground under my feet might give way. I couldn't quite grasp, let alone put into words, what it was that made me feel this way about Burma, but I suspected it had something to do with what Mrs. Clark was talking about now, and what Ahpwa had said the other day. About freedom, and what happens when we take it for granted.

"Who would like to read the first amendment out loud?" asked Mrs. Clark.

A tall, skinny girl with a constellation of pimples on her forehead stumbled through the awkward phrasing. "Congress shall make no law respecting an establishment of religion, or prohibiting the free exercise thereof; or abridging the freedom of speech, or of the press; or the right of the people peaceably to assemble, and to petition the Government for a redress of grievances."

"Who can tell us what that means?"

My hand shot up.

Mrs. Clark opened her eyes wide with surprise. "Yes, Etta."

"It means the government can't tell us what to believe or what to say."

"Very good. And why is that important?"

I paused, the clouds outside the window suddenly clearing. "Because words are like air. Without them, we can't survive. We can't breathe. To take away someone else's words is like, is like... strangling them."

These were the kinds of ruminations I'd been writing about in my letters to Shwe, but even I was surprised to have voiced them out loud. Silence fell over the classroom, twenty-two sets of eyes shifting in my direction, a quick, sideways look at the quiet girl with the new China doll haircut, recently returned after a long absence.

"Thank you, Etta," said Mrs. Clark after several seconds. "Let's move on to the Sixth Amendment. Who remembers what it says?"

After that I kept quiet. No one seemed to hear anything I said anymore. Not even Shwe.

SEVEN

"Wake up already." Parker's voice curls around the edges of my awareness as pain lances my upper arm.

I open my eyes briefly to the blank walls of Sheila's bedroom, the red and black urn atop the dresser slipping, herald-like, into the sticky, whirling images of my dream.

"Etta!" A second spasm of pain jolts me out of my slumber. I reopen my eyes to find Parker pinching my arm.

"Ouch," I protest, shielding my arm with my other hand. She's dressed in a sunny yellow *htamein*, her blonde hair gathered into a bun. I yawn, too tired to sustain my irritation. "You going to work?"

"Already back. It's after 2:00."

I sit up, stiff with guilt. I haven't called Jason.

"Come on. Get dressed," she continues. "I have a surprise for you."

I half groan, half yawn. I'd normally balk at Parker telling me what to do—especially when that plan involves a surprise—but I figure her outing relates to Ahpwa's ashes, and the sooner we sort that out, the sooner we can both go home.

"Fine," I say, "but I have to call Jason first. He must be worried sick."

Since she doesn't have a telephone in her apartment, Parker agrees to take me to the Central Telephone and Telegraph office on the way to her surprise destination. Calling now will mean waking Jason at 3:30 a.m., but with an eleven-and-a-half-hour time difference and no access to phone or internet, I have little choice.

As we plunge single file down the betel-splattered stairwell, a whisper of excitement flits across my chest. What if Parker asked Shwe to drive us again? What if he's waiting for us right now on the street below? Despite last night's revelations, I'm still drawn to him, still yearning to understand the intensity of that long-ago bond. Picking up my pace, I step on Parker's heel and dislodge her sandal.

"Ow, Etta! What's wrong with you?" She looks at me as if I've grown horns, and I wince. What if we never get back to the way we were, what if too much time has passed?

Spilling onto the street, I blink rapidly in the bright sunlight, the pungent smell of fish paste from the nearby market making my head spin. The air is so dense that the market appears hazy and surreal, vendors and shoppers moving in slow motion. Above us, tangled electrical wires and satellite dishes compete for space with laundry and storage on the balconies of the neighboring buildings. I look up and down the street in confusion.

Parker sticks out her hand and a taxi pulls over, the driver an older man with short hair and a receding hairline who regards us with unrestrained curiosity. Not Shwe, I register with equal doses of relief and disappointment. As much as I long to spend time with him, to understand the bond that once connected us, who we were then and who we are now, I can't do that with Parker in tow. I can't reconnect with Shwe in any meaningful way with her watching.

Parker negotiates the taxi fare in surprisingly good Burmese. Not quite as fluent as mine, perhaps, but considering she was only six when Ahpwa forbade us from speaking the language, I'm pretty darned impressed.

"Your Burmese is excellent, Bird."

The gleam of satisfaction in her eyes tells me how hard she's worked to get to this level of fluency. I see now why Parker'd been spending so much time at our childhood home: Ahpwa had been tutoring her. I pull the taxi's dirt-encrusted seatbelt across my torso, ignoring the flecks of dust on my top, only to find that the buckle is jammed under the seat. I'm not jealous exactly, just confused. Why would Ahpwa resume tutoring twenty-three years after expunging the language from our lives? I dig under the seat for the buckle.

"Just let it go," says Parker. For a second, I think she's talking about Ahpwa. Then I let go of the belt and sit back, untethered.

A few minutes later, I steal my first glimpse of the Shwedagon pagoda, its golden spire peeking out between buildings and trees, like a dispatch from my childhood. We pass a shop selling bright blue PVC pipes, then a gold-trimmed monastery with billowing burgundy robes pegged to the clothesline. I recall the photo of U Soe Htet as a novice monk with new understanding. I'm beginning to appreciate how the absence of Burma must make him feel, what Ahpwa must've also endured, that gnawing emptiness, a memory of beauty and belonging too painful and subversive to name.

"Did Ahpwa really want to come back?" I ask.

"Yes." Parker touches my hand.

The taxi stops on the corner of Pansodan and Mahabandoola, in the heart of downtown Yangon. Up and down the sidewalk, stall after stall display hundreds of new and second-hand books. As Parker pays the driver, I pick up a book with a photo of Aung San Suu Kyi on the cover. Six months ago, the mere possession of her photo would have been cause for incarceration; now here she is out in the open, her grace the perfect antidote to the spitefulness of the military. Maybe Burma really is changing. Maybe it is possible to overcome tyranny after all.

"Come on," says Parker, pulling my arm. "I thought you were in a hurry." Several passersby have stopped to watch us, whether out of concern or curiosity, I can't tell. I put the book down, and Parker drags me around the corner to the building's main entrance, a massive portico supported by six pairs of two-story-high white pillars. The four-story telecommunications building stretches across an entire city block, dominating the neighborhood with its redbrick colonial facade. Stepping inside, I wait for my eyes to adjust to the darkness, the high, open ceilings giving the impression of an old warehouse partitioned into rows of semi-open booths.

Parker points to a booth, and I follow her to a large wooden desk stacked with piles of yellowed paper. Sitting on the blue plastic stool in front of the telephone operator's desk with mosquitoes nipping my ankles, I'm transported back to that day with the fortuneteller. Although there's nothing otherworldly about the middle-aged telephone clerk in front of me now, I experience the same sway of emotion, the same sense of being caught out of my depth in shifting currents. I write Jason's number—our number—on a slip of paper and hand it to the operator.

Cradling the oversized receiver to my ear, I wait for the operator to make the connection, a nervous flutter in my stomach.

"Etta, thank God." Jason's voice is thin, faraway. Impossible.

For a second, I'm too choked up to speak. "Jason. I'm so sorry," I say eventually.

Jason. I'm so sorry, my voice echoes back, flimsy and weak.

"My cell doesn't work here."

My cell doesn't work here. The echo unsettles me.

"And Parker doesn't have a phone."

And Parker doesn't have a phone. I stop, flustered by the inadequacy of my words repeated back, how defensive I sound.

"Etta, are you okay?"

The concern in his voice tightens around me. I want to say no, I'm not okay. Everything feels foreign and out of control. Hotter, smellier and more confusing than I remember. But I don't want to worry him. And it isn't completely true either, because there've also been glimpses of comfort and belonging, those fleeting moments when Jason and my life back in Boston seem to slip my mind altogether.

I tell him that I'm just jetlagged, cringing as my lie echoes through the receiver.

"What's it like? What've you been doing?" He stifles a yawn, and I smile, touched by how hard he's trying to sound upbeat. At four in the morning. I imagine him sitting up in our bed, pillows propped behind him. Part of me longs to be back home in the safety of his arms, but another part feels completely detached, the clunky black telephone solidifying the distance between us.

I hold the receiver horizontal to my mouth as I tell him about last night's dinner, my cousins, Parker's apartment, then tilt it back to my ear to hear his response. That's better.

"So how's Parker? Ok?"

I look over at my sister, her legs innocently crossed as she looks up at the cavernous ceiling, trying to pretend she's not listening to my every word. I'd forgotten for a moment that she was there and feel an unexpected rush of tenderness for her. Perhaps I'm not so alone after all.

"She's good. Loves her job." It's true, I realize; Parker has no reservations about being here. "What have you been up to the last 48 hours?" I ask. It's hard to believe that's all it's been.

He talks about friends and work and the apartment, then adds, "But it's not the same without you. And I hate not being able to reach you. Did you even get my emails?"

"No, sorry. I'll try to find an internet café soon. Listen, I'd better go now. The line is really bad."

"Okay. Bye, Etta. I love you."

"I love you too." I forget to move the receiver away from my ear.

I love you too, the phone echoes, and the line goes dead.

As we exit the telecommunications building, Parker puts her arm around me, as if she's the big sister, rather than me. I rest my head against her shoulder, grateful that she hasn't tried to say something soothing and trite as I might have done.

A few minutes later, we're in another taxi, Parker mysteriously tight-lipped about our surprise destination. As a little girl, she could never keep a secret. Wide-eyed and open-mouthed, she'd drop so many hints that there'd be nothing left to tell. But today, she evades my every attempt to extract information, asking instead about Jason, how he reacted to my trip, whether I miss him.

"Of course, I miss him," I snap. But do I really? He might fill my mind one minute and then fall away the next, a phenomenon that scares me more than I care to admit. I go on to recount all the support he provided in the lead-up to my departure, how he organized my ticket, drove with me down to D.C., helped me with last-minute errands.

We drive north again, and the Singuttura Hill comes back into view. That must be it. It's traditional to visit the Shwedagon on the first day in the country. Instead, Parker instructs the driver to continue further down the road past the pagoda, stopping on the right in front of a small, rusted placard. Kan Daw Min Gardens. I follow her through a creaky iron gate, pushing aside an empty beer bottle with my foot as we enter the poorly maintained grounds. Surely Parker doesn't intend to spread Ahpwa's ashes in this rundown excuse of a park?

Inside are four large structures, each more or less the size of an American-style garage. I'm drawn to an ornate, white-tiered monument surrounded by coconut palms, but Parker pulls me away with a cryptic, "Not yet."

I remind myself to be patient as she leads me to the farthest structure on the right, a mausoleum for U Thant, Secretary General of the United Nations from 1961 to 1971, one of Ahpwa's heroes. I know from my lessons with Ahpwa that he negotiated the end to the Cuban Missile Crisis, but what comes to mind is something Ahpwa chose not to share with me, something I read on my own much later in life: When U Thant died, President Ne Win refused to give him a state funeral, leading to massive student protests and the eventual declaration of martial law. Seeing the tomb that caused so much upheaval is interesting, but I can't believe Parker brought me here for a history lesson.

"Why are you showing this to me, Parker?"

"You'll see," she says with a coyness to her smile that makes me want to shake her.

The next tomb is that of Thakin Kodaw Hmai, a famous Burmese poet, who Ahpwa also admired. Is that what this is— some kind of tribute to Ahpwa? I still can't figure out what she's up to but decide to go along with it, reciting one of his poems that Ahpwa made me perform for visitors when I was little.

"*Kaung myo ahtweidwei yenè chunzei myazei saw; daung owei yelo tunzei kazei thaw,*" May a myriad good things with vigor have a chance; may the peacock have its call and dance.

Parker shoots me an injured look, and I see that I've overstepped. I gather Ahpwa didn't cover the poetry of Thakin Kodaw Hmai in her later-life Burmese lessons. I must be more careful.

The third tomb belongs to Daw Khin Kyi, former government minister and ambassador in her own right, but better known as the wife of revolutionary hero, Aung San, and mother of modern-day, pro-democracy icon, Aung San Suu Kyi. Seeing the tombs of all these historical figures is humbling; I know how proud Ahpwa had been of her compatriots—she never let me forget that—but I'm struggling to understand Parker's rationale for bringing me to this particular place on this particular day.

"What's going on, Parker? Why'd you bring me here?"

She gestures to the final tomb, where a stray dog sits watching us.

The area surrounding this tomb is even more unkempt than the others, plastic bags and broken beer bottles strewn among the tumble of weeds that enclose it. While the other three are simple and box-like in their construction, this tomb is shaped like a steeple, with seven ornately carved tiers leading up to a small golden spire on top. I wonder who could possibly be buried here, and why no one takes care of it. Brushing away the debris, I read the inscription.

Here lies Queen Supayalat, Queen of Burma, 1859 - 1925.

Somewhere behind the tomb, a coconut falls to the ground with a thud. I can't believe Parker has thought to bring me here, that she went to the trouble of finding the tomb and organizing this outing. For me. Perhaps she understands me better than I thought. We hadn't played Super Yacht since 1988 when Parker was six years old. I didn't think she remembered the game, much less the queen upon whom it was based.

"Apparently, she spent her final years in Rangoon as a recluse, living in a rundown bungalow provided by the British, and throwing her few, precious belongings at anyone who dared approach without walking on their knees," says Parker. "She even threw her spittoon at the poor doctor who came to treat her on her deathbed."

I shudder at the idea of Queen Supayalat alone and neglected at the end of her life. She'd done terrible, wretched things. Killed her own relatives and terrorized countless others. Yet all I can think about is an old lady alone on her death bed, too proud and scared to let people help her.

I look up at the multi-tiered tomb. "I didn't think you remembered."

"Of course, I remember. I'm not stupid." Parker shoos away the dog, lowering herself onto the edge of the queen's mausoleum.

I sit down next to her, reminding myself that she's brought me here as a gift, a kind of homage to the good parts of our childhood. "I'm sorry."

She picks a twig off the ground and begins drawing circles in the dirt. "I was so jealous of you. All that time Ahpwa spent with you."

A crow swoops down from a nearby palm, passing just over our heads before soaring up to the golden spire at the very top of the Queen's tomb.

"All that time tormenting me, you mean. Making me study Burmese letters till my eyes went loopy, while you were outside twirling around in the sun. I was the envious one."

Parker shakes her head. "I only twirled when you were watching."

The dog circles around the back of the tomb and sits regarding us from a distance of about ten feet. Sometimes, many times, I feel as though Parker and I come from different families, so dissimilar were our childhoods. I always thought she lucked out, having escaped the Burmese lessons, together with the braid drills, recitals, and all the other hoops I had to jump through. But I see now that she had less time with Ahpwa and Mother and Father, less time as part of a cohesive family.

"I prayed for Ahpwa to stop teaching you." She swallows. "And then she did. And you were so sad."

I move closer, wrap my arms around her. "That wasn't your fault," I whisper.

We sit like this for several seconds, the dog now curled up in a ball by our feet.

"It's like we went to Burma one kind of family and came back another," she says.

I keep my eyes trained on the dog as I beat back the smoldering sadness of that time—Ahpwa's breakdown, our parents' divorce, Father's death, then Mother's, all set in motion that one fateful day I betrayed Ahpwa and went to Inya Lake with Shwe. I never told anyone what happened that day, not even Parker. I convinced myself this was for her own good, that I was protecting her. But I can see now that I haven't protected her at all, just as the grown-ups didn't protect me from whatever it was they'd seen or done that day.

Except Parker and I are still here. Unlike Ahpwa and Mother and Father we still have a chance to fix things, to mend what's left of our family story. The question is how? How can we, the living, set straight the deeds and misdeeds of the dead? I look up at the ornate, mildewed tomb. Maybe Parker was right to bring Ahpwa back here, maybe the only way forward is to go back to the past.

In the taxi home, I recall the last time we played Super Yacht and shudder. I've often speculated how Shwe felt that day, whether the same violent urge had also seized him. But until now, I'd never considered Parker, never wondered what she thought or felt in that moment, whether she'd known how badly I wanted to hurt her. I reach out and take her hand.

~

I'm lying on my bed, curled around the bundle of unread letters, the small wooden carving of Yatheik clutched in my hand.

Parker's having dinner with the headmistress of the school where she works, so I'm unsettled to hear footsteps outside my room. Did Parker forget to lock the door? I sit up, my pulse quickening at the risk of an intruder.

Shwe moves into the doorframe. Relief washes over me, followed by a tingle of anticipation.

"Parker asked me to drop this off." He holds up a small blue paperback. No *hello* or *sorry I startled you*. I can't tell if this is a sign of familiarity, or just plain indifference.

I look at the book as if it holds some significance. I can't make out the title but suppose it to be a guidebook. Parker isn't much of a reader, or at least she didn't used to be. I look back at Shwe and see that he's watching me, his eyes like big, brown pools of syrup, as deep and intense as I remember. He surveys the bed, pausing briefly on the purple scarf before spotting the statue in my hand.

"Is that a *nat*?" His face lights up in surprise.

I hold it out, and he steps more fully into the room.

"Made by an old Burmese man I know in Boston."

He takes the statue and turns it over, examining the detail of the robe, feet, and face. "Nice," he says. "You know who it is?"

"Yes," I say, mindful of how fragile this connection is between us, how tenuous the moment. I recall U Soe Htet's words and clear my throat. "It's Yatheik, the hermit spirit who lives in the forest, guiding those who have lost their way."

Shwe hands the statue back to me with a quizzical look. Is he remembering my skepticism about the fortuneteller, the many debates we had about the *nat* shrine near our auntie's house? I wish I knew, wish I could ask. But what if the answer is no, or worse still, what if he remembers only vaguely, the details tepid and flat, like a glass of prosecco left out overnight? What then?

I tell him instead about U Soe Htet, how he went to

America for six months never to return, how he mended Ahpwa's marionettes and still worships *nats* after 50 years in Boston.

He walks over to the window, looking out at the city beyond. "The prison authorities cut down all the trees at one point. To stop us from worshipping *nats*."

I hold my breath, willing him to keep talking.

"You'd think they'd know better. *Nats* can be anywhere, not just in trees."

"How long were you in prison?" I ask quietly.

He doesn't respond, just continues looking out the window.

If only I could find a way past this awkwardness, back to the old Shwe, the old Etta. I examine the Yatheik carving more closely. He's right—the craftsmanship is superb, both the carving and the painting. U Soe Htet must have spent many hours working on it. Thinking about the old man gives me courage.

"These are for you." I hold out the bundle of letters still wrapped in the scarf.

He turns to face me.

"Letters I wrote when we returned to Boston. Ahpwa..." I hesitate. "I thought she mailed them, but I guess she thought it was too dangerous."

As he takes the bundle, his hand brushes mine. He unwinds the scarf and thumbs through the envelopes one by one, inspecting the dates penciled into the corners, the heart stickers and other designs on the backs. For a second, I fear he might give them back.

Instead he clutches them against his hip and says, "Better get back to work."

And he's gone.

EIGHT

One evening toward the beginning of summer, as the high-pitched chirping of crickets sliced through the night air, we sat down to a family dinner. Ahpwa assumed the head of the table as always. She'd prepared another Western-style dinner that promised to leave everyone except six-year-old Parker dissatisfied. Since our return, our meals had become blander by the day. No more spicy curries or pickled veggies, no more noodle soup or fermented bean curd. Even Father, born-and-bred in west suburban Boston, confessed privately that he missed the bite of Burmese cuisine.

But the food was the least of our problems. For weeks now, we'd been tiptoeing around Ahpwa, weighing each word before opening our mouths. Although she'd resumed her previous command over the household, anything could set her off, exposing a new, crazed side of my grandmother that I never could've imagined and never wished to know again. On this particular night, I made the mistake of asking for some homemade chili sauce, previously a fixture at the table, to spice up my tasteless chicken cutlet.

"You want chili?" She rammed back her chair, a wild look on her face. My stomach clenched as she stormed into the kitchen, returning with a jar of the fiery sauce held high above her head.

"Here's your chili." She looked directly at me as she dropped the jar onto the hardwood floor, the glass shattering into dozens of shiny fragments coated with the sticky red paste.

I stared at the gooey mess on the floor in horror. Did she think I was criticizing her cooking? Had I forgotten to say please?

If only I could pinpoint my mistake, I'd make sure never to say or do the same again. Yet even as I weighed possible explanations, I knew there was nothing I could do differently, that it wasn't anything I said or did, but the simple fact of my existence, forever reminding Ahpwa of the one thing she wanted to forget, the one topic fated to upend our lives forever more: Burma. I opened my mouth to apologize, but before the words came out, Ahpwa picked up her plate and dropped that too, tiny missiles of soggy green peas escaping across the floor. For a brief moment, the wildness in Ahpwa's eyes subsided, and I saw instead a kind of relief.

Father placed his hand on my back, but when I looked up at him, he wasn't looking at me but at Mother, imploring her with his eyes. *Do something,* he seemed to say. But she remained unmoving, her hands idle in her lap. Parker swung her head back and forth between Mother and Father, making no attempt to hide her curiosity about who would capitulate first.

Ahpwa picked up the bowl of mashed potatoes, then paused with the bowl in the air, as if waiting for someone to challenge her.

Father's staring intensified.

Mother looked away, a hardness in her eyes that told me she wasn't going to budge.

For a moment, time seemed to stand still. Then Father stood, and with a gentle but firm motion, took hold of Ahpwa's arm and removed the bowl of mashed potatoes from her grip. "That's enough," he said, and escorted Ahpwa out of the room.

"Etta, clean up this mess," said Mother as she ran after Father and Ahpwa.

NINE

Yangon, Myanmar
2011

The drone of the monks' gong reverberates through the kitchen window from the street below, silhouettes of the neighboring buildings black against the yellow sky. I stumble into the kitchen to find Parker already dressed for work and filling a thermos with coffee.

"You're up early." She swings around to look at me, then turns back to fasten the lid on the thermos. On the counter sits a bowl of plump, fragrant mangos.

"Those mangos," I say as the sun cracks through the window.

"Mangos?" She glances around until she spots them. "Yum. Did you get them at the market?"

A moment's confusion gives way to a tight thrill: If Parker didn't buy the mangos, it must've been Shwe. He remembered how much I loved them. I can't think when he could've delivered them, but their fragrance fills me with renewed hope, confirmation that he's read my letters, that he's forgiven me.

"Do you always leave for work this early?" I ask.

"Have to. It's the only way to beat the traffic." She turns to face me. "Plus, I like getting there before the kids arrive. To prepare, you know?"

I nod.

"Hey, you should come by the school later. It takes a while to get there but seeing the smiles on their faces makes it totally worth the schlep." She writes the address down on the back of a Citymart receipt.

"Maybe. I'll see how it goes. I'm still pretty jetlagged." I don't tell her that I'm leaving the day free for Shwe, that I want to stick around in case he wants to talk now that he's read my letters.

Parker leaves, and I move to the living room. It's only 7:00 a.m., and already I'm sweating. Is Shwe even awake yet? It strikes me that I don't know whether he's a night owl or an early riser. It's hard to imagine him sleeping at all. The book he left for Parker the day before lies on the coffee table. A memoir entitled, *Finding George Orwell in Burma*. I plump myself down on the sofa and open the book. Apparently, George Orwell was considered a prophet among certain literary types, who claimed he'd written not one, but three books about Burma: *Burmese Days*, *Animal Farm* and *1984*, the latter two allegories for the unique form of tyranny that existed here until last year.

I read for a while then check my watch. Barely an hour has passed. I get up and look out the living room window. The market is in full swing, vendors displaying their produce on makeshift stands or in baskets placed directly on the dusty ground. Behind the market stalls, shop signs are layered one over the other like a neon collage, some in English, others in the familiar Myanmar circlets, still others in Chinese characters. A fusion of mixed identities.

How pathetic to be waiting for someone who never said he was coming. He probably didn't even read the letters, just put them in a drawer and forgot about them. Or threw them in the bin in anger. Each scenario seems as plausible as the next. When I wrote those letters, I thought I knew Shwe better than I knew myself, thought I could intuit his every sentiment, predict his every move. Now I wonder if I ever really knew him at all.

I slink into Parker's room, seeking distraction. Unlike Sheila, she's made an effort at decoration, draping colorful silk cloths over the windows and pinning vintage prints of old Rangoon to the wall. It would look quite nice if it weren't such a mess. Her open wardrobe reveals a jumble of Western and Myanmar clothing. Still more outfits are strewn about the room in varying degrees of disarray. I poke around the dresser and bedside table, unsure what I'm looking for—some small insight into this woman I know so intimately and yet not at all. A pay stub, perhaps? I tell myself that I'm doing this for her own good, that it's my responsibility as sister to make sure nothing in her life is astray, but who am I kidding? Snooping through her stuff isn't going to bring us closer. I pick a wet towel off the floor and hang it up before hastily leaving the room.

Flopping back down on the sofa, I return to the book. The writer is following Orwell's travels through Burma in the 1930s, making comparisons along the way between the political situation in modern-day Burma and the fantastical state of affairs portrayed in Orwell's books. Like Shwe, she uses a pen name, the consequences of writing about the regime too severe to risk. When military intelligence officers start tracking her, she throws them off by pretending to be a tourist. How does Shwe handle them? Do the authorities really not know he is Moe Pwint? I wish I'd read those articles in Ahpwa's chest more carefully, brought them with me. But how could I have known? I close the book and check my watch again. Another hour gone.

I return to the kitchen, opening and closing drawers until I find a knife. Selecting the best-looking mango—firm but springy to the touch with mottled yellow, orange and green skin—I hold it upright and sink the knife into its flesh. The sweet, tropical fragrance infuses the air, cartwheeling through my memories like a happy schoolgirl. Cutting the mango into strips, I gorge on the fruit until nothing's left but the residual flesh around the pit. I lean over the sink and begin gnawing directly on the pit, letting the juice drip down my chin and onto my neck.

The doorbell's loud techno jingle echoes through the apartment, and my pulse quickens. I fling the skins and pit into the trash, turn on the tap and stick the lower half of my face under the running water, picking mango strings out of my teeth with my fingernail. The doorbell jangles again.

"*Kanaleh*. Just a sec," I yell in English and Myanmar as I run to the living room, still holding the kitchen towel.

Breathless with anticipation, I throw open the door.

"Welcome to Myanmar," says an elderly Myanmar woman dressed in an old-fashioned, latticed *htamein*. "Your sister's told me all about you. I live one floor down. Daw Tin Tin." She holds out a limp hand.

I shake her hand and introduce myself. Parker's told me all about her, too. A sweet, old lady with silver-streaked hair and friendly eyes, she fills her empty days by monitoring the comings and goings of the building's residents. I peek over her head down the empty hallway.

"Is this a bad time?" She follows my eyes down the corridor.

"No, won't you come in?"

"Oh, no. I don't want to disturb you." Her English is impeccable. "I simply wanted to introduce myself and make sure you got the mangos I left for you."

"The mangos were from you?" Disappointment crashes over me.

"Yes, from my farm in Shan State. I left a bowl on the kitchen counter early this morning, before going downstairs to make my offering to the monks."

"Thank you, they're delicious," I say.

Burmese etiquette dictates that I ask her in a second time. Maybe even a third. She must refuse, I must insist; she must refuse, I must insist. Ahpwa would expect no less. But all I can think about is the maddening stickiness of mango juice prickling my neck, and how desperate I am to wash it away. I thank her again and close the door.

I scrub my face and neck with quick, hard strokes. How presumptuous of me to have construed the mangos as a message from Shwe, to have expected his life to change simply because I'm here. He's probably working. Out driving his taxi. Or writing an article. Entertaining one of the women Parker hinted at last night.

I have other priorities, too. I pat my skin dry with the pink, florid towel. I need to find an internet café. Calling Jason from the Central Telephone and Telegraph office was fine for the first day but not something I want to repeat if I can help it. Then there's Ahpwa, although now that Parker's actually asked for my help, the question of where to lay her ashes feels somehow less imperative, or at least less urgent. With a burst of clarity, I realize that the person I'm most concerned about right now is Parker, yesterday's visit to Supayalat's grave having made me see how much she, too, suffered in the aftermath of that 1988 trip. Locating the Citymart receipt where she scribbled the address of the school, I slip on my shoes and head down to the street to look for a taxi.

As the driver peals away from the building, the tension in my jaw begins to soften. What a relief to be out of the apartment, to be free of the indignity of waiting for someone who might never come. I gaze out the window, the reality of being back in Yangon filling me with unexpected wonder: a man cranking the wheel of a hand-operated sugar cane press. Women balancing baskets of goods on their heads. Life being lived out in the open. How could I have forgotten all this?

The taxi drops me at the port. I catch the ferry across the river, then hire a trishaw to take me to the village where Parker's school is located. By the time I arrive almost an hour later, I'm so hot and sweaty I need another shower. How does Parker make this journey twice a day, especially if she's not earning enough to meet her needs? That shouldn't matter, I know, but how can it not?

I poke my head into the classroom undetected, just as the children are returning from recess. There're dozens of them, climbing over and around each other like honeybees as they seek their locus in the hive. I'm fascinated but cautious, curious to see how they behave but wary of getting too close. The children are quite little, six or seven-years-old is my guess, a mixture of boys and girls, their faces painted in varying geometric shapes with buttery yellow *thanaka*.

"Good morning, children!" Parker's clear, melodic tone cuts through the buzz like a gong, delivering the children into their seats.

"GOO MAW NEE, TEE-CHAH," they shout back in unison. Eyes shining with eagerness, bodies fully alert, the children are ready to learn. Or perhaps simply content to watch Parker, whose enthusiasm radiates from her skin like an aura. Even I am unable to look away as she stands, seraph-like, in front of the class. She begins to sing the alphabet song, and the children join in, their mouths open wide as they carol the unfamiliar English sounds, uninhibited.

I suppose I've always been a little jealous of the way Parker moves in the world, the way people are so quickly drawn to her. When she was little, we called her Bird, both after the famous saxophonist for whom she was named, and because she was always singing and flitting about from place to place. It was our father who gave her the nickname. He was the musician and the dreamer, the one who derived joy from matching names and words with people and ideas.

Except when it came to me. "You already have quite a few names, don't you think, Etta Hammond Montgomery Aye Tha Kyaw?" he responded, when I asked at age ten why I had no nickname. Although I knew my Burmese name was listed on my birth certificate, no one ever used it in those days, not even Ahpwa, who only ever called me *Myi*. "Besides, you can't make Etta much shorter. Unless you want me to call you Et?" His eyes twinkled with amusement.

"But Parker is only two syllables, and she has a nickname."

I remember his smile slowly flattening like the inner tube of my bicycle tire that time I ran over a broken bottle. I was too serious, that was the problem. My own father didn't know what to make of me.

Then he leaned in closer and said quietly, "I can't imagine a more perfect name than Etta for you, passionate, pensive and soulful just like your namesake." I was named after Etta James, Father's favorite blues singer. That made me feel a bit brighter, but I still longed for a nickname, still wished I was more like my little sister. The alphabet song comes to an end, and I step into the classroom.

Parker smiles and waves without missing a beat, as if my arrival was part of her lesson plan. "Today we have a very special visitor." She uses a combination of English, Burmese and hand gestures. "Can you say HELLO to my SISTER?"

"HEH-LO, SIS-TAH!" Their enthusiasm is so genuine, so completely unrestrained, it nearly knocks me over.

"Hello, children," I project my voice as emphatically as I can.

Smiles and laughter fill the room. But I'd never be able to summon the same passion and playfulness as Parker without feeling like a fraud. She's always been better with children—making friends easily, babysitting as a teenager, working as a camp counselor during summers—but here in this threadbare school with these eager children, she truly shines.

They sing a few more songs then move on to greetings—

simple exchanges like *What is your name?* and *Where do you come from?* I can see from their upturned faces that they're taking in Parker's every word and gesture, ready to put it all to use the next time they encounter a foreigner. And in a burst of clarity, I see the perfect mutuality of the situation: Just as Parker makes learning fun for them, they make teaching fun for her. No wonder she's willing to work for next to nothing.

At lunchtime, Parker leads me to a small antechamber with an old wooden table and chairs. A young woman appears with two plates of rice and vegetable curry, and we dig in. Parker explains that the meals are provided by the adjacent orphanage which runs the school free of charge, not just for the orphans, but for needy children in the surrounding villages. I can hear in her tone how attached she's become to the place, how enchanted she is with it.

I nod and smile, reluctant to always be the naysayer but worried that she's gotten herself into an impossible situation, that she hasn't thought through the long-term implications of earning less than you spend. That she's counting on Ahpwa's inheritance being larger than I anticipate.

"So what do you think?" She leans forward.

"The kids are wonderful, and you're a great teacher. I'm proud of you, Bird."

"But?"

I hesitate. I hadn't planned on saying anything, not yet, but now that she's asked, it feels dishonest not to share my concerns. Because if I don't say something, who will? "Just wondering how much you're getting paid."

She looks past me, her eyes set firm.

I can see that she's annoyed but tell myself it's my responsibility as big sister to say what no one else will. "Does it even cover your rent?"

"Why do you have to ruin everything, Etta? Why can't you

just be happy for once that I'm happy? Support me instead of finding fault in everything I do?"

I shrink back, surprised. Though not a new conversation, the exasperation in her voice feels sharper, more pronounced, making me wonder if I've gone too far, if, in my efforts to protect her, I've done the opposite.

"Look. I'm working on it," she continues. "Khaing Zar's given me some ideas how to get outside funding, not just to pay teachers, but for books and desks and maybe even a computer or two. I've already presented the idea to Ma Win, the woman who runs the orphanage, and she's all for it. Now I'm looking into potential donors. Once I figure that out, I'll start putting together a proposal." She goes on to describe her and Ma Win's vision for the school, including anticipated timeframe, sustainability considerations and budget estimates, and I find myself pulled in by her energy and passion. I can't remember the last time she showed this much initiative and I'm impressed.

"I'm sorry, Bird. I had no idea. Let me know if I can help in any way," I say, and we hug goodbye.

On my way home, I sit quietly looking out the window of the taxi. Street names have changed, vendors come and gone, yet the essence of the city remains unchanged after all these years. Rundown cars competing for space with pushcarts and rickshaws. People moving slowly but deliberately about their business, careful not to expend too much energy at this, the hottest time of day. For the first time since Parker sprang this trip on me, I consider the possibility that I was wrong about her coming, that maybe Yangon is exactly what she needs.

TEN

The heatwave that gripped Boston the summer of 1988 was so pernicious that the library, my primary refuge from my family, had begun to close early to reduce pressure on the power grid. Ahpwa didn't believe in air conditioning, so I sweated through the long summer days in a state of prickly apprehension, too fearful of another chili jar episode to complain.

At night, I lay awake, breathing fire into the questions that hovered over my days: why Shwe hadn't written, when Ahpwa would return to normal, whether my parents' marriage would survive. Though they never argued in front of us, I picked up fragments of discord about Ahpwa and Burma, whether to share with her the growing unrest or the hopeful advent of a young mother named Aung San Suu Kyi.

After seven consecutive days of temperatures in the 90s and 100s, the heat seemed to have altered the texture of my skin, rendering unbearable even the slightest contact with the sheets. One night in the middle of August, I got up to go to the bathroom and heard my parents in their bedroom, arguing.

"It was bad enough before Burma," said Father. "But this has gone too far. She's becoming more irrational by the day."

Mother's response was too weak to grasp, her words like leaves whirring in the wind.

"She needs more than patience. She needs professional help," Father said.

I pressed my ear to the door but couldn't make out Mother's response.

"I'm sure we could find a Burmese therapist if we tried," he pleaded.

More rustling leaves from Mother.

"I know. I'm not suggesting that you should." Father again. "But something's gotta give. Have you seen what this is doing to Etta, how distant and apprehensive she's become?"

I sank to the ground, the sound of my name stirring up the same old feelings of confusion and dread, my need to understand eclipsed by fear of what such an understanding might unleash. Although I still couldn't grasp the precise causation, I felt certain that both Ahpwa's unusual behavior and this new tension between my parents stemmed back to that day in Rangoon, when I'd gone out with Shwe against Ahpwa's orders.

"I can't do that," said Father. "I'm sorry."

"Then maybe you *should* leave," said Mother, this time clear enough for me to hear.

I sprung away from the door in alarm, then crept back to my bed, where I lay awake for hours, cataloguing my many mistakes, vowing to be a better daughter and granddaughter from here on in, if only my parents would stay together.

The following morning, I found Parker and Father in the kitchen, eating pancakes at the little breakfast nook by the window. A bowl of batter stood on the counter, the stovetop covered in hardened pancake droppings. It was Sunday, a day Parker and I typically spent alone with our father. "I need my dose of delicious," he'd tell Ahpwa, and to my amazement, she yielded to him every time.

Sundays were the one day of the week where I saw myself as an individual with thoughts and needs and desires distinct from those of Ahpwa, the one day of the week where I felt unequivocally American. Whether we spent the day at a park, the beach, a museum or a movie, the day invariably began with a group pancaking effort, the three of us taking turns measuring ingredients, mixing the batter, and flipping the flapjacks.

"We tried to wake you," said Father as I wiped the sleep from my eyes. "But you were out like a light."

For a second, I let myself believe that I'd dreamed the events of the previous night, that life would remain the same degree of miserable, but at least my parents would stay together. The pinched expression on Father's face suggested otherwise.

"Daddy's going away," said Parker as she poured a second helping of syrup over her half-eaten chocolate chip pancakes.

Father held out his arms and I snuggled into his embrace. So, it was true: he really was leaving.

"But we can visit him whenever we want," continued Parker. "It's gonna be fun." She spoke with the same tone of authority she used when playing with her Barbie dolls. *This one will be the movie star, and this one will be her servant. Daddy will move out, and we will be happy.*

I wanted to believe that Parker was right, that our father living apart could somehow be a good development. I tried to picture us laughing and having fun together at the beach, going out for ice cream or playing Frisbee at the park, but the false cheer in his smile told a different story.

ELEVEN

Yangon, Myanmar
2011

Cyber Savvy, the internet café Parker's downstairs neighbor Daw Tin Tin recommends, looks more like a high school computer lab than a café. Sandwiched between a *longyi* shop and jade store opposite Trader's Hotel, the long, narrow establishment is divided into rows of desktop computers separated by wooden panels. Trendy teenagers with spiked rainbow hair make up most of the clientele with a few Western tourists sprinkled throughout. As far as I can see, no beverages are served or consumed in this café.

A small-framed man with wavy, grey hair and glasses greets me in English as I enter. "No Skype, no Facebook, no trouble. Understand? Google okay. No banned sites!"

When I respond in Burmese that Daw Tin Tin sent me, U Zaw Minn breaks into a grin and quietly explains further. Although regulations on internet use are more lenient than they once were, he's required by law to take screen shots of his clients' internet activity every five minutes. I agree to his conditions, and he leads me to a computer in the very back of the room.

"I have a bad cough today. I hope I won't disturb you," he says quite loudly. Then he leans over and whispers in my ear, "For some reason, I always get a tickle in my throat right before I take the screen shot."

As I wait for my email to load, I open a second tab and type Moe Pwint, the pseudonym that Shwe uses, into the search box. I'm hoping that his writing will provide a clue to the man he's become.

I click back on the first tab to find four messages from Jason—one for each day since I left Boston. I start with the oldest message and work in reverse chronological order, the way he wrote them and intended them to be read. Most are pretty short—a few questions about how I'm doing, followed by a quick summary of what he's been up to. Three contain links to articles he thinks I might find interesting, all of which redirect to a page that says, "THIS WEBSITE IS BLOCKED BY MYANMAR POST AND TELECOMMUNICATIONS."

The café owner coughs, and I close the tabs immediately, chuckling at his quiet ingenuity. When I was in my twenties, I wondered how the Burmese could cope under such harsh government restrictions. The answer, I now understand, is that they simply carry on living like the rest of us, adjusting their behavior to the reality of their situation and incorporating whatever small acts of defiance they can along the way.

The final message from Jason describes his recent visit to U Soe Htet, who regaled him with more tales of my grandmother. According to Jason, the former professor reconnected with Ahpwa at a Southeast Asian Food Fair in Harvard Square in 1975. Although she was unable to place him, he recognized her immediately as the enchanting young woman who'd come to speak at his school back in Burma. Determined to capture her attention, he played up both his stature as a university professor and the ease with which he navigated American culture. But it wasn't until the conversation turned to her fondness for marionettes that he knew he'd won her over. Out of respect for my grandfather, Ahpwa refused to marry U Soe Htet, but their love was what the old man described as "a powerful engine." The last time he saw her was in 1988 just before our trip to Burma.

Questions swarm my mind as my eyes race down the screen. How could Ahpwa and U Soe Htet have been together so long without my knowing? Why did they separate after our trip to Burma? But also: Why did U Soe Htet tell all this to Jason and not to me? As grateful as I am that he's checking in on the old man, I can't help feeling a little envious of their growing connection. Yet I know that U Soe Htet is responding to Jason's sincerity and his constancy, the very same qualities I also love about him. And that Jason wouldn't take the time out of his schedule to visit the old man if not for me.

I draft a long response describing the city, the dinner with my cousins, and my outing to Parker's school, telling him that I love him and miss him and will see him soon. Hitting send, I click the other tab to check the results of my Google search on Moe Pwint. One after another, each link leads to the same warning indicating that the website in question has been blocked by Myanmar Post and Telecommunications. As I close the tabs, a whisper of apprehension hovers over me. Has Shwe not reached out to me because he doesn't want to, or because he can't?

~

The city is colorful, crowded, chaotic. I walk southeast, stopping now and then to peek into a shop or admire an old building, looking vaguely for a sign of what to do with Ahpwa's ashes. Unlike the other day with Parker, no one follows me with their eyes or turns their head as I pass. I float through the streets as if invisible, watching and listening unobserved to the sights and sounds of Yangon.

A flash of red, the cry of a vendor, a whiff of fish paste, around every corner is a memory. I find myself looking for Shwe— not the man he is today, but the teenaged boy I once loved, that passionate, curious youth who made me look beyond the surface of these same streets. How did he react when he arrived at our auntie's house the day after the march to find me and my family gone? Was it sorrow he felt or anger, understanding or betrayal? And now?

"*E kya kwei! E kya kwei! E kya kwei!*" The call of a local doughnut vendor brings me back to street level.

Suddenly ravenous, I follow the distinctive aroma of *mohinga* to a teashop under the shelter of an old banyan tree. As with most banyan trees around Yangon, the host tree and strangler fig have long since fused into a single, unified being. A small *nat* shrine, about twelve by eighteen inches, is fastened to the tree alongside a framed photo of democracy icon Aung San Suu Kyi.

An eagle-like woman with sharp, black eyes stands behind an assortment of aluminum pots, simultaneously stirring and shouting orders at a boy washing dishes. I smile at the woman, then sit on one of the tiny stools, my knees level with the equally low table. The boy rushes over to take my order. Up close I see that he's quite young—nine or ten at the most—yet haggard. I resolve to tip him generously when I leave.

Aside from two couples, the other patrons are all men, some sitting alone, others in a small group of two or three. The boy brings me a bowl of steaming hot *mohinga*, and I slurp up the pungent noodles, while concentrating on snatches of conversation around me. Leaning forward, I catch something about NLD—the National League for Democracy—and the upcoming by-elections. One man says the opposition party should boycott the elections, while the other thinks that would be a mistake. Mosquitoes buzz languidly around my ankles. A tall, sinewy man, dressed for business in a button-down shirt and green and black checked *longyi*, seats himself at the table next to me.

"And where do you hail from?" he asks in heavily accented English.

"How do you know I'm not from here?" I respond in Myanmar.

"You are the only woman seated alone." He sweeps his arm through the air. "Few Myanmar women would feel so at ease." This must also be why U Zaw Minn of Cyber Savvy initially spoke to me in English.

Ko Martin is a human rights lawyer from Mandalay who came to Yangon five years ago to be closer to his girlfriend, now his wife. When he learns that I, too, am an attorney, he begins to speak very quickly, barraging me with question after question about the American legal system. As I describe the world of corporate labor law, the boy fills our cups with fresh tea, humming a popular Myanmar song as he works. The cook hasn't shouted at him for some time. Feeling more relaxed than I have in days, I ask Ko Martin about his work.

"Our profession involves great risk here in Myanmar. When we take on a case against the government or one of the cronies, we too are harassed, sometimes even detained. There's no distinction between the accused and his lawyer. We are viewed as one and the same as those we represent. Both in the eyes of the government, and the public." Ko Martin fishes the last few rice noodles out of his bowl then fixates on me with steel grey eyes. "We could use someone like you."

"What do you mean?" A flicker of curiosity catches under my ribs.

"Someone with a legal background, who speaks both languages. Someone who can foster outside support for what we are trying to do." He lowers his voice. "And whisper in the ears of the Americans when we are in trouble."

I look at the photo of Aung San Suu Kyi that's pinned to the tree and shiver. She made the ultimate sacrifice a woman can make, keeping the opposition movement alive by choosing to remain under house arrest in Burma rather than returning to her husband and children in England. I think, too, of Shwe and all the other

Burmese dissidents around the world who've endured unknown horrors for the sake of Burma's freedom.

"There is no money, of course," continues Ko Martin. "Few of our clients can afford to pay us much more than a bag of rice."

"It's not the money," I say. Despite the warnings I'd heaped on Parker yesterday about working for little to no money, I understand the pull to do something meaningful without regard for compensation. And unlike Parker, I've paid off my student loans, which means that any inheritance from Ahpwa's estate will translate into savings.

Ko Martin looks at me expectantly.

"I'm only visiting. I live in Boston."

"My mistake. I presumed incorrectly that you were here to stay. Do come see me if your circumstances change. There are many ways to help, both big and small." He hands me a tattered business card as he gets up to leave.

As I watch him walk away, I wonder what it would be like to stay in Yangon, to share an apartment with Parker and work with Ko Martin, committing to a cause bigger than myself, maybe even finding middle ground with Shwe, somewhere between the puppy love of my teenage years and this hollow awkwardness that seems to now define us. But how could I leave the life Jason and I have built together? How could I betray him like that? As I stand up to leave, the cook resumes shouting, and the boy stops humming. I slip him some *kyat* and step back into the shriveling heat of the city street.

TWELVE

Boston, Massachusetts
1989

Father moved into a one-bedroom apartment near his office in Back Bay. Under different circumstances, I might've enjoyed the buzz of the city, but I was too focused inward to notice anything outside our little bubble of three. Per the terms of the separation, Parker and I spent Saturday nights at the tiny apartment, jostling for space on a pullout sofa bed that smelled like a furniture showroom. Though a high-schooler, I didn't mind missing the few social gatherings I was invited to, at least initially.

Sunday mornings, we ate breakfast at a neighborhood diner. Parker ordered chocolate chip pancakes, but I switched to eggs. I figured we'd reestablish our old pancake ritual once Father got settled, but weeks turned to months, and we continued going to the diner. Parker pointed out how much rounder and fluffier the diner's pancakes were than ours, as if this was something to celebrate, some kind of upgrade. She wasn't wrong. Our pancakes had been on the dense side, more often than not misshapen by wayward drips, especially when she was in charge of the griddle. But to compare them to the diner's felt disloyal, as if naming the flaws in our pancakes somehow negated the whole ritual, and by extension our father's role in our family.

Father responded to Parker's culinary analysis with a show of amusement, but I sensed a growing gloom behind his forced smile. If only we could resume our old rituals, he'd feel better, happier. One Sunday in January, as frigid rain thrashed the streets, I cleared my throat. "How 'bout we stay here and make our own pancakes instead?"

His gaze settled briefly on my face like a butterfly alighting on a delicate flower, and for a second, he seemed to consider my suggestion. Then he shuddered, as if shaking off the emotion. "I don't have a griddle here, Sweetheart. Besides, the diner makes them so much better. Isn't that right, Bird?"

Parker nodded enthusiastically.

I wanted to grab her bony shoulders and shake her, make her see that this wasn't about pancakes or where we ate breakfast. It was about the very essence of our family, the unique blend of customs and rituals that defined us, helping us to find our way in the world. But Parker was only seven, too young to understand what was at stake.

Later that week, I snuck down to Ahpwa's kitchen in the middle of the night and stole the griddle. We never used the pan anymore, so it was unlikely she would care, or even notice. Yet I couldn't shake the feeling that I was doing something wrong, that taking the pan was crossing a line, loving Father a betrayal of Mother and Ahpwa. That if Ahpwa discovered my deceit, she'd prevent me from taking the pan, just as she prevented all other efforts to bring harmony back into our lives.

I stashed the griddle in my overnight bag under my pjs and a pair of jeans, tiptoeing through the remainder of the week so as not to attract attention to my latest crime. Saturday afternoon, I slipped into Father's car with a rush of relief. But when I pulled out the pan to show him, he just shook his head, the sadness in his eyes extinguishing any hope that our family might one day return to normal.

In time, the diner became familiar enough—an acceptable stand-in ritual, however fluffy the pancakes. We even laughed sometimes, most often in response to one of Parker's elaborate tales. But I stopped looking forward to Sundays the way I had before Burma, stopped caring whether we went to a movie or museum or stayed in the apartment watching reruns on tv. My only care was to prevent Father from sinking any lower than he already had, an aspiration in which I ultimately failed. Within two years, he was gone. The death certificate said cardiovascular disease, but even back then, I knew otherwise: My father died of a broken heart.

THIRTEEN

I slip on one of Parker's simple *htameins* and head to the National Museum on Pyay Road. I tell myself I'm going for Ahpwa, seeking inspiration about where to lay her ashes. But really, I just need to get out of the apartment, escape my growing agitation about Shwe—why he hasn't come to see me, whether he's okay. Although rather drab-looking on the exterior, the museum has a startling collection of artifacts from Myanmar's two-thousand-year-plus history. What draws me in, however, is the exhibit dedicated to King Thibaw and Queen Supayalat, the most striking of which is the Royal Lion Throne.

Thirty-four and a half feet high and covered from top to bottom in pure gold and precious gems, the throne sends goosebumps up and down my arms. To think this is where the royal couple actually sat. I imagine them perched together on the central platform surrounded by ministers and advisors, Thibaw with his legs crossed in front of him, Supayalat tucking hers demurely behind her, deferring to him in public only to later strongarm him into her way of thinking. Did he not see how manipulative she was, or did he recognize her shortcomings and love her anyway?

As I stand in front of the throne, a silver-haired man dressed in a formal, white *tike pone* jacket and navy *longyi* approaches and asks, in English, if I have any questions.

"Is it true?" I respond in Myanmar. "Was Thibaw really so weak, and Supayalat such a tyrant?"

"Certainly not! This—" He raps on the teak wall panel. "This is what it was all about."

According to U Aung, the museum keeper, the British wanted control of the lucrative teak industry, but King Thibaw refused. Unable to obtain logging rights through legitimate channels, they decided to overthrow the monarchy. In order to garner the necessary public support back home, they set in motion an elaborate smear campaign, painting a picture of the royal couple as incompetent, immoral and sadistic. Thibaw, a devout Buddhist who never touched alcohol, was portrayed as an ineffectual drunk, while Supayalat was vilified both for her inhumane treatment of servants and for the alleged role that she played in the 1879 massacre.

"Alleged?" I ask. How I wish Ahpwa could hear this alternate version of events. The museum keeper's defense of the queen would have pleased my grandmother, I know, maybe even offered her some relief.

U Aung nods emphatically. "Many believe the massacre was not orchestrated by Supayalat at all, but by her mother Hsinbyumashin. Regardless, the killing of potential heirs was standard practice in the Konbaung dynasty. Had such a massacre not taken place, any one of Thibaw's relatives would most certainly have tried to usurp the throne." By way of proof, U Aung describes the final days of the monarchy—how the British used a decoy of one of Thibaw's only surviving cousins to spread confusion among the king's subjects, creating the conditions for a British takeover and the eventual exile of the young royal family to a remote village in India.

Given the context of 1886 Burma, I begin to see the queen as more of a victim than a perpetrator, vilified for her connivance when, if anything, she wasn't conniving enough. Maybe her only fault was being stronger and more charismatic than her quiet husband, being a woman. I recall our childhood game of "Super Yacht," Parker's red knees and the guilty thrill I got from stepping all over her golden locks.

"What about the *shiko*?" I ask. "If the queen was not so wicked, why did she force her subjects to serve her on their knees, making them prostrate themselves so she could walk on their hair?"

"But this was tradition! If she hadn't acted the part, her subjects would not have respected her," says U Aung with such passion and certitude that any other explanation seems suddenly preposterous.

By the time I leave the museum, my previous convictions about the queen have been upended. The only thing I know for certain is that the story is more complicated and nuanced than I allowed, a realization that comes as a kind of epiphany, a revelation that I can't wait to share with Parker when I get home.

~

Cyber Savvy owner U Zaw Minn receives me with another big grin. "Ma Aye Tha. "So good to see you again. Same station as before?"

"Yes, please." I'm touched that he remembers my name after only one visit.

"You recall our regulations, correct?" he asks quite loudly in Myanmar.

"Yes, of course. No banned sites. I will be careful."

"Good, good. Now tell me, how is our friend, Daw Tin Tin?" he asks as he escorts me to the back of the café. When I tell him that she seems well, his grin widens. Grasping both my hands in his, he asks me to please give her his very, *very* best the next time I see her. I promise to do so as soon as I get home.

Sitting down at my cubicle, I compose another long email to Jason, describing the museum's various exhibits in elaborate, if somewhat impersonal, detail. It'd be different in person. If Jason were here with me, I'd tell him all about the loquacious museum keeper and his alternative theories on the queen. I don't doubt Jason would find it interesting. But given how little I've told him about Queen Supayalat, or our childhood game of Super Yacht, it feels too complicated to explain in an email. I'll tell him when I get home, when I'm curled up on the sofa next to him, with Burma finally behind me.

I open a new tab and type Moe Pwint into the search box. Nothing but the same, banned sites. I try Shwe's blog instead. To my surprise, it comes up right away. I scroll slowly down the page, drinking in Shwe's meditations on the world around us, a perspective at once familiar and unfamiliar, comforting and disturbing. His writing is contagious, each post a perfectly crafted morsel of truth that makes my blood pump faster and stronger, stirring in me a kind of enraged compassion I haven't felt since my college days. An entry on the safety conditions of the city's construction workers makes me reconsider the barefoot men I've seen dangling, helmetless, from bamboo scaffolding on the new skyrises sprouting up around town. Another piece on the plight of orphaned monks arouses my sympathy for the column of young, robed boys passing our building each morning. These are the tamer entries.

Others take more direct aim at the government: an exposé of state-sponsored corruption in the mining industry; profiles of garment workers imprisoned while striking for an extra dollar a day in wages; an editorial on government complicity in the persecution of minority populations across the country. Shwe's blog reinforces the same depressing fact again and again: that the government continues to place the priorities of the rich and powerful above the needs of those less fortunate. I marvel at how insightful he is, how sharp and articulate, able to zero in on the most poignant part of people's lives.

Part of me brims with admiration, inspired by his willingness to speak out in his own name for what's right, exposing the truth just like he always wanted to do. But another part worries that he's going too far, that by so brazenly testing the limits of the new press freedoms, he's putting himself in danger. Scrolling through the last few entries, I note the dates and frequency of posts with increasing urgency. Until recently, he posted every other day, sometimes daily. His last post was the day before I arrived, a full five days ago. Where is he?

~

Daw Tin Tin's apartment is furnished with a tasteful combination of Myanmar artwork and colonial-era teak furniture. Standing in her front entrance, I thank her again for putting me on to Cyber Savvy and tell her how happy U Zaw Minn was to hear that she'd sent me.

She blushes, which makes me like her more. "Please wish him every happiness also from me when you see him next."

When I tell her that I will likely return to Cyber Savvy the next day and the day after that, she expresses surprise. I explain about Jason, how anxious he gets when he can't reach me, how sudden my trip was, how we're getting married next year.

"Why didn't you tell me you were engaged? You must tell your Jason to call you here, on my telephone." She places a conspiratorial hand on my arm. "Between you and me, the line is officially disconnected. But the telephone company's so incompetent, they forgot to turn it off. We must be careful not to make any outgoing calls, though, or they'll catch on and charge me for twenty years' worth of telephone bills!"

We share a laugh at the absurdity of the situation, and I take my leave, climbing the final set of stairs to Parker's apartment.

Parker's not home yet, so I set the table and heat up some fish and sour leaf soup that I bought at the market earlier today. The tart and earthy Roselle leaf is difficult to find in Boston, so I'm trying to eat it as often as I can. It's hard to believe I only have one week left. When Jason booked my ticket, I asked him to make the return flexible in case I wanted to come home early. Now, the idea of leaving sends me into a panic. Here it is day five, and I've made little to no headway with Parker or Ahpwa, let alone Shwe.

Parker whooshes into the apartment, going straight to her room.

"How was work?" I call out from the living room.

"Okay. I mean, the kids are great. I'm just frustrated that I have zero time to research donors," she shouts back. "I think I'll go to the U.S. Information Service on Saturday to see what I can find out. Oh, and Sunday's that Miss Butterfly contest. Are you gonna go?"

Ugh. I try to think of an excuse, which is next to impossible considering how little I have to do each day.

"It's ok." She comes back into the living room in a tank top and shorts. "I know you don't like that kind of thing."

My chest swells with gratitude. More and more lately, Parker seems to be the one rescuing me rather than the other way around.

As we sit down to eat, I tell her about my trip to the museum, what I learned. "Do you ever wonder why Queen Supayalat did all those terrible things? Or whether she even did them at all?"

"Not really." Parker slumps down in the kitchen chair. The commute is harder on her than she's admitting.

"I mean, what if it's not true? What if she was the victim of an elaborate smear campaign?" I explain the museum keeper's theory.

She scrunches up her face in doubt. "I dunno, Etta. She always seemed a little unhinged to me."

"But what unhinged her? That's the question. Would history have been kinder if she'd been quiet and demure, sitting by the king's side without speaking her mind or acting on her concerns?"

She gives me a look of concern, as if, like Queen Supayalat or Ahpwa, I too might begin throwing precious objects across the room. "Are you okay?"

I think about the revelations of the past several days. Reading the Emma Larkin book. Finding out that Shwe also uses a pseudonym. Queen Supayalat's forgotten tomb. My own love letters hidden away for a quarter of a century. Shwe's blog. Ko Martin. The consequences of speaking out. The consequences of silence. Assumptions we make based on facts that may or may not be true.

"Have you seen Shwe?" I ask suddenly.

Parker thinks for a minute, her forehead crinkled in concentration. "Not since dinner the day you arrived, come to think of it."

Our eyes meet.

"What'd you do, Etta?"

FOURTEEN

Boston, Massachusetts
1998

Mother passed away my first year of law school. We'd never been close, her having abdicated every aspect of my rearing to Ahpwa, but her death unsettled me. With both our parents gone, Ahpwa and Parker were all I had left, and at 75, Ahpwa was starting to slow down, too. The idea of Parker and me all alone on this side of the world frightened me. We Burmese are meant to live in large, extended families, our lives all intertwined, everyone on top of each other and knowing each other's business. For the first time in a decade, I began to fantasize about returning to Rangoon.

By that time, Burma was completely cut off from the outside world. Ever more virulent anti-press laws meant that precious little information was leaked. Those who left the country were considered traitors, risking constant harassment or even imprisonment if they tried to return. Anyone with foreign connections was viewed with suspicion. And US sanctions against Burma, beginning with the Reagan administration and strengthened by each subsequent president, had made the Burmese government especially suspicious of Burmese Americans.

Afraid to return, I began instead to quietly educate myself about the country, supplementing my knowledge of ancient kingdoms and traditional arts with more contemporary history and politics. I learned that journalists had been apprehended and imprisoned for such trivial offences as owning a fax machine or possessing photos of Aung San Suu Kyi. That The Lady herself had been temporarily released from house arrest, though her movements, like those of many other NLD members, remained restricted. That students continued to protest, and universities had been closed yet again.

Did I think of Shwe in this context? Yes and no. Though we hadn't spoken in a decade, I knew somewhere deep in my gut that he was the kind of person who'd buck against such restrictions, go out of his way to fight authoritarianism, whether by owning contraband or engaging in more seditious acts. But this knowing was more of a dull ache than a sharp, biting fear. I knew Shwe in spirit, yes, but not in the specific, and it was this divide, this complete ignorance about the adult Shwe, that allowed me to set apart my new understanding of Myanmar from the Burma of my memories.

No longer living at home, I stopped by the house regularly to make sure Parker and Ahpwa were faring okay. On the cusp of 16, Parker had begun to show increasingly poor judgement in the months following Mother's death, drinking and smoking weed more often than I considered healthy. But it was Ahpwa who concerned me more. With Mother gone, I worried she might lose it again, return to the volatile, dish-smashing days after our return from Burma. What would happen to Parker then?

One afternoon, several months after Mother's passing, I came by earlier than usual to find Ahpwa in the kitchen assembling ingredients for dinner as she listened to the Burmese news on the old shortwave radio. The scent of fish sauce lingered in the air.

Ahpwa greeted me with an unusually placid smile. "I'm glad you came by. There's something I want to talk to you about." She seemed different somehow, her posture a little looser, eyes wider, less focused. Was I too late? Had she already flipped?

I sat down at the table and thought suddenly of Mother— how patiently and discreetly she'd managed Ahpwa all those years. How hard that must have been. "What is it, Ahpwa?"

She ducked into the pantry, returning with an armful of

onion, garlic and ginger pressed against the front of her apron, a jar of tamarind paste in her free hand.

"I know things have been difficult for you, *Myi*..." She trailed off, and something shifted inside me, the petals of a flower slowly opening.

"But don't make the same mistake as me, don't let the bad destroy the good."

I watched, uncomprehending, as she chopped the onion in half and turned it on its side, flicking away the skin in a single motion before transforming the bulb into thin, half-moon slivers. When she looked up, I saw that she was crying, and I wondered whether it was the onion or tears of sadness. That's when it hit me. She'd called me *Myi* again. A decade after it began, *America the Beautiful* had come to an end.

*

FIFTEEN

I pick up the last remaining mango from the kitchen counter, its flesh yielding to the pressure of my fingertips. An eternity seems to have passed since I gave the letters to Shwe, a lazy, almost dreamlike interval during which I've tried to keep busy, tried not to think about him. But his absence is like a cramp in my side that won't go away. The mango is past ripe, a sweet, almost fermented smell emanating from its skin.

When Shwe didn't return right away, I thought only of what his absence said about us, assuming his disappearance was related to my letters, that they'd made him angry or otherwise upset. Another, more worrying possibility begins to take shape in my mind: What if he *can't* get back to me? The more I think about it, the more certain I feel that he's in trouble, that someone or something is preventing him from returning. I imagine increasingly outlandish, yet somehow plausible, scenarios: that he's passed out in a gutter outside some seedy bar, that he's been kidnapped by one of the Golden Triangle drug lords, that he's back on the cold, damp floor of the prison's dog cages.

I have to find him, make sure he's safe. But how? I don't even know which part of the city he lives in, not to mention the street or building. I might've asked Parker, but she's already left for school, and of course, neither of our cell phones work here. Recalling that Khaing Zar works in one of the UN agencies based at the Inya Lake Hotel, I set off immediately. Surely his sister'll know his whereabouts.

As we enter the hotel grounds, my taxi driver—a chatty, spindle of a man—extends his arm out the window, tracing the building's outline against the sky as he demonstrates its resemblance to a giant submarine, complete with a cylindrical-shaped conning tower on its roof. The closer we get, the more animated he becomes, explaining that the building was designed by the Russians in the late 1950s as a gesture of Cold War solidarity with socialist Burma.

Intricate teak carvings and other traditional artwork lend the hotel lobby a dreamy, old-world feel. I pause to admire a floor-to-ceiling display of antique bells and gongs, awed as much by the simplicity of its design as the solemnity of the individual pieces. Yet I can't help wondering whether a certain nuance is not lost by assembling them all together like this, the cultural and historical essence of each piece sacrificed for overall effect.

Khaing Zar receives me with the same warm smile and ease I observed at the restaurant the other night. Dressed in a fresh lavender *htamein*, she glides through the office confident and carefree, not at all how I'd expect her to behave were she concerned about her brother. After a quick tour of the premises, in which she introduces me to several of her colleagues, we settle in her private office, where I ask, finally, about Shwe.

"Don't worry." She places her hand on my arm. "I'd know if he were in trouble."

"Then, where is he?"

"My guess is the monastery. We'll know if he comes back with his head shaven." Her eyes flash with amusement.

"Shwe? A monk?" I can't believe it. While I know it's customary for Burmese men to enter the monastery at several points throughout their lives, I assumed Shwe would shrink away from such convention, that, like me, he'd be more comfortable on the fringes of his faith rather than at its epicenter. But I don't know what I was thinking. Shwe doesn't shrink away from anything.

"Yeah, he does that more often than you'd think."

It's Khaing Zar's nonchalance, more than anything, that soothes me. The casual way she jokes and speculates about her brother lending a sense of normalcy to his behavior that I hadn't considered. To her, he's neither mesmerizing nor mysterious; he's just Shwe, her somewhat damaged, prone-to-brooding older brother.

Knowing he's safe, I offer to take her to lunch at the hotel's restaurant, where I ply her for advice on what to do with Ahpwa's ashes.

"Why not bury her in America?" says Khaing Zar, matter of fact. "She lived there much longer than she lived here."

"That's what I told Parker," I say with a sniff of vindication. But do I still feel the same? Now that we're here, now that Parker and Ahpwa and I have made this journey halfway across the world, I see that my grandmother never let go of Burma, that even at the peak of *America the Beautiful* when she wanted nothing to do with her heritage, the Golden Land continued to call to her. Like the thick, elastic bands she used to press her homemade tofu, she was stretched too thin, the pressure of competing cultures pulling her apart.

"In Buddhist tradition, death is just one stage in the cycle of life," continues Khaing Zar in that gentle, soothing tone of hers. "Funeral rites are not for the dead, but for the living, to help us come to terms with our loss, especially during the first seven days after our loved ones pass."

I nod, thinking back to the days immediately following Ahpwa's death, before I began to pack up Ahpwa's things and met U Soe Htet and fell under the spell of the marionettes. Despite Jason's best efforts, I went to the office every day, convincing myself that I couldn't afford to take more than a couple hours here and there, that doing so would somehow jeopardize my career, when in fact, it was a week like any other, full of meetings, contracts, and briefs that any one of my colleagues could have assumed on my behalf. At the time, I thought I'd managed my loss well.

"Funerals did play a bigger role in the past," Khaing Zar goes on, "but when the government moved the cemeteries and crematoria outside the city in the '90s, we made new rituals."

"They moved the cemeteries?"

"Sure. They do as they please," says Khaing Zar with a wave of her hand. "This is the reality of living under an authoritarian regime. Contrary to what the rest of the world may think, we don't let it break us. We adapt, we carry-on, yes. What choice do we have? But that doesn't mean we accept, and it certainly doesn't mean that we forget."

I think about the difference between adapting and accepting, between carrying on and forgetting. When I was growing up, Ahpwa held so tightly to her traditions that I almost suffocated. Until the day she let it all go. How might her life have been different had she stayed here? I look out at the hotel gardens, artfully landscaped with tropical flowers and trees. U Soe Htet longs to feel the Burmese sun on his face, the soil between his toes. What form did Ahpwa's yearning take? What did she ache for?

Our lunch arrives, a club sandwich for Khaing Zar and *nangyee thoke*, a noodle salad made with thick, round rice noodles and curried chicken, for me. I ask about San San, the nanny who looked after us all when we came to visit.

Khaing Zar tidies the layers of her club sandwich before responding. "She stopped working for us soon after your family left. The result of a disagreement with my mother."

"What kind of disagreement?" I spoon toasted chickpea flour and slices of hard-boiled egg onto my noodles.

"Better ask Shwe. Or San San herself. I can tell you where

she lives if you want to see her," she says, and I write down the address.

The salad is fresh and peppery. I feel at ease for the first time in several days. Shwe's safe, Parker's showing initiative and Ahpwa's ashes seem somehow less urgent. As we eat, Khaing Zar begins to confide in me about the challenges faced by the World Food Programme in Myanmar, how difficult it is to work with the government, but also how rewarding it can be when you finally reach those who are suffering. It's an area I know little about, so I ask lots of questions, how funds are obtained and distributed, how beneficiaries are selected. She goes on to talk about the widespread distrust of the UN, its portrayal in the state media as an instrument of Western imperialism and suppression of Burmese interests.

"So, how does the family feel about your working for the UN?"

"Shwe's supportive, of course. He gets it. But the rest of the family..." She doesn't finish her sentence.

I think back to dinner that first night—Thandar's necklace, Phyu Phyu's dress, the stilted conversation—and meet Khaing Zar's gaze.

"What about them?"

"Do you really not know?"

As her eyes bore into mine, I hear Shwe's rebuke 23 years ago. *Sometimes you're really stupid, Aye.* Confusion spirals into alarm as I piece together what I know. Shwe's grandfather. Military repression. Human rights' violations. Censorship. Incarceration. Tyranny. I put down my chopsticks, grasping, finally, the implications of Ahpwa's brother being a general in the military regime.

"General Myint Oo?"

"Shh." She glances around the restaurant.

SIXTEEN

Boston, Massachusetts
2001

Jason and I'd been together eight months, and I'd met his parents twice. The first time, they'd driven up to New England to see the autumn leaves and insisted on taking us out to dinner. The second time, Jason and I'd flown down to Pennsylvania for his nephew's birthday, spending the weekend in separate bedrooms at his parents' house. My reluctance to introduce him to Parker and Ahpwa was becoming a sore point.

I considered my options. Though Ahpwa had mellowed in the years since Mother died, she could snap at any moment. What if she started smashing dishes again? How would I explain that to Jason? Parker continued to make some questionable decisions, but none of them came close to Ahpwa's potential to throw my life into mayhem. After a year of waiting tables at various restaurants and bars across Boston, she'd finally enrolled in college and seemed to be getting her act together. I decided to give her a chance.

Heading into our late twenties, with two steady incomes, Jason and I had begun to frequent concerts, art galleries and museum exhibits, but I figured Parker would turn up her nose at anything too posh. So, when the weather grew warm, I invited her to join us for a free concert at the Hatch Shell. I'd take care of the food and the blanket. All she had to do was show up.

"Sure, I'll drop by," she said. "Okay if I bring someone?"

I should've paid more attention to her response, but my mind had cartwheeled into planning mode. I spent the next several days selecting the right foods for the picnic basket. Was Camembert too pretentious? What about Brie? I wanted so badly for the two of them to like each other. I even threw in a couple of bottles of white wine despite Parker being underage.

Jason and I arrived an hour early to stake out a good spot. It was a beautiful summer day, the breeze from the river tempering the heat of the afternoon sun. He stretched his long legs across the blanket, and I laid down, resting my head on his lap as I soaked up the last rays of sunshine. We were too busy laughing and talking to notice the time at first. But as the sun sank lower in the sky, the ground seemed to grow harder, the air buggier. Watching Jason swat at a mosquito, I wondered what she'd think of him, whether she'd notice the flecks of green in his hazel eyes or how his face flushed when he looked at me. I thought he looked sexy in his blue polo shirt and khakis, but could see that she might find him too straight-laced, too conservative.

I'd shown him photos, so he knew how different Parker and I looked—her being blond and blue-eyed like our father—but I wasn't sure I'd prepared him for how different we were in temperament. The more he crossed and uncrossed his legs, the more my anxiety soared, each shift in his position triggering a new round of speculation as to what he might be thinking.

"I didn't actually tell her to come early," I reminded us both.

He rolled his head from side to side, stretching the muscles in his neck.

"Should we eat?" I asked.

"I can wait." His voice was its normal, even timbre, but he looked so awkward sitting on that blanket, so restless and uncomfortable, that I felt sure he was secretly annoyed, putting up a happy front for my sake. I was beginning to feel sorry for myself when I remembered the wine. Digging through the picnic basket, I found the bottle of pinot grigio, slick with condensation, and proceeded to remove the cork under cover of a napkin.

"I hope it isn't too warm." I handed him a plastic cup of wine.

"Not bad." He took a sip then set the cup down on the blanket.

The Hatch Shell had been a poor choice, I saw suddenly. Jason was too long-limbed to spend an entire evening on a blanket, with or without the wildcard of my impetuous little sister.

Parker and her friend showed up 45 minutes into the concert.

"Whoa, chill music," said the friend, nodding his head slowly. He was unshaven, with stringy brown hair that covered his ears. His name slipped my mind almost the same moment I learned it, but his smell was unforgettable—a nauseating blend of patchouli, marijuana and fried chicken.

I looked at Parker in dismay, all my hopes of a happy introduction crumbling in her bloodshot eyes and see-through sundress. "You come 45 minutes late, like this?"

"Why do you always have to be such a kill-joy?" she answered back.

We glared at each other with undisguised contempt.

"Dude. Relax," said the friend.

"Don't call me *dude*," I said.

"Shh," said Jason, his eyes wide with admonishment as he glanced around at the other concertgoers.

The music swelled around me. I needed to get it together. This new relationship with Jason was too precious to risk losing my temper. After an awkward pantomime of greetings, I doled out snacks and we squeezed onto the too-small blanket for the remainder of the concert.

Later that night, as Jason and I walked back to his apartment that would soon become ours, I offloaded all my concerns about Parker, blaming her irresponsibility and inconsideration for the perforated evening as if I had played no role in the debacle. He listened graciously, asking all the right questions then paraphrasing back what I'd said. I took his attentiveness as confirmation that he agreed with me, that I was in the right, and from that point onward, went to considerable effort to carve out separate occasions to spend with each.

SEVENTEEN

After delivering Daw Tin Tin's greetings to U Zaw Minn, I sit down at my regular computer and open two tabs. In addition to checking my email, which I neglected to do yesterday, I want to find out more about General Myint Oo.

Jason's written twice. The first message is long and chatty, bringing me up to date on the various goings-on of friends and work colleagues. The second he sent just hours ago, likely right before going to bed.

> *Dear Etta,*
>
> *Are you okay? I've been checking my email all day for a message from you. I don't know how to explain it, but you seem so far away and unreachable. Maybe it's the story of U Soe Htet and your grandmother getting into my head, but I feel like I am losing you. Please call or write soon.*
>
> *Love Jason*

Alarmed by this new, desperate tone, I respond right away. *I'm sorry. I love you. Things don't work the same here, but I'll try to write more often.* I tell him about my lunch with Khaing Zar and give him Daw Tin Tin's number, with the proviso to call only in case of emergency. Although she said he could call any time, I don't want to take advantage of Daw Tin Tin or feel beholden to her.

Next, I begin a short email to my boss. She'd been surprisingly understanding about my need to come here, her only ask that I send her a weekly update. But what can I possibly say with everything so up in the air? While I still hope to return as planned in one week's time, I can't imagine leaving before I see Shwe again. And who knows when that will be? As a precaution, I decide to tell her that I might need a few more days.

Closing my email, I check the results of my Google search on General Myint Oo. Official government-sponsored webpages paint him as a fearless and patriotic leader, celebrating the many donations and other good deeds he performed at the end of his life. The remaining links, including those from opposition media such as Mizzima and Irrawaddy, lead to the same, automatically generated warning indicating that the website in question has been blocked by Myanmar Post and Telecommunications.

I consider sending Jason a second email asking him to look into General Myint Oo. He wouldn't be able to send any links, of course, but if he found anything of interest, he could cut and paste the text into an innocuous-looking email message, which might get through. I imagine trying to explain all this to him—both the why and the how. He'd be happy I asked, grateful to finally be included in my mysterious quest, this journey that's taken me so far away from him. But do I really want Jason learning the dirty history of my family before I understand it myself?

~

San San lives in a working-class neighborhood on the outskirts of Yangon, where makeshift shacks are stacked one upon the other like the slipper seashells I used to collect at the beach as a child. A man stands in front of his shack, his *longyi* hiked up to his groin as he lathers soap over his bare chest and legs. I quickly avert my eyes only to realize that he doesn't care whether I see him bathing. I'm the one embarrassed, not him.

San San's place is three doors down, a small but tidy lean-to, with two plastic chairs sitting out front. Knocking on the door, I recall the last time we saw each other, how kind and understanding she'd been to Parker and me, how she'd seen my despair at leaving Shwe and agreed to deliver my message to him.

"*Yau bi la?*" she says as she opens the door. So, you've arrived?

While common enough, the greeting chips at my confidence. *Yau bi la* is something you say after a separation of an hour or a day, not a quarter of a century.

"*Yau bi,*" I answer. Yep, I'm here.

Aside from a few more pounds around the waist, she's just as I remember, the same delicate features and bright complexion, the same quick smile and nod of the head. What surprises me is how young she looks. At thirteen, I viewed her as an adult, but I see now that she's not much older than I am. We embrace awkwardly, and she invites me in.

The living area is cluttered but clean, a sack of rice and bundle of straw mats standing incongruously beside a small fridge and gas burner. In the center of the one-room shack is a set of mismatched chairs and an old wooden table that looks vaguely familiar. She makes some tea and asks about Mother and Father and Ahpwa. I struggle to provide a narrative of their lives beyond the simple fact that they are dead. She doesn't mention Parker, so I presume that they've already seen each other.

As I sip the thick, sugary brew, San San tells me her story. She grew up poor but happy and loved, her semi-educated parents both tailors by profession. On the eve of her 15th birthday, military police stormed her house and, without warning or explanation, stole her parents away. For a while, no one seemed to know what they'd been accused of, or where they'd been taken. They were simply in the wrong place at the wrong time, without the necessary connections to extricate themselves. Eventually news came that her parents had been taken to a hard-labor camp in the north. "As far as I know, they are still there," she adds.

The eldest of four, she dropped out of school to support her siblings. After a few false starts, she was hired as a nanny by Shwe's mother, who treated her well for the most part. She'd been working with them for two years when my family came to Burma.

"So, what happened? Why'd you stop?"

She looks at the wall, where a web of mildew spreads outward from an exposed PVC pipe. "A misunderstanding, you might say." I gather from her evasiveness that she doesn't want to go into the details of her dismissal, so I ask instead about her family, whether she married, had children.

Brightening, she whips out a glossy photo album full of photos of her daughter, Su Su, and son, Thant. Su Su is very beautiful with the same delicate features as her mother, though there's something unsettling about the way she stares at the camera, as if challenging the photographer in some way. I guess her to be in her early twenties. The boy, Thant, is much younger, with an earring in his left ear and spiked green hair, which makes me laugh. I don't see any men in the photos so assume there's no father to speak of.

"I'd love to meet them one day." I look up from the album.

San San beams. Then she picks up my hand and examines my engagement ring.

"You will marry soon?" she asks.

I tell her that the wedding is scheduled for next year and she nods without expression.

"And how is it between you and Shwe these days? Back then you were like two seeds of a tamarind pod, and everyone knows that saplings of the same fruit can never be far from each other."

I smile at her twist on the old proverb. Coming from anyone else the question would be an intrusion, but San San was witness to Shwe's and my relationship from day one. And like many domestic staff in a busy Burmese household, she knew everything that went on under that roof.

"We haven't talked much, to be honest. He disappeared not long after I arrived," I say. "Khaing Zar says he's gone to the monastery."

She meets my gaze with an expression that I can't decipher. Sorrow? Longing? Regret? "That's what he does. Goes inside himself. Same like after you left, reading and writing all day long. I knew it meant trouble, but your auntie, she didn't understand."

"What do you mean?"

"He was so serious. Like an old man. I tried to distract him, to comfort him." Her eyes wander down to the table. "But your auntie became angry."

"I don't understand. Are you saying that Shwe is the reason you were dismissed?"

San San shrugs, and I follow her gaze to the open photo album on the table. I can feel her watching me and waiting. For what, I don't know.

Calmly at first and then with mounting disbelief, I realize what it is about Su Su's stare that unsettles me. I know those eyes better than I know myself. I turn the page of the album, and there is Su Su in graduation gown and cap, standing between San San and Shwe.

~

Parker's sitting at the kitchen table surrounded by papers when I get in.

"Are you okay? You look like you've seen a ghost."

I stare at her blankly, wondering if she knows about Su Su.

"I went to see San San."

"Oh yeah, I visited her when I first arrived. So fun to see her after all these years."

I'm guessing from the lightness of her tone that she has no idea about San San and Shwe. For a second, I think I should tell her, in the spirit of being more open, then realize that it's not my information to share. What business is it of Parker's, or mine for that matter?

"How'd your research go?" I ask instead.

"Mixed. Turns out traditional government donors like USAID steer clear of orphanages. Too much like charity, you know? But I think I've found some smaller foundations that might be interested." She bites her lip, then holds out a stack of foundation profiles and guidelines that she borrowed from the library.

We spend the next hour organizing the information into categories. I suggest she establish criteria to narrow down her search, and she comes up with three: specialization in children's issues; focus on Myanmar as a priority country; and a clear and structured application process. After much discussion, she zeroes in on four small foundations that meet these criteria. I give her some pointers on how to put together the proposal, which she jots down in a small notebook, and for the first time in days, I feel like I've accomplished something.

PART THREE

ONE

Gliding around the kitchen in my newly purchased apron from the market below, I simmer some pork belly in a marinade of dark soy, chicken stock and sugar. I'm making *pone yae gyi* as a surprise for Parker. Rich and earthy, the pork and fermented black bean dish adapts easily to her milder palate by reducing the amount of chili. She's off at the Miss Butterfly Contest with Thandar, but since it's Sunday, I wanted to reestablish our tradition of dedicating the day to family by preparing something special for when she gets home.

I've just finished chopping the onions when the doorbell sounds, and I startle, the strident techno-jingle a sound I still can't get used to. I look at my watch. Parker must have "forgotten" her keys again. We can't agree on this: She hates me locking the door, and I don't feel safe leaving it open. But we're getting along well enough these days that the disagreement is more playful than hostile. I run to the door, drying the tears from the onion with the back of my wrist. But it isn't Parker.

It's Shwe, his head shiny and bald, cheeks slightly hollowed, and around his neck, the botched pink and purple scarf I'd given Ahpwa as a child. I'm so stunned, I can't decide whether to shout at him for disappearing or throw my arms around him in delight, to tease him about his shorn head or ask about the letters. In the end, the scarf wins me over, the utter absurdity of wearing it in this heat making me laugh out loud. Here at last is the boy I adored all those years ago, the quirky, irreverent kid who could turn a dreary day into a kaleidoscope of possibility.

"Mmm." He sniffs the air theatrically, and I invite him to stay for dinner. We don't embrace, but that's okay. It's enough that he's here, that he's come back.

209

He hangs the scarf on a hook next to the door. The colors still strike me as garish and immature, but now that I see it fully extended, all those dropped stitches and yarn-changes blend into the contour of the knitting, enhancing rather than detracting from its appearance.

I put Shwe to work chopping ginger and garlic, while I pick through the saw-herb leaves and cube the sautéed pork belly. Working side by side like this with him fills me with a splintery new hope. That the past still means something. That we'll find our way back to a more natural way of relating. Yet, I'm wary of the space between us, going out of my way not to get too close, not to accidentally brush my hand against his.

I tell him about my excursions around the city, and soon, we're exchanging views on the extent to which Yangon has or hasn't changed over the years.

"The city's lost its soul," he says. "First Naypyitaw, then Nargis."

"I don't know," I begin, "there's something about this place I've never experienced anywhere else. A kind of rawness, an impression of life being lived fully ..." I trail off, suddenly shy about my choice of words, uncertain how to finish, whether to say *that I remember,* or simply end the sentence there.

He shakes his head. "People only care about themselves. There's no sense of community, no commitment to anything bigger than meeting our everyday needs."

Something in me recoils against this unfair description of Yangon and its inhabitants. I picture Ko Martin, the lawyer in the teashop, and U Aung, the museum keeper. The little girl who stopped to help her sister on the side of the road.

"Maybe cities have a natural ebb and flow. People need to focus on their own needs for a period before returning to the greater good." I'm not entirely sure what we're talking about anymore but notice that he stops chopping to listen to what I have to say. I tell myself that this as a good sign, that at some point in the future, we'll be able to talk about the past, too. Even if that feels impossible now.

I put the rice on to boil and start sautéing onions while Shwe describes life in the monastery—fasting from noon to dawn, walking through the streets to collect alms, sleeping on a hard, wooden platform. The aroma from the fried onions envelops us, and my mouth begins to water. Shwe talks about meditation, how his favorite part of monastery life is being able to practice any time of day or night, often for hours on end, how by stilling his mind, he's able to stay focused on what matters.

"Clears away the fog, you know?"

He passes me the chopped garlic and ginger, and I stir them into the onions, letting them simmer for a minute before adding the pork and stock. I don't meditate anymore, but there was a time in my early twenties, before I met Jason, when I practiced daily. I can't remember why I stopped. I suppose I found the inward focus unsettling. Mixing in the fresh *pone yae gyi* paste from the market, I begin to wonder what Shwe means precisely, whether the fog he mentions is related to me, or something else altogether.

I cover the pot and turn up the heat, then spin around to face him. "So, you read the letters."

"Yeah." He lifts the lid of the pot and inhales deeply, then walks over to the window. "Seems like a lifetime ago."

"What do you mean?"

"How naïve we were."

Naïve as in natural and innocent, or naïve as in ignorant and immature? The word richochets through my mind, sapping what's left of my confidence.

The door to the apartment opens and closes, and Parker sweeps into the kitchen like a gust of wind.

211

"Whoa. What happened to your hair?" She rubs her hand over the top of Shwe's head.

I cringe, knowing how taboo it is touch someone's head in Buddhist culture. But Shwe doesn't blink. Instead, he gives Parker a carefree kiss on the cheek, and in that simple, casual gesture, so unlike how he relates to me, seems to cancel out any progress, however small, that he and I have made.

The pork mixture boils over, upsetting the lid and bubbling down the sides of the pot. I swing back to the stove to turn down the heat.

"So, monastery, huh? What was *that* like?" asks Parker.

I stir vigorously until the mixture reduces to a simmer.

"Oh, you know. Hectic." His tone is light, almost bouncy.

She swats his arm. "I don't think I could handle the fasting."

"I don't think you could either," he responds, laughing.

I prepare the condiments in tight-lipped silence while they carry on in short, playful quips back and forth. As much as I want the three of us to bond as a family, I can't help resenting Parker for interrupting the first real conversation I've had with Shwe in 23 years.

I dish out the steaming hot pork and we sit down to eat, the rich, earthy aroma of *pone yae gyi* tempering my wounded pride.

"Yum" says Parker. "You didn't put too much chili, did you?"

"If anything, she didn't put enough," says Shwe, adding some fresh chilis to his dish.

As I listen to their banter, my jealousy softens to curiosity. True, they share something I will never have. Their relationship is easy and light, unshackled by the past. But is that what I want from either of them?

TWO

Shwe returns the following morning just as I'm leaving the apartment.

"Where you headed?" He gestures to the bag on my shoulder.

I tell him my destination: an Indian button shop I read about in one of Parker's magazines, the singularity of its focus reminding me of old Rangoon, where every product had its own store, and the world seemed less complicated.

"25th Street, right? How're you getting there?"

"Umm . . . taxi?" I say with a nervous laugh.

He laughs too, and a few minutes later I'm sitting in the front, left passenger seat of Shwe's taxi, travelling south on Pyay Road.

Rows of old-fashioned black Singer sewing machines line the shop, alongside giant spools of thread and buttons of every size, shape, and color. I sort through a basket of delicate glass buttons while Shwe chats with the owner, showering him with questions about the Indian community's views on everything from sanctions to Aung San Suu Kyi to the potential for interfaith dialogue. The owner's wife brings us two cups of thick, sugary tea and a plate of Indian sweets as colorful as the buttons. Then Shwe and the owner exchange contact details, and we say our goodbyes.

Back in the taxi, we cruise down Strand Road and turn up Pansodan, the cracked domes and mildewed facades of the old colonial buildings still dominating the cityscape despite having been abandoned when the capital moved to Naypyitaw.

A middle-aged man holding a briefcase waves us down.

"You mind?" asks Shwe.

I shake my head, and he pulls over. As much as I'd love to spend the day with him alone, to finally talk about us, what we felt when we were kids and what it means now, to ask about Su Su and General Myint Oo, I can't deprive Shwe of his living.

The man with the briefcase is heading to Kamayut Township in northern Yangon. He and Shwe negotiate a price and the man gets in, acknowledging me with a nod. Yangon taxi drivers often ride around with a companion in the front seat, so my presence doesn't surprise him. As we set off, Shwe glances repeatedly in the rearview mirror.

"What's in the briefcase?" he asks after a few minutes, and for a fleeting, irrational moment, I'm worried that the man might be concealing an AK47 or its Myanmar equivalent, the EMERK rifle I'd seen in video footage in my twenties.

"Pathogenicity screening for H5N1," answers the man.

I glance at Shwe, who looks back to the rearview mirror for clarification.

"Kits for testing poultry. To stop the spread of avian flu," the man, a veterinarian working for the Department of Livestock, explains.

We spend the next twenty minutes discussing animal husbandry practices, the efficacy of random testing, and the likelihood of an avian flu epidemic in Myanmar, and I begin to understand why Shwe likes driving a taxi so much. It's like a series of first dates without the pressure of commitment. We leave the vet on University Ave, not far from Parker's apartment, and for a desperate moment, I worry that Shwe intends to drop me off as well. Scanning the throng of pedestrians, I notice a couple of elderly tourists consulting a map.

"There!" I say, with a little too much enthusiasm.

"What?"

"Those two, they need a taxi," I say almost at the same time as the woman puts her hand out to wave us down.

"Wow, you're good," he says, and I can tell from the lightness of his tone that he's as pleased as I am to continue driving around together. There's much still to say, but right now all I really care about is keeping this going for as long as possible.

The couple climbs in the back seat. Establishing that they're from Germany, Shwe strikes up a conversation about their recent elections as he transports us to the Nga Htat Gyi Pagoda in Bahan Township. After a quick peek at the giant seated Buddha, Shwe and I stop at a teashop for some of the best *mohinga* I've had in years, then pick up another client heading to the airport. It's dark when he drops me back at Parker's apartment.

~

I've just put my bag down when I hear a telephone ring on the floor below and know instinctively that it's Jason. Sure enough, Daw Tin Tin arrives at the door a few minutes later, slightly out of breath.

"I have the most delightful young man on the line for you." She squeezes her eyes together in an exaggerated blink that reminds me of U Soe Htet.

"Oh no. So sorry for the inconvenience—" I begin.

"Don't be silly, dear. It's no bother whatsoever."

As I follow Daw Tin Tin down the narrow stairwell, my mind stumbles through possible emergencies: What if one of his parents is ill? Or U Soe Htet? What if Jason himself has had an accident?

She leads me into her living room where a mint-green, rotary telephone sits on a table of its own, the recumbent receiver connected by a mass of coiled cord. I sit down on the antique armchair next to the phone, trying not to let my apprehension show.

"I'll give you some privacy, dear," she says as she backs out of the room.

I clamp the receiver to my ear. "Jason! Is everything okay?"

"What? Yeah. Oh, sorry. I know you said only to call in case of emergency, but I got worried when I didn't hear from you."

I can see him coming to this decision, not through a tortuous, analytical route like I might, but quickly and decisively, *yes, I'll call her today*. It's sweet but a little annoying considering I asked him not to use this number so freely. But what really concerns me is how distracted I've become. In the excitement of driving around Yangon with Shwe, I forgot all about Cyber Savvy and my regular emails to Jason. "Sorry I couldn't make it to the internet café today."

"Or yesterday," he adds.

"Yesterday?" At first, I think he's confused by the time difference—6:30 p.m. Yangon time being 7:00 a.m. Boston time—then I realize with a jolt that he's right: I haven't emailed him since before visiting San San. I explain about my visit to our old nanny—how far away she lives, how strange it was to see her after all this time, how young she looked. Then move on to the button shop and the sitting Buddha, making them sound like longer excursions than they really were. Jason seems satisfied with the explanation, but I remain troubled. No matter how much I talk up the fullness of that day, I can't shake the simple fact that Jason slipped my mind.

He tells me about a new project he's involved in at work and his plan to visit U Soe Htet later in the week, how he keeps forgetting to give him the photos I found in Ahpwa's chest but promises to remember next time. The more we talk, the more I melt into the conversation, safe and protected, as if I'm back in Boston, curled up next to him on our new sofa.

"I can't wait to see you this weekend," he says, finally.

I think about my walks around Yangon and the changing shape of my relationship with Parker, about Shwe's return and the unexpected joy of spending the day in his taxi, even if we haven't yet sorted out the past. How can I return home when I've only just arrived? But at the same time, how can I not?

"You're not coming, are you?"

The disappointment in his voice tugs at my conscience. I don't want to hurt Jason, but I need more time. I tell him the truth, which is that I don't know.

THREE

Over the next few days, Shwe's clients bring him to the neighborhood around the same time every morning, while I conjure up a variety of errands requiring a taxi—not an easy task considering there's a market below Parker's building. As we explore the city, our conversations meander through the decades, crisscrossing the time we were last together without quite touching on us.

I talk about what happened to my family after Burma—Ahpwa's break, Father's ultimatum, Mother's lack of fortitude—terrain I've turned over and over in my head yet rarely spoken of out loud. I share with him how alienated I sometimes felt growing up in the whitewashed suburbs of Boston, and how freeing it feels now to walk through the streets of Yangon, anonymous. It's as if the windows of Shwe's taxi provide a fresh vantage point for looking at my life, a new awareness that is crisper and clearer, more linear.

On day four, we abandon all pretense of clients and errands.

Driving over U Htaing Bo Road, Shwe tells me about his early days as a journalist, working undercover to evade the Ministry of Information's Press Scrutiny Division. "I wrote my stories out by hand, dispatching them in crates of dried lentils to Mae Sot or one of the other border crossings. Once the piece arrived, some poor scribe at Mizzima or Voice of Burma had the task of deciphering my handwriting. I don't know how they did it." He shakes his head. "First translating my scribbles into print, then sneaking those stories back into Burma. I'll never forget the first time I read one of my own pieces in print, the satisfaction I felt that the truth was finally being told. That I was part of the movement making it happen."

The way he talks about his work fits the image of him I've held in my heart over the decades. I'd known all along that he was destined for a life of consequence, that all that intensity and rumination had a purpose. The taxi, too, feels like a logical extension of his teenage self—always talking, listening, connecting with the people around him. As I watch him casually navigate the traffic, his crumpled shirt slightly open at the chest, it strikes me that even Parker's claim that he's a lady's man makes sense, yet another expression of his unbridled passion for life, or in this case, women. That he fathered a child with San San is not a deviation but a reflection of who he is.

"The government hates Moe Pwint," he adds with a snicker of satisfaction.

I stiffen. "Do they know who you are?"

"Nah, they haven't been able to prove a connection. Every time they arrest me, it's for something petty like possession of a banned publication or unsanctioned assembly. Not that they need an excuse to arrest people."

I shudder, resisting the image of Shwe back in prison even as I know it's a possibility.

"How old were you the first time?"

He turns left onto U Wisara Road. "Seventeen." His tone is cool, matter of fact.

I started college at the same age, commuting back and forth from home because Ahpwa forbade me to live in the dorms. At the time, this seemed the ultimate injustice.

"What about your grandfather? Couldn't he do something?" Despite what Khaing Zar intimated over lunch, I still want to believe that Ahpwa's brother was a good man, or at least a good grandfather.

Shwe turns to look at me, his expression somewhere between pity and disdain.

My eyes wander down to the scar on his arm, the one I'd noticed that first day at the airport, almost before we'd spoken.

"Could've but didn't." I answer my own question but remain unsettled. As cold as Ahpwa could be, she would never have allowed anyone to hurt me. Was Shwe's grandfather really so uncaring, so heartless?

The taxi slows to a crawl as we enter the heart of downtown, trucks unloading their goods in the middle of the road, pedestrians crossing the street at will. Shwe turns onto a side street so narrow that the taxi straddles baskets of vegetables that vendors have placed in a line down the middle of the road. There's so much more I want to ask—about Su Su, about prison, about Shwe's grandfather—but I can see that I need to tread more carefully.

"I had a look at your blog."

"Yeah?" His tone lifts. "What'd you think?"

"It's good. Really good. When did you start?"

"Right after Nargis," he says, referring to the devastating cyclone that hit Myanmar in 2008. "The government was so overwhelmed by all the death and destruction, and so oblivious about the internet, that we could publish whatever we wanted. We didn't even need to mention politics. Describing everyday life was damning enough."

"And now?" I ask.

"Supposedly we're free to publish anything, but I still use the lentil method to send out my more controversial pieces, just to be on the safe side." He drums his fingers on the steering wheel. "One of these days, though, I just might put them to the test."

A new edge to his voice sends goosebumps up and down my arms. It's almost as if he wants to get caught, as if exposing the corruption and deceit of the government outweighs any physical or psychological harm he might incur in the process.

~

I'm sitting on Parker's sofa about an hour later when I hear the telephone ring through the floor. I run downstairs just as Daw Tin Tin opens the door on her way to get me. Despite all my warnings and caveats, Jason seems to have incorporated a daily call into his morning routine—making it part of her and my evening routine. Though she claims to be happy for the diversion, *delighted,* in fact, to have such a charming young man ring her each night, I bristle at the inconvenience of the situation, at the clumsiness of my life in this moment. If only I could talk to Jason without having to impose on someone else, if only my life weren't so disjointed.

Daw Tin Tin makes the usual fuss about giving me my privacy and disappears into the shadows. At the sound of Jason's voice, my mood begins to loosen. I tease him about Daw Tin Tin having a crush on him, and we're soon back to an easy exchange. In some ways, I feel closer to Jason than ever, the concentrated window of the phone call forcing us to communicate more directly, even if the topics themselves are on the superficial side.

I look forward to telling him what I've seen and where I've gone, and find myself energized by his many questions. When he asks who I went with, I say simply that I went with my cousin. I don't hide the fact that I've done all this with Shwe, nor do I offer additional details. I tell myself that the two have nothing to do with each other. Shwe is simply part of who I am, has always been part of who I am, even if Jason doesn't know this about me.

"So, I gave U Soe Htet those photos you left," says Jason.

I recall the two photos with a flutter of curiosity, the first an image of U Soe Htet as a much younger man holding the Yatheik marionette, the second a young man I'd never seen before.

"And?"

"One made him laugh and the other made him cry."

"Which one made him cry?" I press the receiver to my ear.

"The other man."

I tug at the tangled telephone cord as I piece together what I know. But there's something here that doesn't add up, some missing piece of the puzzle that I can't quite grasp.

Allowing Jason to tell me the story in his own time takes all my self-control. Apparently, Ahpwa visited U Soe Htet's family while we were in Burma in 1988. Although U Soe Htet never had the opportunity to hear about the visit from Ahpwa herself, his sister had described it in a letter that arrived weeks later. Ahpwa had been exceptionally kind and attentive to his family, especially to one of his nephews, who was studying hard at the University in the hope of one day joining his uncle in America. According to Jason, Ahpwa even agreed to sponsor the young man's trip to Boston. This nephew is the young man in the photo that Ahpwa kept in her chest, the photo that made U Soe Htet cry.

"What was his name?"

"Lwin Soe," answers Jason.

I frown. The story doesn't fit my memory. Ahpwa could've visited U Soe Htet's family without my knowing, of course, but I would've known had she sponsored someone to make the trip all the way to Boston. Before 1988, we often hosted Burmese newcomers. Sometimes they stayed a night or two, other times only long enough for a cup of tea. Ahpwa would make me recite a poem or some other Burmese text I'd been forced to memorize. I didn't care much for the recitals but enjoyed sitting around the table afterward, listening to stories of old Burma. Over the years, all sorts passed through—men, women, young, old, rich, poor— but like so many aspects of our family life, those visits came to an abrupt stop with *America the Beautiful*. Either Lwin Soe never made it to America, or Ahpwa reneged on her promise.

"What else did he say?" I ask.

"Nothing more about Lwin Soe. But he talked a lot about your grandmother, how she broke things off as soon as she got back to Boston." There's a hint of hostility in his voice when he speaks of Ahpwa, a bitterness to his tone that unsettles me.

According to Jason, Ahpwa telephoned U Soe Htet shortly after we returned to Boston, saying only that she couldn't see him anymore and that she was sorry. He tried to reason with her, but Ahpwa would say no more. Eventually, U Soe Htet gave up, channeling his passion into his academic career, which flourished. But Jason was convinced that the question of why Ahpwa left him still pained the old man.

"My theory is that it was about status," he says, "after meeting his family, she realized what different socioeconomic classes they came from."

"Did U Soe Htet actually say that?" Jason's interpretation strikes me as unfair, over simplistic.

"Not exactly. I just put two and two together." A cautious, slightly higher pitch to his voice tells me that he knows I'm annoyed, even if he doesn't yet understand why.

"Well, she wasn't like that."

He's silent for a moment. "So tell me what she was like. Talk to me."

I shrink back into Daw Tin Tin's chair, wincing in self-reproach. Why am I upset with Jason? His theory is not so far-fetched, given how hierarchical Burmese society can be. But Ahpwa wasn't a snob. Even before *America the Beautiful*, she'd let herself be seduced by the American love affair with rags to riches stories, eschewing all notions of social stratification.

"I mean, maybe it was like that for some people," I concede. "But not Ahpwa."

"So why do *you* think she broke up with him?" he asks.

"I don't know." The fury in my chest has begun to recede, but I'm ready for the conversation to end.

He exhales. A sigh?

"Okay, I'd better get to work anyway. Let's talk tomorrow."

I return the receiver to its base but remain seated in the chair, trying to understand what might've happened to Lwin Soe, but more immediately, why I got so defensive, and Jason so frustrated.

Daw Tin Tin peeks her head into the room. "Everything ok, dear?"

I look up, surprised at first, then with resigned acceptance. I should've known she'd be listening to my conversation.

I sit down on the bed, Ahpwa's urn in my lap. How little I knew her, really. How little I bothered to get to know her. So many years we lived, ate, and read together, yet I knew next to nothing about her and U Soe Htet, let alone know why she left him. To me, she was just Ahpwa—high-handed and controlling Ahpwa—who choreographed my every move like one of her old marionettes. I was so tangled in resentment that I never stopped to consider what she might have felt, what hopes and regrets she had as a woman.

Returning the urn to the dresser, I stare into the mirror pulling my hair back at the nape of my neck, the way she wore her hair before we went to Burma, before she cut it all off. I can see why people say I look like her. I have the same round face and broad cheek bones, the same piercing eyes, and shiny black hair. Is this what worries Jason—that I'm too like Ahpwa, that I'll do the same thing to him that she did to U Soe Htet?

FOUR

Shwe and I head south on Baho Road, our passenger this morning a middle-aged Kachin man on his way to one of the city's few Baptist churches. He and Shwe are discussing an increase in tension between the Tatmadaw and the Kachin Independence Army in the northern most region of the country. I try to follow but am distracted by the heat, sweat dripping down my collar bone as last night's call with Jason plays over and over in my head. The photo of Lwin Soe remains a puzzle, but what really concerns me is Jason, this new edge to our phone calls that leaves me nervous and unsettled. For the first time in days, I ask myself what I'm really doing here in Yangon, how much longer I can stay without damaging my relationship with Jason.

"You okay?" says Shwe, after dropping our passenger at the church.

"Yeah, just a lot on my mind."

"Want to talk about it?"

Talk to Shwe about Jason? The idea is so outlandish that, for a second, I'm giddy with possibility. If only my life were so cohesive, so undivided. But Shwe and Jason belong to two distinct hemispheres. To merge the two is to risk turning the world upside down. No, I can't talk to Shwe about Jason. But maybe Shwe can tell me something about U Soe Htet's nephew.

"Do you know a man named Lwin Soe? He'd be maybe five, ten years older than us."

He thinks for a minute. "Nah, I don't think so. Wait—is this the same guy Parker was asking about?"

I spot a young, white woman with short, red hair waving at us from the side of the road. "Look. There."

Shwe doesn't seem to hear me, then pulls over at the last minute.

"Hi, Shwaaaaayy. So good to see you! Oh wow, your hair," says the woman as she slides into the back seat. Dressed in casual business attire with a necklace of misshapen orange and white jade beads, she looks to be in her mid-twenties. I'm guessing she works at one of the many non-governmental organizations providing humanitarian aid to Myanmar.

"Hey, Jennifer," says Shwe.

"Who's your friend?" she asks.

"Oh, this is my cousin, Ma Aye Tha Kyaw." He speaks to Jennifer in English, but for some reason introduces me by my Burmese name, then winks at me and adds, "She doesn't speak English."

I'm about to object when Jennifer turns to me.

"*Min...ga...la...ba.*" She articulates each syllable of the common greeting with great care. "*Twei...ya...da...wun...tha...ba...dei.*" It's nice to meet you.

I glare at Shwe, but he just smiles and keeps driving.

"*Twei-ya-da wun-tha-ba-dei.*" I respond reluctantly, but Jennifer's interest in me has already faded.

"I haven't seen you in ages. Where've you been?" She presses closer to the driver's seat.

I look sideways at Shwe, trying to gauge how he feels about this woman, whether he likes her as much as she clearly likes him. Whether they've slept together.

"Oh, you know," he answers, cool as a cat. "How 'bout you? What're you up to?"

As she talks about her work, I imagine his hands traveling down her skinny waist, over her pasty hips, knowing suddenly that this is what would follow if I weren't here. Embarrassed, I turn toward the window, staring blankly at a young woman selling fried dough on the side of the road. As Jennifer and Shwe talk about some mutual friends, the woman places the basket of fried dough onto her head and sets off down the broken footpath. I don't know why it bothers me so much, the idea of Shwe and Jennifer. I have Jason, after all. But the more I try to put the image out of my head, the clearer it becomes, except now, instead of Jennifer's pale waist, it's San San's smooth, bronzed hips.

Shwe pulls into the parking lot of Pearl Condo where Jennifer lives, waving her away when she opens her purse.

"Well, don't be a stranger," she says with a disappointed smile.

We watch in silence as she walks up a set of stairs then turns to wave one more time before disappearing into the building.

"Really?" I say.

He shuts off the engine.

My ears pound with indignation. I know I should mind my own business, refrain from saying more, but I can't seem to stop myself. It's as if everything I've loved and lost has come to a head in this moment, the sense of enchantment I held in my heart since adolescence perforated by Shwe's tryst with Jennifer.

"So, if I weren't here, you'd have gone up to her apartment?"

"Sure. Why not?" He meets my gaze, and for a moment, I think he understands. Then: "I like Jennifer. She's interesting. Fun to be around."

His words hit me with stinging clarity. I'm neither interesting nor fun. Whatever connection we once enjoyed has come to an end. Or perhaps never existed in the first place.

"Because you're not some hormone-crazed teenager anymore. You're a grown man. A father."

He shrinks back at the word father, and immediately, I wish I could take it back.

"You saw San."

He stares out the front windshield. The parking lot is dusty and chaotic, cars parked according to some indiscernible pattern, people meandering this way and that. Two young boys emerge from Jennifer's building and sit down on the steps with a bag of chips. Shwe's expression is blank.

"You were just a kid," I begin. But it's too late. By bringing up Su Su in the heat of an argument, I've spoiled the possibility of a more nuanced conversation about her existence. I can longer ask how he feels about her, if he regrets having had a child so young or is content with the way his life turned out, what kind of relationship he and Su Su have now. Here I thought Shwe and I were finally getting closer, but I can see now that we hardly know each other.

He shakes his head and starts the ignition. As we exit the crowded parking lot, I worry that I've blown it, that this will be the last of our trips around town together. Yet, it's not anger I sense, but something more subtle: I've disappointed him.

~

I spring down the stairs the moment the telephone rings, eager for the sound of Jason's voice. If nothing else, the argument with Shwe has reminded me how much I miss Jason, how patient and easygoing his temperament, the soothing effect he has on my own mood. Yet, the closer I get to Daw Tin Tin's, the more I worry that he, too, is growing tired of my evasiveness, that if I'm not careful, I might lose him as well.

We meander through the usual topics of work, family and friends. He's not especially solicitous, but hasn't given up on me either. As he describes the Red Sox game that he and U Soe Htet attended the other day, I begin to relax, stretch the telephone cord as far as it will reach to examine one of Daw Tin Tin's larger pieces of lacquerware—a multitiered offering bowl with concentric rings of tiny, mythical animals. According to the museum keeper, Burmese lacquerware is the finest in Asia. Each piece must be polished and repolished until every last imperfection is removed, hardening in an underground cellar in complete darkness for long intervals. I think about the time and labor this entails, the patience and commitment.

"Any idea when you'll be back?" says Jason. "It's been almost two weeks."

My chest tightens. I hate disappointing him but don't see how I can leave right now with so much unresolved.

I lift the top of the offering bowl from its base. Inside is a gold watch and a pair of reading glasses, both decidedly masculine in appearance. So Daw Tin Tin hasn't always been alone.

"Maybe next week?" I say.

The uncertainty of my response echoes through the telephone line.

"Why? What're you doing that's taking so long?"

I drop the lid back on the offering bowl. This is the first time since the day I sprung this trip on Jason that he's asked me directly why I'm here.

"Just trying to figure some stuff out. I'll explain when I get home. I promise." I tell myself that this is true, that I fully intend to tell Jason everything. Just as soon as we can speak face to face.

I return to my room, pausing in front of Ahpwa's urn and U Soe Htet's carving. To preserve my relationship with Jason I need to return to Boston. But to leave Yangon now with things so up in the air with Shwe feels hasty, worse even than when I left in 1988. Not to mention the fact that I've made no progress in finding a place for Ahpwa, or convincing Parker to come home. I pick up my brush and run it over the top of my head, my hair parting down the middle just as it always has. Maybe I'll grow it long again. A change might be nice.

Parker appears in the doorway, a look of aversion on her face, as if she's just bitten into a floury apple.

"Hey. How's the proposal coming?" I ask.

She leans against the side of the doorframe, arms crossed as she studies me through narrowed eyes. The heat pricks my face.

"Is everything ok?" I ask, concerned suddenly that my advice about which foundations to go with was faulty, that I've let her down again.

"Just trying to figure out what you're up to," she says finally.

I look at the hairbrush in confusion. "What do you mean?"

"What're you doing with Shwe? Why'd you really come here?"

"What are you talking about?"

"He's not the same since you came. First, he disappears. And now…now you've got him chauffeuring you around like your own personal driver. It's not right, Etta."

"So, you spend a few weeks with him and think you know everything there is to know?"

She winces, and I realize I've gone too far. Who am I really mad at?

"I'm sorry. I didn't mean that."

Parker takes a deep breath, and I can tell that she, too, is trying to keep her cool.

"It's just. Does Jason know you're spending all your time with Shwe?"

I place the hairbrush back on the dresser and turn my whole body to face her. In all the years Jason and I have been together, I can't think of one nice thing she's ever said about him.

"Since when do you care about Jason?"

"I don't." She pauses. "But I thought you did."

FIVE

A pair of giant *chinthe* guard the entrance to the Shwedagon. Leaving our shoes at the foot of the steps, we climb the enclosed stairway barefoot, just as we did 23 years ago. Shielded from the searing sun, the marble floor is cool and sticky under my feet. I wonder vaguely about the stickiness, then decide it's better not to know. At least there's no sign of betel nut sputum anywhere that I can see.

In contrast to the street, the atmosphere inside the covered stairwell is hushed and unhurried, as if part of a dream. We slow our pace instinctively, walking side by side without speaking or touching. The ascent is gradual, each set of stairs followed by a large, open landing where vendors peddle assorted religious ware, from flower garlands to alms bowls to Buddha statues. Midway up, an old woman beckons to me. She's a head shorter than I am, with kind eyes and silver hair tied back in a scarf.

"You mustn't go empty-handed, dear." She thrusts a bunch of delicate, white roses and some incense into my hands.

I look at Shwe, and he nods. I assumed our daily circuit around Yangon would come to an end after my tantrum about Jennifer. Instead, he showed up at the usual time this morning, insisting we come straight here without picking up any customers.

"Why, what's the hurry?" I asked.

"I realized that you hadn't been. That's all."

He didn't elaborate, but I can tell by the set of his jaw he has an agenda. Perhaps he's had enough of driving circles around the past. And what better place to confront it than the venue of our first outing together 23 years ago?

As I fumble through my bag for some *kyat* to pay the flower seller, a young boy appears in front of me holding a dome-shaped, bamboo birdcage almost as big as he is. In the cage are as many as one hundred tiny swallows lined up on perches like school children on bleachers. For a small donation, the boy will set one of the caged birds free, and I will get merit for saving a life, atone for any sins I have committed. I pay the woman for the flowers and incense and turn back to the boy.

His head is shaven like a monk, with open sores above his right ear and on his crown. Scabies probably. He raises up his spindly arms, hoisting the cage high in the air so I can see. The birds shuffle, lifting and repositioning their claws to maintain balance, ready to fly away the moment the opportunity presents itself. Never mind that the boy will catch them again after a few short-lived moments of freedom.

I'm about to ask how much to set *all* the birds free when Shwe pulls me away. I never fully embraced all those Buddhist tenets Ahpwa taught me, and he knows it. Maybe that's why he was so eager to bring me here—the most sacred site in Myanmar—to see if I've reformed. We continue our ascent in silence, the final stairwell longer and steeper than the previous ones.

Emerging from the covered stairwell onto the open platform, we slow to a standstill. In front of us, the main stupa gleams gold, its top-most vane shimmering with over 6000 diamonds, rubies, sapphires and other precious gems. How angry Ahpwa used to get about the Brits having turned the pagoda into a military installation during their occupation of Burma. The idea of their big, black boots tramping over this sacred ground offends me now too. For even if my own faith has wavered over the years, the depth of her devotion was never lost on me. If only she'd had the chance to come back to Burma just one more time, to unwrap her secrets and lay them out in the sun. Parker was right about that much. But to leave her ashes here forever?

Dozens of smaller shrines, statues and pavilions surround the main dome. Each cardinal direction indicated by a golden stupa, as are the four corners of the platform, with 60 smaller stupas lining the perimeter of the pagoda. I look up, hoping to catch a glimmer of the 72-carat diamond that adorns the topmost orb. Most people agree that it's too high for the naked eye to see, but Ahpwa insisted you could see it from the right perspective. She does belong here in many ways. Yet I can't stop thinking that there was more to my grandmother, that her faith was only part of who she was.

Shwe touches my arm. "I'll be right back."

I remain standing in the middle of the outdoor platform as he approaches a small, standalone shrine, about five feet high and three feet in diameter. A statue of Buddha perches on the edge of a gold-rimmed basin while a gilded dragon guards the drain below. Other devotees gather around the shrine saying prayers and making offerings. I mean to look away, to give Shwe privacy, but find myself watching him, studying the way he pours water first over the Buddha and then over the dragon, his lips moving continuously. There's something here I want to understand, both about Buddhism and about Shwe, where his faith comes from and what it means to him, how he integrates his beliefs without losing his self.

"Come," he says afterward, pulling me to the left. "We have to walk clockwise."

Continuing around the main stupa, past countless Buddha statues, shrines and other pavilions, I'm amazed how little has changed in 23 years. On the surface, at least. Shwe points to the giant bell we rang together in 1988, the one my father helped me sound. I remember the way he hiked up his bright blue *longyi* as he walked, how he came to my aid when I failed to ring the bell, how lucky and grateful I felt to have him as my father, not just because he was cool, but because he paid attention to me in a way no one else did. What I didn't know at the time, what I could not have known, was that he'd never be quite the same again. After Burma, he withdrew, emotionally at first, then physically too, moving out of our house, divorcing Mother, and finally, succumbing to the heart attack that took his life. But that day at the Shwedagon, he was the perfect father, exactly what I needed to navigate the maze of cultural landmines that defined my life. Suddenly, I'm choked with grief, missing my father more than I have in years.

Shwe puts an arm around my shoulder, and I lean into him, feeling as if I'm thirteen again, ready to surrender to this boy who seems to understand what I feel even before I do. We continue walking in silence. Sadness still clings to me, but it's a nourishing sadness, one that fills me up rather than draining me. Maybe being here with Shwe is exactly what I need to restore balance to my fragmented life, to reconcile past with present, and present with future. Parker's wrong about Shwe and me. It's not intimacy we seek but clarity, not romance but resolution.

A pair of Western tourists walk uncertainly toward us, then turn abruptly, changing direction.

"Why do we walk clockwise anyway? I never understood that," I say.

He stops walking. "It's like life, Aye. You can't go backwards, only forward. Don't you see?"

I try to recall what he said in the kitchen when we were making *pone yae gyi*, back when he first returned from the monastery, and I worked up the courage to ask about the letters. Something about that period when we were teenagers being another lifetime. I wonder if this is Shwe's way of telling me that it's time to move on time, to let go of the past.

"Are you saying that the future is more important than the past?"

"Both are important." He begins to walk again. "Who we are today comes from our thoughts of yesterday, while who we are tomorrow comes from our present thoughts."

As we turn the corner, a gathering of saffron-robed monks prostrate themselves before a golden Buddha statue, a halo of neon lights flashing over its head. On the other side, fair-skinned tourists huddle under the shade of an ancient reliquary, reading their guidebooks and applying sunscreen. The Shwedagon attracts a curious mix of pilgrims and tourists, yet I don't seem to fit either category. I grew up eating and breathing Buddhism, studying the history, tenets, and culture ad nauseum. But my analytical side always got in the way, demanding proof before conviction. I never truly practiced, never opened myself to its possibilities.

Shwe stops in front of another small shrine, similar to the one he stopped at before, and I step back to allow him some privacy.

Instead of approaching the shrine himself, he gives me a gentle push, nudging me forward.

A birdlike creature with the head of an eagle and torso of a human sits at the bottom of the shrine, beckoning to me. Garuda, the symbol of those born on a Sunday. This is my shrine, the one I was meant to visit after our trip to the fortuneteller so many years ago. Even then I had my doubts, resisting the possibility of some mumbo jumbo sabotaging my future, our future. I turn back to Shwe, gauging what this ritual means to him, whether the closure he seeks is for him or for me.

He gestures to the flowers and incense that I've been holding since we arrived, and I step forward, a tangle of emotion in my breast—about Shwe, about Buddhism, and about myself. Is it wrong to make an offering if my faith is not complete? Does following the divination of a fortuneteller make me a believer? Is this the real reason I came back to Yangon: to find out if the fortuneteller was right?

A middle-aged woman wearing an elegant turquoise *htamein* gives me an encouraging smile. "Like this." She lays her flowers and incense in front of the Buddha, then dips the red plastic cup into the basin of water and pours it over the statue five times. When she's finished, she hands me the red cup.

I dip the cup into the water, empty it over the Buddha, then dip it into the basin again. "Five times, is it?"

"Either that or one per year of life," she says with a twinkle in her eye.

"Five sounds good." I smile back at her. This isn't so hard.

"Now eight times over Garuda."

As I watch the water flow over the statue and out the drain below, my chest begins to lighten, as if returning to the Shwedagon with Shwe, fulfilling the fortuneteller's prescription, has satisfied a need I hadn't realized I had. I don't know how things will end with Shwe, whether Jason and I will survive our growing alienation, or even where to lay Ahpwa's ashes. I don't have the answers yet, but like the good luck birds, I'm ready to fly as soon as the opportunity presents itself.

~

I'm halfway through a *Myanmar Times* article about the popularity of ChickenKing, the city's first American fast-food chain, when the doorbell chimes. Throwing open the door, I'm surprised to see Daw Tin Tin standing in front me, her hair twisted into an elaborate knot at the nape of her neck, much like Ahpwa's.

"Oh hello, dear," she says in her smooth English accent. "That delightful Jason of yours asked me to let you know that he has an early morning meeting at work so he won't be able to call today."

My initial reaction is one of relief. I'm still digesting today's visit to the Shwedagon, still weighing the significance of having fulfilled the fortuneteller's prescription 23 years later. How can I speak of this to Jason when I don't understand it myself? Yet, I can't help feeling somewhat slighted, as if he could've rescheduled his meeting but decided against it to prove a point, to punish me for all the times I didn't get in touch with him.

I thank Daw Tin Tin and invite her in.

She refuses, as usual, but lingers in the doorway. "He really is such a charming young man, you know."

"Yes, I know." It's sweet how much she likes Jason, but also a little unsettling.

"Not one to let get away," she adds as she turns to leave.

"I agree," I say as evenly as possible, but as she walks back down the corridor, I begin to worry that she knows something I don't. Has Jason been talking to Daw Tin Tin about our relationship?

SIX

The military cemetery where General Myint Oo is buried is located on the outskirts of Yangon, about an hour's drive from Parker's apartment. After much cajoling on my part, Shwe agreed to take me there with the proviso that he won't go in himself. I didn't have the guts to ask him before, but after yesterday's trip to the Shwedagon, I feel bolder, as if making the offering at our respective shrines has somehow liberated us from each other, while at the same time bringing us closer together.

I couched my request as part of Parker and my mission to find a final resting place for Ahpwa, and while that's partly true, my desire to visit the General's grave is more complicated. I need to find out what really happened in 1988: why my family came to Rangoon and why we left so abruptly. I've always known that it had something to do with Shwe's grandfather, that Ahpwa was concerned about her little brother. Khaing Zar's intimation over lunch last week cemented that belief.

What I still can't understand is why: What was it about her brother that made Ahpwa take her family halfway across the world, only to tear us away three months later? Shwe said no at first, offering to get one of his taxi friends to take me instead. But transport isn't my problem; it's Shwe I need. He's the only one who can take me on this journey, the only one who understands.

Getting out of Yangon is the usual shock of potholes and car horns, beggars wordlessly beseeching us. As we queue to cross the bridge, a young girl selling strands of flowers emerges from between the columns of cars. Shwe buys three strands and hangs them from the rearview mirror, infusing the car with the heady fragrance of jasmine. We chat about this and that—a new restaurant that's opened downtown, the upsurge in construction around the city, the traffic.

Over the bridge, the horizon stretches out before us. Soon we're surrounded by acres of rice paddies, so green and lush I feel as if we've entered a painting. As we speed past, men, women, and children toil among the paddies, bent over with their straw hats and baskets under the hot Myanmar sun. I'm struck once again by the clash of beauty and suffering, the impossibility of the two existing side by side. I open the window and breathe in the clean, fresh air, gathering courage.

"Shwe?"

"Mmm?" He fiddles with the radio.

"Tell me about him?"

Ahead, an overladen truck leaves a trail of black smoke in its wake.

"That wasn't part of the deal," says Shwe, his voice flat.

"I need to know the truth if I'm going to make any sense of it."

"Sense of what?"

"What happened to my family."

He rubs the back of his neck, the dragon tattoo stretching and contracting as he pulls at his skin. The distance between the taxi and the truck narrows. I notice a man sleeping on the bulge of burlap that keep its cargo intact, the entire frame of the truck listing ominously to the right.

Shwe looks at me sideways. "What exactly do you want to know?"

"Everything."

He swerves onto the opposite side of the road and for a second, I can't see beyond the black cloud of exhaust that engulfs us. Then he presses his foot to the gas and accelerates past the truck, realigning to the correct side of the road just as another car comes in the opposite direction.

242

"I suppose I always knew he was important," he begins. "I could tell by the way people treated us. Kids at school, teachers. I could do whatever I wanted. And for a long time, I thought that was pretty cool. But it was lonely, too. Those other kids were polite on the surface, but they kept their distance. At first, I thought it was me. But as I grew older, I began to notice the way parents and teachers looked at him when he showed up at a school event, how they'd point with their chins, then whisper something to the person next to them. So, I started to pay more attention. Watching, waiting, listening. I was just beginning to figure out who he really was was when your family arrived in 1988."

"Why didn't you tell me?"

"I guess I wasn't ready to say it out loud. Telling you would've made it real."

We pass through a small village, banana plants and papaya trees interspersed among the thatched roofs. He's quiet for a minute, then continues.

"It wasn't until *tada phyu* that I knew for sure." *Tada phyu:* the white bridge at Inya Lake. He looks at me, seeking permission to go on.

I nod, my mouth too dry to speak. It's the first time I've heard White Bridge mentioned out loud, the first time Shwe and I have spoken of that day.

"I recognized the insignia on their uniforms. Even a few faces I'd seen at his house."

I keep my eyes peeled on the road, at once understanding and not understanding, wishing suddenly that I was back home in Boston, that I'd never returned to Yangon, never asked to know the truth.

"He was their commander, Aye. They didn't take a piss unless he ordered them to."

A flash of red. A swell of nausea. Students running in

every direction. Riot police chasing them down like animals. The screaming. The billy clubs. The flowers stained with blood. Shwe rubbing my back. I cover my mouth with my hand, feeling dirty and depraved, contaminated by a deep-seated pathogen I've always suspected but never wanted to admit.

Shwe pulls over, turns off the ignition.

I roll down the window, gulping in the thick, tropical air until I can almost breathe again. Only then do I look around, taking in the concrete wall and black iron gate in front of us. We've arrived at the military cemetery where General Myint Oo is buried.

Shwe tilts his head back, gazing up at the sky. I stare at the entrance to the cemetery, turning over a long-forgotten image of Ahpwa: She's sitting in a borrowed wheelchair at the Frankfurt airport as we wait for our final flight home from Burma in 1988. Her chignon has begun to fray, loose hair forming an unsightly bubble on the back of her head that fills me with secret satisfaction. How many times had she criticized the state of my hair, made me feel small and ungainly because I couldn't keep my braid neat? But my satisfaction soon gave way to alarm. I'd never seen my grandmother lose control of anything before, and the notion terrified me. What would happen to our family without Ahpwa in control?

The black iron grille of the cemetery gate comes into razor focus. I may not have found the right place for Ahpwa, but I'm beginning to understand what happened to her, the pain she must've endured on discovering what her little brother had become, the guilt she must've harbored at the deaths of those students, deaths she thought she might've prevented had she never left her brother, had she never left Burma.

"Let's go home," I say. "This isn't where she belongs."

Shwe reverses out of the parking spot, and we set off in silence, passing back through the rice paddies, past the villages and banana plants and papaya trees until we reach the outskirts of Yangon.

"What happened to you the night we left? The night of *tada phyu*?" I ask as we approach the bridge.

He makes a sound somewhere between a grunt and a laugh. "I lost it. Screaming and calling him a murderer until they locked me in a shed at the back of the house."

I imagine restless, inquisitive Shwe confined to a small shed, pounding the walls in anger and frustration as he struggled to make sense of what we'd seen that day, what his grandfather had commanded of his troops. How I wish I'd been there for him, to hold him and comfort him.

"They let me back into the house eventually, but I wasn't allowed outside for weeks. No more school. No more hanging out at the teahouse. No more watching the sunset over the lake." He stops at a red light. "I didn't even know your family had left."

Those first days after my family returned to Boston nearly broke me, images of my final hours in Rangoon cutting through my mind as I sat alone in our cold, dark house with no one to confide in, no way to unburden myself. How I despaired over not having said good-bye to Shwe, convincing myself that I'd failed him, that in allowing Ahpwa to take me away, I'd broken our promise to be true to each other, to put each other above the demands of the grown-ups, above their lying and misdeeds. To discover now that he didn't know I'd left strikes me as a cruel joke, my childhood obsession spinning on a false assumption. How trivial my letters now seem in comparison to what Shwe experienced, how small and insignificant.

I place my hand on his arm, and he turns to look at me. Our eyes lock, and for a fleeting moment the old Shwe is staring back at me, his syrupy, brown eyes pulling at my heartstrings. Then the light turns green, he looks back at the road, and the moment is gone. Layers of concrete and noise rise up around us. The traffic slows, and I stare out the window, readjusting to the rhythm of Yangon.

A crow lands in a puddle on the side of the road, hopping from one leg to the other as it looks around greedily. Aside from the small pockets of green around the lakes, crows seem to have taken over Yangon these past twenty years, scaring away the smaller, more elegant birds with their swagger and din.

"So, what'd you do? How'd you pass the time?" I ask when the traffic starts to move.

"Taught myself English," he says. "I already knew a little, of course. But it wasn't until I met you that I understood its power, the directness and clarity it lends to your thinking. Its ability to reach the rest of the world. I picked up its cadence from listening to you talk with your father but lacked the vocabulary to speak or write as effectively as I wanted. Turns out my mother's grandfather was an avid reader, so we had a ton of English books in the house. There was even a set of 1939 Encyclopedia. Most of the volumes were full of mold, or half-eaten by white ants, but I didn't care. I devoured everything. San San even managed to smuggle in an English dictionary."

San San. I shouldn't have been so quick to judge. They were just kids, offering and seeking solace in a time of chaos and distrust.

"You *read* the dictionary?"

"Cover to cover. And the Encyclopedia—all 20 volumes. The more I read, the more determined I became to expose the truth about what was happening here."

The hardness in his voice sends a shiver down my spine. Shwe is laid back about so much in life, but when he talks about politics, his personality changes. He becomes so tenacious, so completely consumed, as to be almost reckless.

"And you succeeded. Look at how Myanmar has changed."

He gives me a look of exasperation verging on contempt. "Only as much as they've allowed it to. This was no revolution, Aye, just an elaborate PR campaign to avoid the inevitable. Those crooks in government knew their time had come, so they swapped their military uniforms for civilian clothes and *voilà*: The world crossed Myanmar off its list of causes. So much for democracy. So much for truth."

Truth. For a second, I think this is aimed at me. Then I look back at Shwe and see that he's somewhere else, that his truth is far bigger than mine.

~

Daw Tin Tin's phone trills through the floor. I dash down the stairs, emerging from the narrow stairwell just as the old woman opens her door. She receives me with the same knowing smile she always wears, a smile that, more and more, leads me to suspect that she's formed some opinion about me, though I have no clue what that might be. But I have too much on my mind to worry about what Daw Tin Tin thinks or doesn't think.

As she leads me into the living room, I consider what to say to Jason. Although we spoke only two days ago, the world looks different now that I know the true nature of my family. Jason so good and clean, will he really want to marry the great niece of a man responsible for the death of so many?

"Etta. Sorry I couldn't call yesterday."

Hearing his voice is like looking at an old photograph; I feel stirrings of comfort and pleasure but can't distinguish past from present. I remain standing, asking all the usual questions about work, weather, parents, friends. But the words stick in my mouth like putty. I have too much to say to engage in small talk.

As Jason recounts the latest news from home, I comb my mind for an anecdote I might tell him about the last couple of days, something harmless and light. But it's no use. Since learning about General Myint Oo, I see only darkness. How can I tell him what my great uncle did, what he was, without Jason associating that depravity with me, even if unwittingly?

"I found out what happened to U Soe Htet's nephew, Lwin Soe. Why he never came to the States," he says.

"Really?" I wonder vaguely why he's still pursuing the question of Lwin Soe, whether it's for me, or for him.

"It's pretty awful actually. Turns out he was killed not long after meeting your grandmother. Beaten to death by security forces during a student protest. U Soe Htet—"

"What protest? Where?"

"Near some river. Or maybe it was a lake. I can't remember the name. The students were unarmed, but the military police went nuts, clubbing people to death."

My vision begins to waver, the details of Daw Tin Tin's lacquerware collection blurring beyond recognition.

I take a step forward to steady myself and bang my knee on the coffee table, the force of impact knocking the handset from my hand.

"Etta? Etta, are you okay? Etta?" Jason's voice rises from the floor. Small and faraway.

Daw Tin Tin peeks her head through the door, a look of concern on her face.

"Sorry. I lost my balance." I pick the handset off the floor. "I'm fine, really."

Daw Tin Tin retreats.

Jason remains quiet.

"I'm fine," I repeat.

Still nothing.

Then: "I don't believe you."

"You don't... What?"

"I don't believe that you're fine." His tone is slow and measured. "I don't understand why you won't talk to me, Etta."

I lower myself into the chair. I let myself believe that Jason hadn't noticed, that he'd accepted my jaunty travel tales and half-truths. But he knows me better than that, of course, maybe better than I know myself. I wish I could start over, tell him everything from the beginning—not just about Burma and my family, but about me, how what happened altered my perception of myself, my persistent, irrational fear that things might have turned out differently if only I'd been better, stronger, wiser. But to explain now is to lay bare all the facts I neglected to tell him throughout our time together, and this, I know, will feel like a betrayal to him, every omission and evasion over the years a breach of trust, a violation of our commitment to each other.

I close my eyes, unable to see a way out. How can we share a life together if I can't share this with him? I shake my head, which of course he cannot see, ten thousand miles of miscommunication between us.

"It's just sad what this country has been through." I wince.

He doesn't respond right away, but I hear the frustration in his breath, the disappointment.

"Okay, Etta," he says. "I have to go. I'll talk to you soon."

The phone clicks before I have a chance to respond.

"Jason?"

The other end of the line is dead. The steadiest, most forgiving person in my life has just hung up on me. It's so out of character for him that for a second, I think it's a mistake, that some technical fault caused the line to drop, and he'll call back any minute. Yet as I reflect over the last several weeks, how self-absorbed I've been, how immature really, dismissing Jason's needs so I can run around Yangon like a teenager, I'm surprised he hasn't hung up on me earlier.

I want desperately to call him back, but how? Daw Tin Tin's made it abundantly clear that her phone cannot be used for outgoing calls. And the Central Telephone and Telegraph office doesn't open until morning.

Shwe's sister opens the door dressed in a satiny house coat, a familiar jazz tune filling the air. She holds a glass of red wine in her hand. Apologizing for stopping by unannounced, I explain briefly about Jason and ask if she has a phone I could use.

"Sorry, I use the one at work. You're welcome to come by my office tomorrow if you like." She gives me a sympathetic smile, and I notice that she has the same dimple as Shwe except hers is on the other side of her face and slightly higher up. "You look like you could use a glass of wine. Want to come in?"

I look at my watch. I need to speak to Jason as soon as possible, but what option do I have? Even Cyber Savvy is closed at this hour. Besides, he's probably at the office by now, rushing from meeting to meeting. Do I really want to dump all this on him while he's working? Wouldn't it be better to call tomorrow morning when he's back home?

"A glass of wine sounds wonderful." I slip off my shoes.

With its ebony carvings, Persian rugs, and handwoven wall hangings, Khaing Zar's apartment is a tribute to the many places she's worked. As I wander around admiring each item, I realize why the music sounds familiar. She's listening to Etta James.

"You know I'm named after her?" I say as Khaing Zar pours me a glass of merlot.

"Who? Etta James?" She stops pouring and looks at me in surprise. "I always assumed Etta was a Westernization of Aye Tha."

"Other way around. Father wanted to call me Etta, and Mother found a way to make it work without upsetting Ahpwa."

She hands me my glass, and we sit down on opposite corners of the sofa, angled inward so we're facing one another.

"I gather she was a difficult woman."

"You might say that." I give her a sad smile. "But I think I'm beginning to understand her a bit better now that I know the truth about her brother."

"How so?" she asks.

"I always knew she felt guilty about leaving him. That much was clear growing up. But I assumed her guilt was limited to his well-being, that she worried he was unhappy or unwell." I pause. What I like about Khaing Zar is that I can say whatever's on my mind, which in turn helps me to figure out what I believe. "Now that I know what he'd become." I take a shaky breath. "The blood on his hands. I think she felt something worse than guilt. She felt responsible for those lives."

She studies me for several seconds, her bare feet tucked behind her on the sofa. "You know, when I was little, I used to fantasize that I was part of your family. I had this idea in my head that your lives must be perfect, that growing up in the land of freedom and democracy meant you'd escaped the darkness of those times."

I picture our childhood home, the two cars in the driveway, maple tree in the front yard, how absurdly safe my life was when contrasted with what was happening here during those same years.

"We were lucky." My voice cracks.

"Were you?" she asks.

A high-pitched hissing fills my ears as I meet her gaze.

"At least those of us who were here had each other," she continues. "We understood what others were going through because we experienced the same."

I swirl the wine slowly around my glass. *You don't know how lucky you are*, Ahpwa told me time and again. Even now I find it impossible to place any significance on my own suffering in relation to what happened here. Maybe that's what *America the Beautiful* was all about—Ahpwa trying to convince herself that, living in the land of freedom and democracy, we'd escaped the horrors of Burma's military regime. But Khaing Zar's right. Democracy doesn't preclude loneliness and suffering. Freedom of speech is of little comfort if no one is listening.

"How do you stomach it?" I ask. "How do you live with the fact that someone in our own family did all those terrible things?"

"Listen, Aye." She sets her wineglass down on the table. "What the General did was horrific. A crime against humanity. One day, maybe, the history books will find him guilty. But we aren't the ones who committed that crime."

"So, we have no responsibility, as his relatives?"

"Of course, we have a responsibility. Every human being on this planet has a responsibility, regardless of who their relatives are. To reduce the suffering of others. To promote peace and understanding. To be the best version of ourselves that we can possibly be. But having a responsibility is not the same as being responsible. We didn't kill those people. Nor did we benefit from what he did. Those were his actions, his decisions. Not mine. Not yours. And not your grandmother's."

The wail of a saxophone swoops around us, a searchlight in a stormy sea. A memory of Ahpwa after our return to Boston comes into focus. She's sweeping the kitchen with such force that the bristles of the broom have bent backwards. At the time, I assumed her anger to be directed at me.

"I wish Ahpwa had known that. How different her life might've been. How different all of our lives might've been."

"Then don't repeat her mistake," she says with a new firmness to her tone.

"What do you mean?"

"Stop blaming yourself for what happened to Shwe. There's nothing you could've done."

I close my eyes as a fresh wave of helplessness washes over me.

"You're right, I know. But I can't shake the feeling that he's in danger, almost as if he wants to get caught."

She nods slowly. "I wouldn't say he wants to get caught, exactly. But in Shwe's mind, being in danger means he's making an impact, pushing the right buttons to achieve change. Honestly, I don't think he could live with himself any other way." She looks at me to see if I understand, then adds, "But he's careful. Most of the time."

I look down at my wine, a deep, ruby red in color. "I just hate the idea of him behind bars again. Or worse."

"Listen, Aye. The only one who can protect Shwe is Shwe. He has to decide how he wants to live his life, just as you have to decide how to live yours."

~

Parker's lying on the living room tiles in her bra and underwear when I return.

"Trying to keep cool," she explains.

After a moment's hesitation, I peel off my clothes and lie down next to her, the tiles fresh and smooth against my skin. Our schedules have been so out of sync the past couple of days that we've barely spoken since our blow up over Jason. I realize that I miss her, that I've grown accustomed to this new easiness between us and don't want to lose it again. Though we still argue plenty, that sting of alienation I felt in Boston has receded. Our relationship feels stronger, richer, more like it used to be. But if I want that to continue, I need to be honest with her. I need to stop protecting her from the truth, beginning with what I've learned about the General. I look up at the ceiling fan, spinning ominously above us.

"Did you ever wonder why we came here in 1988?" I ask.

"Only all the time," she says. "The only thing I can think of is that Ahpwa wanted to figure out if she was still Burmese. But there must have been more to it to make such a long journey with all of us in tow."

"That's what I always thought too, and I'm sure that was part of it," I say. "But I learned something today that makes me think there was something more specific pulling her back. I think she needed to check up on her brother, find out if the rumors were true."

"What do you mean?" Parker turns to face at me.

I tell her what I now know about the General, what kind of man he was, how he commanded the special forces that caused all that bloodshed.

"That's horrible." She says after several seconds, then places her hand on top of mine. "But thank you for telling me."

We lie there for several seconds, watching the fan go around and round. The tiles have drawn the worst of the heat from my skin, leaving me restored if not quite refreshed. Parker, too, seems more relaxed, thoughtful.

"I still don't get why we *all* came, though. If what you say is true, she could've come on her own. She was still strong enough back then. Or come alone with Mother. Why drag us all here?"

"Good question. Also, why for so long? She really must've been expecting good news to uproot us all for what was meant to be a whole year."

Taking that much time off work would've been tricky, let alone finding someone to take care of our house, and convincing the school to let Parker and me take a year off. As a child, I never considered such details, but looking back now, I can see how much work it must have been for our parents to organize. It would've been easier if we'd stayed behind with our father, just as it's easier for me to be here now because Jason is home looking after our apartment.

"I thought maybe it was to save their marriage," says Parker.

I look at her in awe. When did Parker become so perceptive, and why has it taken me so long to notice?

"I never thought about it that way," I say. "But I bet you're right. He came here for her, to prove how much he loved her, and to understand the hold that Burma had over our family."

"But it didn't work," says Parker.

"No. It didn't."

I used to think my parents would've stayed together if only we hadn't gone to Burma, that the strain of the trip had been the cause of their discontent. Looking back now, I see that the trip only hastened the inevitable.

SEVEN

I arrive at the Central Telephone and Telegraph office just as the cavernous hall shudders to life. It's 7:00 a.m. here, 8:30 p.m. in Boston. Locating the same operator Parker selected on my first day, I sit down on the tiny stool and hand her a slip of paper with the number of our landline. As she places the call, I go over what I'll say when Jason answers, how I'll introduce the topic of my family's immorality. Do I start with, *When I was thirteen...,* or launch right into, *My grandmother's brother was a murderer...*? I'm still trying to work out how one relates to the other when the operator confirms what I've already begun to suspect: Jason isn't picking up.

Overhead, a pigeon flutters out from under the eaves, flying the length of the building in search of open air. I'm kicking myself for needing to have this conversation by telephone, in this warehouse-like building, in front of this stranger. I write Jason's cell on a second slip of paper and hand it to the operator. Calling his cell will be expensive, but money is the least of my concerns.

Still no answer. I try not to think anything of it. He's probably out with friends. At a movie or a concert. I leave a message on his voicemail apologizing for yesterday and asking him to call me at Daw Tin Tin's as soon as he can so that I can explain.

Cyber Savvy is a short walk from the Telegraph Office, so I head there next, hoping Jason's written. Though not yet 8:00 a.m., the air is heavy with humidity, sweat dripping down my neck. I look up at the sky, wondering when the rains will bring relief.

"Ma Aye Tha Kyaw," says the café owner, grasping my hand with both of his. "I haven't seen you for some time. Tell me, how is Daw Tin Tin?"

We chat about Daw Tin Tin as he walks me to my usual cubicle.

"You recall our regulations?" he asks anew. And for the first time since I started coming to Cyber Savvy, I realize that he's not speaking to me at all, that this is a script he recites to protect himself against the possibility that one of his customers might be a government agent. He trusts me because Daw Tin Tin sent me.

"Yes, don't worry." I sit down in front of the keyboard, unexpectedly nostalgic for the period when I came here every day, before I gave Daw Tin Tin's number to Jason, and Shwe and I began our daily circuit of the city.

"And our signals?" he whispers with a forced cough.

I nod in acknowledgement and turn to the monitor. A nub of anxiety forms in my gut. Just how angry is Jason?

I scan my inbox: a message from my boss, an e-statement notification from my bank account, and an invitation to an art exhibit on Newbury Street, alongside several items of spam ranging from ads for penile enlargement to urgent requests for my banking details. I stare at the screen in disbelief. He hasn't written. Choking back a growing sense of panic, I delete the spam, file the bank notification, and respond to my boss, thanking her for her patience and understanding. Finally, I open the invitation to the art exhibit. I know the gallery well. We've attended many exhibits there over the years, often combining the outing with a dinner at a favorite restaurant.

One exhibit stands out in my memory, a collection of experimental artwork by emerging New England artists. We'd gone straight from an alumni cocktail party to the gallery, arriving just before closing. Fueled by the extra glass of wine, we decided to purchase one of the pieces I'd been drawn to, a bold, abstract painting that seemed to quiver with energy. And because it was the end of the evening on the last day of the exhibit, the gallery owner lifted it off the wall right then and there, wrapped it in bubble wrap and handed it to us. Amid fits of laughter, we lugged the painting along to a restaurant, leaning it against our table as we ate.

Seeing that this latest reception started just over an hour ago, I catch my breath. Is that where he is now? Did he go alone? I've been so wrapped up in my new surroundings that I failed to appreciate how lonely he must be, waking in an empty bed each morning, making a single cup of coffee in the coffee maker, eating his meals solo at the kitchen table. Worse still, I've failed to tell him how important he is to me, how much I depend on his gentle presence in my life. With growing apprehension, I close the gallery invite and compose a new message asking him, once again, to call so I can explain.

Before leaving, I type in the URL for Shwe's blog, curious to see what he's been writing since we began spending time together. He's written several new entries, beginning with a profile of Yangon's Indian community that includes a direct quote from the owner of the button shop. Another post reflects on the challenges of controlling avian flu in poverty-stricken communities, quoting an anonymous source from the Department of Livestock. I wonder when he took his notes, or whether he just has an excellent memory. Above all, I'm chuffed that our outings together inspired him enough to blog about.

The final entry, posted just yesterday, describes an incident that took place at the grand opening of the American fast-food chain, ChickenKing. According to Shwe's blog, a hydrogen balloon exploded at one of the stalls, injuring several onlookers. But the real focus of the story is a young family of four who ended up in the hospital with third-degree burns with no compensation whatsoever from ChickenKing. By the time I finish reading the story, my concern about Jason has warped into a splintering rage against the fast-food conglomerate.

~

"I saw your story about the family burned by the hydrogen balloon," I tell Shwe an hour later as we drive up Kabar Aye Pagoda Road looking for passengers. I'd just returned from Cyber Savvy when he arrived at Parker's apartment to pick me up for our daily excursion.

"Yeah? What'd you think?" His eyes shine with eagerness.

"It's shameless the way they're treating that family. So unfair, so wrong. But your writing, Shwe, it's excellent, really powerful."

He checks the rear and side mirrors, then flashes me a mischievous look. "But am I a good driver?" He swerves to the left, then loops across the opposite lanes in a dramatic, fluid U-turn that makes me clutch onto the door handle.

"What the hell are you doing?"

"Taking you to see them," he answers.

"Who?"

"The family."

With its redbrick façade, arched entryways and Roman-style window trimmings, the hospital is grander than I expected. Shwe tells me that the facility was once the premier hospital in southeast Asia.

"Come on. What are you waiting for?" He holds open my door as I gaze up at the beveled domes topping each tower.

"I don't know about this, Shwe. Are you sure it's okay?"

He nods, nudging me forward with his hand on the small of my back.

The interior of the hospital is notably less grand than the exterior, paint peeling off the walls, antiquated appliances and other disused medical equipment cluttering the marble floors. I follow him into a long, open gallery of beds, each just a couple of feet from the next.

The family has been assigned two single beds in the corner of the large hall. A plate of bananas and fried snacks sits on a table between the beds, which are made up with colorful *longyi* material. The father stands to greet us, his right arm and torso wrapped in bandages. We learn that the rest of his body was shielded from the fire by his four-year-old son, who he'd lifted up to see the display. The son lies motionless on one of the two beds, bandaged from head to toe.

On the other bed lies the man's wife, her face, neck and arms wrapped in gauze. The six-year-old daughter crouches at the top of her mother's bed, staring at me with wide, frightened eyes. Apart from a small bandage on her hand, she's physically unharmed, having been protected by the counter that she stood behind. The only part of her exposed to the explosion was her hand, which reached up to touch her mother's arm.

I kneel down on the floor next to her.

"Hello," I say with a smile.

Her fingers inch closer to her mother's abdomen.

"Has anyone been to see you from ChickenKing?" Shwe asks the father.

The man shakes his head. "You are the only one who has come."

I stand. I never liked ChickenKing, but if something similar had happened in the States, I'm certain the company would go to great lengths to ensure that this man's family was given the best care possible—anything to avoid bad publicity or a potential lawsuit. But neither of these seem to be a concern here.

"What about the company where you work? Have you heard from them?" asks Shwe.

The man nods. "I must return to work tomorrow, or they'll give my job to someone else." I follow his gaze from his son to his wife to his daughter. "Every day I stay here is another day of lost wages. My wife was selling samosas on the street, but what can she do now? And who will take care of them when I go back to work?"

I look back at the little girl, who continues to stare at me, unmoving. Surely, he does not intend to leave this terrified little girl to look after her bedridden mother and brother? "Isn't there anyone else who can help?" My voice sounds unnaturally high, almost shrill.

Shwe shoots me a look of warning. Don't add to this man's burden with your do-goodism and naïveté, his look says.

But the words are already out of my mouth. "An uncle or an aunt? A neighbor?" I say in almost a squeak.

Unlike Shwe, the father doesn't seem to notice my growing hysteria. "My brother's family brought us some food and these cloths for our bedding." He shakes his head. "But they have so little. I don't know what more they can do."

Afraid to open my mouth again, I look to Shwe.

"Here." He gives the father a wad of kyat equivalent to fifteen dollars.

I follow suit, handing the father all the money in my purse, about forty dollars. The money is nothing to me, but for them it might last as long as two weeks. The father blushes and grasps our hands, whether in gratitude or shame, I can't tell. I kneel down again to say good-bye to the little girl. She still doesn't move, but I want to think I see the hint of a smile in her eyes.

"What will happen to them?" I ask on our way out.

Shwe shrugs. "They'll find a way, but they'll be forced to live in conditions you or I can't possibly imagine."

"Can't they sue ChickenKing?"

He laughs.

I recall what Ko Martin, the lawyer, told me that day under the banyan tree. The Myanmar judicial system functions not to protect the underprivileged but to safeguard the interests of the rich and powerful. In other words, no one cares about this family. Not ChickenKing. Not the government. And not the courts. Even a human rights lawyer like Ko Martin would be too busy for so unexceptional and apolitical a lawsuit. The only way for this family to have their case heard is to bribe a judge. And when you don't have enough money for food, the pursuit of justice becomes an extravagance, a squandering of resources too risky to entertain.

~

"Sheila's coming back next week," says Parker. She's sitting on the sofa, reading the Emma Larkin book, her feet up on the coffee table.

"Sheila?"

"My roommate? The woman whose room you've been staying in?" Parker glares at me in obvious disbelief.

A moment's confusion gives way to a rush of possessiveness. I knew all along that this situation would come to an end, that Sheila wouldn't stay in Australia forever and I couldn't stay here forever, that one way or another I'd have to vacate the room. But somewhere along the way, I lost track of time, all those hours driving around in Shwe's taxi belonging to some parallel reality, a world where Sheila's room is my room, Parker's apartment, our apartment. I've enjoyed living with Parker, having Shwe and Khaing Zar nearby.

It strikes me with sudden, sobering clarity that Jason is the only thing missing from my life here. I try to imagine what it would be like to have him here with me. He doesn't fit, of course, but the thought of him leaves me a little shaky. Maybe Sheila's return is a sign. Maybe it's time to go home.

I fall asleep on the sofa, waiting for the sound of Daw Tin Tin's phone from the floor below, that sharp, startling ring that I've grown to depend on.

EIGHT

I wake early, apply a flash of lipstick, and head down to the street dressed in the only business clothes I brought with me—a red fitted jacket with matching pencil skirt that Jason calls my "power suit." I can't think why I packed this suit but am grateful that I did. Wearing it makes me feel stronger, reminding me who I am and what I'm capable of as I confront this unsettling day.

I can't quite believe Jason didn't call last night but am trying not to let my mind run wild. He'll get in touch when he's ready. I have to trust that. I have to trust him. Until then, the only way to distract myself is to do something wholly unrelated to either of us. And what better cause than the injured family so casually dismissed by ChickenKing?

Hailing my first solo taxi since Shwe's return from the monastery gives me a fresh burst of confidence. This is something I need to do on my own, without Shwe's judgement or interference. As much as I've learned from him in the time we've spent together, both about myself and my family, I'm realizing how differently we approach life's injustices, his tack to expose and confront, while I prefer to wage battle from within.

The taxi driver turns down Bogolay Zay, coming to a stop in front of an open stairwell between a pirated DVD store and a barbershop. I dig Ko Martin's tattered business card out of my purse and doublecheck the street number. Yes, this is it, the office of the lawyer I met in the teashop. In addition to finding out more about his work promoting the rule of law, I want to get his blessing for the rather unorthodox scheme I devised in the middle of the night to help the burn victims.

After three alarmingly steep flights of stairs, my black pumps pinching my feet, I poke my head through the open door. Ko Martin stands abruptly, knocking over his cup of tea, which threatens to saturate the many files stacked on his desk. As he snatches papers out of the path of the encroaching puddle, I scan the room for something to mop up the spill.

Illuminated by a single, exposed lightbulb that hangs from the middle of the ceiling, the one-room office is dominated by two clunky, teak desks each facing the middle of the room. In one corner stands an upright fan, in the other, a folding table topped with an electric kettle, a jar of sugar, and several packets of Royal Myanmar 3-in-1 instant tea mix. I grab a stack of stiff, single-ply napkins from next to the kettle and begin mopping up the spill, apologizing for having startled him.

"Nonsense." He waves away my words. "I am delighted that you have come. I did not think, that is, I did not know..." His voice trails off.

I understand suddenly that Ko Martin is one of those people who becomes excited in the moment, fashioning pipedreams out of a chance meeting, then just as quickly discarding them when they don't pan out. He never expected to see me again after our encounter in the teashop, would likely have forgotten about me altogether if I hadn't stopped by today.

"May I offer you some tea?" He hesitates. "Or a cold drink? I know Americans prefer their beverages chilled."

I look around the room uncertainly. The combination of the stairs and the heat have left me parched, but I see no fridge or icebox.

"A cola perhaps? Or an orange soda?" he adds.

He's so eager to please that I agree to an orange soda.

"Excellent!" He walks over to the open window, attaches a 500-kyat note to a long string, then lowers the string down to the street. "Ma Lu, one Max+ Orange please. Foreigner cold," he shouts over the windowsill. A minute later, Ko Martin pulls up a small, plastic basket containing a bottle of Max+ Orange.

The soda is cold and sweet, a welcome contrast to the wearying heat. Unsure where to start, I ask him to tell me more about his work. He talks for a while, gesticulating passionately as he details the range of human rights abuses that result from an absence of rule of law—lawyers harassed, judges bribed, prisoners held without cause, the powerful acting with impunity. "My dream is to start an association. An alliance of legal professionals working together to raise awareness about the importance of rule of law and the role that lawyers can play. But there is much to do and little time."

"Are your cases always political in nature?" I ask.

"Yes, of course." He gives me a polite but impatient smile. "That is what I do."

"What about more routine lawsuits? Personal injury, for example? Would you ever represent someone who's been wronged, say, by a corporation?"

He gives me an inquisitive look, and I tell him the story of ChickenKing and the family in the hospital.

Ko Martin shakes his head sadly. "This is a perfect example of why we need to strengthen the rule of law in Myanmar. To protect the rights of the people. To prevent this kind of exploitation by the rich and powerful. I wish I had time for cases like these, I really do, but they are everywhere. The child who gets hit by a bus. The window washer who falls from shoddy scaffolding. The garment worker wrongfully terminated from her job. If I start down that road, I'll have no time for the real work, the transformational work of changing our legal system, which in the long run is the only way to prevent further abuse. It's like the old proverb about babies in the river."

"I don't think I know that one. Is it Burmese?"

"No, this one comes from your neck of the woods. You see a man throwing babies in the river. How do you respond? Do you jump in the river to save the babies from drowning, or tackle the man who's throwing them in?"

Both, I want to say. But I see his point. He's one person with limited time and resources. If he wants to effect real and lasting change, he needs to focus on the higher profile and more political cases, ones that will set a precedent and lead to lasting change.

"So, there's nothing that can be done?"

"On the contrary, there is a great deal to be done." He appraises me with pointed expectancy. "I said it before, and I'll say it again, we could use someone with your background and your expertise."

I shift awkwardly in my chair. This was not at all what I intended when I set out this morning, and the possibility makes me a little lightheaded. What if I did stay here to work with Ko Martin?

"Of course, the conditions are not quite what you are accustomed to."

I follow the sweep of his arm, noticing for the first time the water stains on the ceiling, the diagonal crack in the wall that runs from one corner of the floor to the opposite corner of the ceiling. Ko Martin's meager room pales in comparison to the swanky law offices of Webley, Chin and Scott. Yet I can see myself seated at the second desk, drinking Royal Myanmar 3-in-1 instant tea as I solicit potential donors or appeal to the diplomatic community for support, pleading on behalf of students, journalists and other activists, who risk their lives to speak the truth. People like Shwe. The idea cartwheels through my imagination until I remember Jason with a thud and remind myself that I don't live here, that this isn't my real life.

"It's not that," I say. "It's just that I have to leave soon."

"Oh, I beg your pardon. I must have misunderstood the purpose of your visit today." He smiles politely. "Why then did you come?"

I open my mouth to confess the scheme I conjured up in the night to intimidate ChickenKing into action, then close it again, realizing that he won't approve, that when it comes to upholding and respecting the rule of law in Myanmar, Ko Martin is a purist.

Bo Gyoke Road is the usual jumble of potholes, open drains and unblushed humanity. I hop over a dark, shiny puddle onto the freshly refurbished sidewalk in front of ChickenKing. On the opposite corner is an Indian temple, across the street, the sprawling colonial building that houses the city's largest market. The storefront and interior of the restaurant are much like any other ChickenKing in the world, complete with red-paneling, white block letters and images of chicken in its many forms. I know from the *Myanmar Times* article that the restaurant has seen record sales since opening, and today looks to be no different. Though not yet 9:00 a.m., a line has already formed on the sidewalk.

The corporate office is located around the corner with a separate entrance far from the lip-smacking customers. After meeting with Ko Martin, I almost didn't come. But to do nothing when I have the power to do something doesn't seem right. An attractive young woman sits in the front office, reading a dog-eared copy of *Animal Farm* from behind her computer monitor. She flips the book closed and jumps to her feet.

Leaving my ethics in the street-side puddle, I introduce myself, in English, as an associate from the Boston firm Webley, Chin and Scott and ask to speak with the brand manager.

"Please, take a seat." Her accent is hesitant, self-conscious.

A minute later, she ushers me into the brand manager's office. In contrast to the interior of the restaurant, his office furnishings are sleek and modern—all grays and blacks with nary a paper visible. The manager himself is a baby-faced, young Myanmar man, who wears his nerves like an accoutrement to his ill-fitting Western suit. I'm betting this is his first real job out of business school, and that he won't want any trouble.

"Good morning." He straightens his tie.

Putting on my best courtroom face, I introduce myself in quick-fire legalese, citing the "case" of the hydrogen balloon. His eyes widen in alarm as I expound on the latest thinking in corporate citizenship and social responsibility, while hinting at the increasingly serious consequences of ignoring these concepts. No such case exists, of course, nor have I been asked to represent my firm in any way while in Yangon.

As I speak, he checks his agenda again and again, as if hoping to find there an explanation for who I am, how seriously to take me. I feel a pang of guilt using American legal tactics so shamelessly on this unsuspecting middle manager, then I picture the little girl sitting on her mother's hospital bed and decide that my methods are justified.

"You are from which law firm again?" His brow crinkles with worry.

"Webley, Chin and Scott. We are based in Boston, Massachusetts." I wince inwardly. What I'm doing is completely unethical. If any of the partners were to find out that I'm using the firm's name in this context, I could face disciplinary action, or worse. I tell myself that things are different here, that if the rule of law were applied evenly in Myanmar I wouldn't have to resort to such tactics.

"And you came to be involved in this case how?" says the manager, his voice rising in pitch.

"We've been monitoring social media for the past few weeks and noticed that the case was picking up momentum. I thought it prudent to advise you of this new development before the situation escalates beyond the capacity of a quick resolution. In our view, this is something you'll want to resolve sooner rather than later." Surely, my colleagues back home would approve of a few scare tactics.

"Thank you," he says, as if I am doing him a favor. "I will look into this straight away."

I nod and write Daw Tin Tin's number on my business card. "Here's my card. Please let me know if there's anything I can do to assist you in this case."

I skip out of his office, confident that the burn victims will soon receive compensation, even if I went about it the wrong way.

~

On the ride home, I begin to worry about what Jason would say about my ChickenKing stunt, whether he'd find my behavior heroic or unethical. Like Ko Martin, Jason has an unwavering sense of right and wrong: If I believe in the rule of law, I should uphold and respect it no matter what. In other words, the end does not justify the means, especially when the means in question—skirting the rule of law—directly undermines the ends.

Most of the time, I find this aspect of Jason's personality admirable, a quality I wish I had more of. But unlike Ko Martin, Jason has never lived here, his knowledge of Myanmar limited by its distorted portrayal in the media, not to mention the guarded half-truths I've fed him over the years. The country is hard to understand from within, let alone from 10,000 miles away. So much of what matters takes place under the surface, so much remains unsaid, that what seems at first glance to be logical and true often turns out to be the opposite.

What alternative does that family have? What argument could Jason put forward to justify inaction in the face of such obvious need on the part of the family and such indifference on the part of ChickenKing? The taxi driver makes a sharp turn, and I thrust my hand onto the empty seat next to me to keep from falling over. Argument is the wrong word, I realize. Jason wouldn't argue with me. He'd have some questions, of course, but he'd listen to what I have to say, study my face as I explain my rationale. He might even come around to my way of thinking in the end. With sudden urgency, I try to calculate how long it's been since he hung up on me. One day? Two days? Surely, that wasn't the end. Surely, he wouldn't give up on me just because I don't want to talk about Lwin Soe. Yet in my heart, I know I deserve worse.

~

Shwe's standing outside Parker's building, chatting with some construction workers from the plot next door when I return. In the short time I've been in Yangon, the colonial homestead next door has been razed to the ground. Bulldozers and diggers have now appeared, and the air is filled with the clank and churn of excavation. He surveys my make-up and business attire, the black pumps, so wholly unsuitable for the climate, not to mention the broken sidewalks.

"Business meeting?"

"Sort of. Not really. I just had to see someone—" I look away. Shwe won't approve of my ChickenKing stunt either, though not for the same reasons as Jason or Ko Martin, not because he cares about rule of law, or ends and means, per se. Shwe would be more concerned about the power dynamics. He wouldn't like that I used my Western credentials to manipulate the ChickenKing manager—my business attire and legalese just another form of imperialism in his eyes.

He studies me for several seconds, then touches my arm. "You okay? You don't look good."

The touch of Shwe's hand sends a rush of warmth to my face and chest. For the briefest of moments, I imagine succumbing to this feeling, allowing his touch to drive away all my loneliness and uncertainty about Jason. Would that be so terrible? Is allowing myself to be comforted by Shwe a betrayal of Jason? Ever since I returned to Yangon, I've been trying to understand the pull of this childhood bond, to control it and contain it, fearful of where it might take us, where it might take me. Until now, my love for Jason has kept me from responding to that pull. But does he even count anymore?

I put my hand to my head, a cloud of dust and debris from the neighboring construction site swirling around us. "It's so noisy."

He gestures to his taxi parked half on the sidewalk half on the street a few yards away. "Go for a drive?"

A drive, yes. What better way to clear my head? I look down at my swollen feet bursting out of the tight, black work pumps. "I need to change though."

He nods, and we fall in step, Shwe holding open the door as I walk through. I exhale as the noise from the construction site recedes to a muffled clatter. But as we enter the narrow stairwell, I wish we'd stayed on the street. Though Shwe and I have come down these stairs together countless times, going up with him behind me feels reckless and unnerving, like visiting a fortuneteller, or passing through a dragon's lair. I search for something to say but am too distracted by the curve of my suit, the bareness of my neck.

"I'll just be a minute." I head straight to my room and close the door behind me. I need time to figure out what this is. What I want from Shwe, and what that means for Jason and me. Whether there still is a Jason and me. As I dig through the dresser for something to wear, my eyes keep returning to Ahpwa's urn and U Soe Htet's statue, the tragedy of their ruptured love affair sticking in my throat like a bad decision. All because she didn't trust him enough to tell him the truth, didn't trust his love. I understand now why Jason's become so obsessed with their story. We can't go on the way we have been.

I throw on a casual *htamein* from the market and return to the living room, ready to face Shwe. To my surprise, he's set out a full tray of tea on the living room table and is sitting back in his favorite armchair, whistling a breathy tune I can't identify. Maybe I was wrong about his intentions. But then what is this?

"I thought we were going for a drive," I say.

"Sure. But first, you're going to tell me what's going on." He looks at me with his usual intensity, and I see that what Shwe is asking is far more complicated than an afternoon tryst. What he wants is the truth.

I look down at the teak floorboards, escaping into their endless swirls and knots. If only I were more like Parker, able to spew out emotions on command.

I imagine telling Shwe everything.

That General Myint Oo killed U Soe Htet's nephew.

That I bullied the manager of ChickenKing.

That I'm terrified Jason has given up on me.

I take a deep breath and begin to talk, tears pricking my eyes. He moves to the sofa, puts his arm around my shoulder, and a weight lifts from my chest, a heaviness I've been carrying for years, decades even. I have the impression that he understands not only what I've said, but what I haven't said, what I can't yet see myself. Just as when we were teenagers, there's no need to explain but also nowhere to hide. I'm an open wound, raw and tender to the touch.

The more I reveal, the closer I come to understanding what it all means: the marionettes, the letters, the shrines. Why I can't let go of Shwe. What it is that binds us together. I look up at his smooth, wide lips, the dimple on his left cheek. How nice it would be to kiss those lips again, to go back to that time before everything began to fall apart, back to when we were teenagers, and my biggest concern was whether Shwe and I could spend the day alone together. I lift my face towards his.

With an almost imperceptible shake of his head, he shifts position, and the moment falls away, all that intimacy and understanding evaporating just as quickly as it formed.

The doorbell chimes.

For a second, neither of us move.

Then it rings again, and Shwe stands.

"*Kanaleh,*" he calls out as he walks toward the door. Just a sec.

I don't know whom I'm expecting. A vendor, perhaps. Daw Tin Tin. Sheila returning from Australia. I'm too busy assessing the damage of that almost kiss to pay attention, too busy weighing the humiliation of his rejecting me against the regret I might have felt if he hadn't.

Until I hear a voice that I know better than my own.

"Hi, I'm Jason."

"Shwe. Good to meet you."

I look up to see Shwe and Jason standing on either side of the doorway.

"Come on in. I was just leaving," says Shwe, disappearing into the corridor.

275

NINE

Part of me wants to run after Shwe, to claim my place in the left passenger seat of his rusted taxi, ask him to drive somewhere far away, back through the rice paddies and beyond, to a place where no one can find me. Except now here is Jason, standing, improbably, in the doorway of Parker's apartment, having followed me halfway across the world. The walls of the apartment shift in and out of focus as I try to make sense of what I'm seeing. Jason here. In Yangon. With me.

Then suddenly I'm standing in the doorway, Jason's long, protective arms wrapped around me as if nothing has changed, and our relationship is just as it was before Ahpwa died, as if we are the same people we were before I returned to Myanmar. I close my eyes, savoring the intimacy of his embrace, the luxury of his body around mine, before pulling away.

"How are you here?" I cringe at the inadequacy of my question.

"Good to see you, too." He studies me as if interpreting a painting, searching for meaning in every line and shadow of my face.

I step back, too conflicted to meet his gaze. For almost ten years we've shared a bed and a life, cooking our meals together, making a home, planning our future. I've planted tomatoes with his father and made peach pie with his mother, spent weekends in Vermont with his college friends. He trusted me, trusted us. Then Ahpwa climbed onto a chair for a can of coconut milk, and all my childhood beliefs came tumbling down with her, shifting the foundation of our relationship.

"You caught me by surprise, that's all. I wasn't expecting to see you so soon." I trail off, fighting an urge to flee.

"When exactly *were* you expecting to see me?"

I look away.

"That's what I thought." He picks up his bag and carries it over the threshold of the apartment.

I stare at the suitcase in confusion as I try to envision Jason in Myanmar. Driving around town with Shwe. Drinking wine with Khaing Zar. Sharing an apartment with Parker. I don't see how any of this can continue with Jason, and yet here he is, having come all this way.

"Seriously though, how'd you find the apartment?"

"Daw Tin Tin met me at the airport." He gives me a sheepish grin.

Our eyes meet, and I smile.

The longer I look into his eyes, the less alone I feel, the connection between us seeming to restore itself without any conscious effort on my part. Jason is like a vital organ, so integral to my existence that I forget he's there, forget he's not part of me. I can't imagine life without him. At least I couldn't until recently.

I scan the room until my eyes settle on the pot of tea, wondering briefly where Shwe went, what he might be thinking or doing right now. "Tea?"

He follows my eyes to the living room table where the teapot sits flanked by two empty teacups. There's still a slight depression on the sofa cushion where Shwe and I sat just minutes ago. I look back at Jason in alarm, but he's not looking at the sofa. He's looking at me, his gaze incisive and probing, as if trying to tease out the intimacy between us.

My heart lurches. A moment ago, I was ready to run off with Shwe, escape to a place where past and present are not in opposition. Now here's Jason, reminding me of the life we share together, making this time with Shwe feel like a digression, a misplaced fantasy from my adolescence threatening to hijack my present.

"You must be hungry. Let me find something to eat." I retreat to the kitchen, staring into the near empty cupboard until the pounding in my chest begins to ease. Then I grab a pack of black sesame snacks and take a deep breath. Jason's visit is unexpected, but maybe that's okay, maybe his being here is exactly what I need.

Returning to the living room, I'm taken aback to see Jason sitting in the same spot Shwe occupied just minutes ago. I settle cross-legged on the sofa facing him. He pours two cups of tea, adding an extra dollop of sweetened, condensed milk to each.

I raise my eyebrows in surprise.

"U Soe Htet," he responds, his tone open, lighthearted.

I shake my head and smile, Jason's relationship with U Soe Htet filling me with wonder. Two months ago, I could not have imagined such a friendship, would never have believed that Jason could be so eager to embrace U Soe Htet's customs, to understand his convictions. All for me. I should be flattered. Yet I can't help worrying that Jason's become *too* invested in the old man's story, that he's equating my grandmother's actions with my own, conflating their circumstances with ours.

"So." Jason stretches his arm over the top of the sofa, brushing the ends of my hair with his fingertips.

A sliver of longing travels the length of my spine. To be held. To be safe. To be loved. But as badly as I want to respond to his touch, I need to resist, maintain a clear boundary between us until I can figure out what it is that I want, where I want to live, why I came here in the first place. The answer feels closer than ever. If only I had more time.

"What's going on?" he says.

I stiffen. "With Shwe? He's just a cousin."

A look of confusion flashes across Jason's boyish features. "With *you*. What's going on with you, Etta? Why are you still here?"

I survey the room as if the answer lies within the bare walls of the apartment. It's funny how much the lack of décor bothered me when I first arrived. Somewhere along the way, I stopped noticing, and now it's begun to feel like home, the backdrop to the life I share with Parker and Shwe and Khaing Zar, a life that Jason knows nothing about, just as Shwe and Khaing Zar know nothing about my life in Boston.

"I guess I'm just trying to figure some stuff out," I say. Yes, that's what I need to do, figure stuff out. This is a good answer, an honest answer.

"Like what?"

His persistence, so unlike Jason, leaves me unsettled. It occurs to me that he's been preparing for this, probably sought advice from his friends, from our friends. Can I blame him? He needed someone to talk to, and I was inaccessible, unresponsive. But I can't help feeling excluded, pushed aside, as if a line has been drawn, however unintentionally, on one side stands Jason and our friends, and on the other side, just me.

"It's all right, Etta. You don't have to answer now. I'm here for a week. I thought maybe we could take a trip, do some sightseeing." He pauses. "Then you can decide what you want to do."

Jason in Myanmar for a week? I feel like one of the good-luck swallows at the Shwedagon, carried from one place to the next yet unable to spread my own wings.

"Ever been to Mandalay?" he asks.

"Mandalay?" I'm still turning over the gentle but firm deadline I've been issued to decide by the end of the week if and when I will return.

"Yeah, you know, '*On the road to Mandalay...*'"

I widen my eyes in surprise as he recites Rudyard Kipling.

"Don't laugh," he says. "I've wanted to go there ever since Mr. Leonard's ninth grade poetry class."

I rest my head against his hand, amused that he still remembers a poem from high school, and thankful for his ability to make me smile even when I don't want to. Maybe his timing isn't so bad after all.

~

We're back in the living room, pouring over the Myanmar Airlines schedule in the newspaper, when Parker returns from work. To my fascination, they greet each other with a warm hug and what appears to be genuine enthusiasm.

"So what have you been up to? Etta says you're working?" he asks.

She perches on the armrest of the sofa, filling him in on her work at the orphanage school, including her quest to obtain longer-term funding. "I know it's not the most sustainable project in development terms, but these kids need so much. It seems wrong not to try to help."

He asks some follow-up questions on budget and feasibility, and she responds with detailed explanations, demonstrating just how much time she's spent researching and analyzing the various options. I can tell by the way Jason cocks his head to the side that he, too, is impressed.

By late afternoon, Jason can't keep his eyes open, jetlag having finally caught up with him. I find an extra pillow and remind him to use bottled water to brush his teeth, then say goodnight, relieved to avoid the awkwardness of going to bed together. While part of me yearns for his touch, to be held and caressed and aroused, making love to Jason right now doesn't feel right, or fair, given how confused I am.

Returning to the living room, I collapse onto the sofa and begin flipping through his guidebook. My visit to ChickenKing

281

earlier this morning seems to have taken place light-years ago. Likewise, my time with Shwe feels like a story from someone else's life. With Jason's arrival, the experiences of the last couple of weeks seem smaller and less defined, as if my vision has been recalibrated to a wider lens.

Parker wanders in from the kitchen eating a piece of toast smeared with peanut butter. No plate, of course. I keep quiet. This is her apartment, after all; if she doesn't mind crumbs on the living room floor, that's her prerogative, not mine.

"So, Jason?" She raises her eyebrows.

I brace myself for whatever willful misconception she's about to proclaim about him.

"I'm impressed," she says.

"You are?"

"I always got the sense your relationship was too convenient for him. The way you moved into his apartment, adopting his friends, his lifestyle, you know?"

As she takes another bite of peanut-butter toast, the old instinct to defend Jason flares. I picture our apartment back home, all the furnishings we selected together, the woolen rug and Roman blinds, the "new" sofa, now a year old, every surface holding a memory, years of decorating and deliberating, making decisions as a couple. Maybe I did slip too easily into his world, but what she doesn't see is how willing he's been to adapt that world, going out of his way to make the apartment ours rather than his.

"But following you all the way here. That says something," she adds.

My irritation splutters into uncertainty. "We *are* engaged..."

She doesn't respond, and in the silence that follows, I turn her words over, examining not only their meaning but the intention behind them, understanding, perhaps for the first time, that any misconceptions she may have about Jason are born out of concern rather than spite, love rather than malice. She might still be wrong about him, but it's not out of dislike for Jason; it's because she wants to be sure he sees the real me, loves the real me.

I open the guidebook to the section on Mandalay. Jason has starred and underlined several passages, including one on the Royal Palace where King Thibaw and Queen Supayalat once lived. Staring down at his notations, I realize that Parker has touched on my own hidden insecurity about him, a nagging fear that if our relationship were to become too complicated, he might lose interest or motivation, that his love for me extends only as far as what is comfortable. And yet, here he is.

Parker clears her throat. "So, what about Shwe?" Her tone is curious but gentle, absent of confrontation.

A tangle of emotions lodges under my breastbone. Shwe left so quickly, I don't know what to think or feel. Whether he's upset that I tried to kiss him or disappointed because Jason has come. I thought we were on the verge of a new understanding these last few weeks, that with Shwe by my side, I could finally figure out what it all means, why I can't let go of the past. But does he really hold that power? Do we really know each other so well, or is it simply that we share the same memory? That our lives intersected at a pivotal moment, what we saw and felt that day at the lake continuing to echo across the years, contaminating what might otherwise be virtuous and good?

Part of me worries that Jason's arrival will send him back to the monastery or into the bowels of some dark, seedy bar. Yet I can just as easily imagine him carrying on as if nothing had changed, chasing story leads across the city in his beat-up taxi just as he did before I came and would continue to do if I were to leave. I still don't know with Shwe; that's the problem. I don't know whether he's still hurting from the betrayal of his grandfather or so hardened that he can no longer feel pain, if the bond I feel is current and real, or a remnant of the past, a figment of my imagination that continues to haunt and seduce regardless of time or distance traveled.

I look up at Parker in desperation. I can scarcely articulate these thoughts to myself let alone explain them to another person. But this isn't just anyone, this is Parker.

"He took off when Jason arrived. Can you check on him? Make sure he's all right?"

"Of course." She sits down next to me.

"I just want to make sure he doesn't do anything reckless."

She nods, and the softness of her expression tells me that she understands, that she'll do what she can.

"We leave for Mandalay tomorrow morning. Then back to Yangon for a couple of days before—" I realize that I don't know what comes next, whether I'll accompany Jason back to Boston, or he'll return alone. Both seem equally plausible and implausible.

"Before you return to Boston." Parker states what I'm unwilling to admit.

I open my mouth to correct her, then close it again.

"Sheila's due back any day now," she continues. "So you better put your stuff in my room before you head off to Mandalay."

A void of disbelief and loss opens up around me. Whether or not I return to Boston with Jason, the room is no longer mine. This apartment, this experience with Parker has come to an end, our time together slipping away in plain sight.

"What about you? How much longer do you plan to stay?"

"I think I'll stick around for a while. I wouldn't feel right leaving Ma Win and the kids right now. Not until they're in a better financial position, anyway. But once that's done..." She pauses, and the certainty drains from her freckled face. "I've been thinking about going back to school."

"Really? In what?"

"Education?" An eagerness in her tone tells me how important this is to her, how badly she wants my approval.

"That's wonderful, Bird! I'm so happy for you." As I stand to hug her, my heart swells with admiration. Parker has found her calling. Not only is she doing okay, she's thriving. She no longer needs me to take care of her, only to love and support her. Maybe it is time for me to go home.

TEN

The crenulated walls of the fortress rise from the surrounding moat like a fairy tale. I squeeze Jason's hand in anticipation. I've been dreaming about Queen Supayalat for as long as I can remember, recreating her rise and fall over and over as I tried to understand who she really was, what drove her to make the choices she made, to kill her cousins and steal her sister's husband. To visit the Royal Palace now with Jason by my side strikes me as significant, though I don't yet know in what sense, whether this is a beginning or an ending, time to let him into my Burmese world or time to release him from my family's immorality.

As we approach the entrance, he reads various facts and figures aloud from his guidebook. The citadel forms a perfect 1020-acre square at the center of Mandalay Hill with three gates along each of the four, two-kilometer-long walls. Due to a large military installation that now shares grounds with the Royal Palace, tourists may only enter through the east wall. I don't give this much thought until I notice the large red banner above the ticket counter:

THE TATMADAW AND THE PEOPLE COOPERATE
AND CRUSH ALL THOSE HARMING THE UNION.

The sight of two soldiers standing sentry at the palace gates, EMER-K rifles at the ready, turns my insides cold. Tatmadaw is the Burmese name for the Myanmar Armed Forces. While I know in theory that the military still rules the country, I've encountered little evidence of its presence in Yangon. Or perhaps chose not to see it. An image unfolds in my mind—a man lying face-down on the ground, one side of his face pressed into the dirt, hands cuffed behind his back. I saw the footage on the news a couple of years back, a Burmese man being apprehended by the military police. Except now, the man I picture in my head has a scar that runs the length of his forearm, a dragon tattoo on the back of his neck. I shudder.

"You okay?" Jason's voice, tender and concerned.

A busload of elderly Swedish tourists push past me, holding out their money as they queue to enter the palace, oblivious to any danger posed by the armed guards. Suddenly all I want to do is leave this country, return to the sanctuary of my Boston life, where monuments aren't guarded by armed soldiers, and memories don't lurk around every corner, punching me in the gut when I least expect it. I reach for Jason's hand, soothed by his quiet presence.

"Let's just wait for these tourists to go through," I say.

He gives me a cautious second look then tightens his hand around mine.

Inside the gates, the red and gold roofs of the palace buildings shimmer in the afternoon sun. Jason begins snapping photos, and the soldiers soon slip from my mind. As my gaze travels over the intricate carvings and gilded structures, I picture Queen Supayalat as a little girl growing up on these very grounds, running around the palace with a pack of cousins, playing *htote si toe,* or hide-and-seek, or just plain tag. I wish, suddenly, that I could protect that little girl from what's to come, extend her childhood just a little longer before her mother plots her ascendency to the throne, fating these same playmates to be clubbed to death in velvet body bags and trampled by elephants.

Wandering up the watch tower with Jason, I try to imagine how she felt back in November 1885 when she stood on this same platform and beheld the British flotilla coming down the Ayeyarwaddy River to overthrow their kingdom. Did she regret having advised Thibaw against negotiation, or did she remain steadfast in her views, defending her stance even as she and her family were cast out of the palace on a bullock cart? What guided her actions as a queen and as a woman?

Jason touches my arm, and I startle. We continue on, stopping in front of a life-size recreation of King Thibaw and Queen Supayalat. Jason looks up from his guidebook.

"Sounds like the last king and queen were real tyrants."

I bristle. I've followed the story of Queen Supayalat and King Thibaw my entire life and still can't distinguish truth from myth. For him to pass judgement so quickly and emphatically makes my skin prickle with irritation.

"It's a little more complicated than that," I say.

"Most things are. But this is my only source of information." He holds the guidebook up in the air, and in the stiffness of the gesture, I see again the counsel of his friends, the threat of a growing rift. Then a glint of golden-brown stubble across his jaw catches the afternoon sun, and my self-righteousness buckles. How can I expect him to know the alternate history of the Konbaung Dynasty when I only just learned it myself? Why come here with him if not to share what matters to me?

We sit together on a shaded bench, and I tell him everything I've learned about the royal couple: the smear campaign orchestrated by the British, the royal family's exile to India, the slow but steady deterioration of assets and honor. The more I talk, the more important it becomes to me that Jason understand the traditions of the Konbaung Dynasty, the competing interests and expectations that dominated their lives, Thibaw's capitulation, Supayalat's unceasing defiance.

"Nice to see you so passionate about this," he says when I'm finished.

I stiffen again, his comment striking me as condescending, smug even, another ill-informed opinion, except this time it's about me. I shoot him a look of warning.

Instead of recoiling, he moves closer, placing his hand on top of mine. "Look, Etta, I don't understand exactly what's going on with you, but I'm here if you want to talk. When you're ready."

I resist an impulse to deny that anything's wrong and rest my head on his shoulder instead.

As we sit silently on the bench, enjoying the reprieve from the sun, a young white couple dressed in tee shirts and elephant pants approaches the effigy.

"Apparently the last king was a total wimp, dominated by his bloodthirsty wife," says the man in a looping Australian accent.

Jason elbows me, a conspiratorial gleam in his eyes, and I squeeze his hand, surprised at how natural it feels to have him here by my side, how fitting, as if the events of the past month have come to their logical conclusion, Shwe leading me out of the darkness before disappearing once again into my childhood memories. Jason might not share my connection to Myanmar, but that doesn't mean he can't see my longing. Or that we can't love each other.

Our hotel has two restaurants, one Chinese and one international. We opt for Chinese the first night, sharing a laugh when the waiter brings Jason a fork and me chopsticks. I order the closest approximation of what we might get back home: spring rolls, chicken with cashew nuts, stir-fried snow peas. As we compare the dishes to those of our favorite Chinese restaurant back home, I picture the route we take to get there, the clean, open sidewalks and tidy, tree-lined streets, electricity cables tucked somewhere I don't need to think about, pavement free of betel nut sputum. Is this what I want: to return to my old life?

The hotel room is freezing, AC remote unresponsive. Still jet-lagged, Jason gets under the covers and falls asleep almost immediately. I slip on my shoes and return to the lobby in search of new batteries for the remote.

"Please wait," says the night manager, disappearing into the back room.

I sit down at the guest computer to check my email. The internet connection is faster than Cyber Savvy, and it loads quickly. Nothing of note. The night manager still hasn't returned, so I type in the URL for Shwe's blog.

He's posted a new story. An exposé predicting widespread bloodshed against the Rohingya Muslim minority in Rakhine State if authorities aren't held accountable. I catch my breath at the recklessness of posting this story under his real name, at his complete lack of concern for his own safety. The government won't take kindly to such an eloquent and pointed accusation, especially since it's all true. Khaing Zar was right about her brother. Poking and prodding the status quo is who Shwe is. He wouldn't be satisfied if he weren't testing the limits of authority because that would mean he wasn't doing enough.

Being with him these past few weeks was like riding that human-powered Ferris wheel back in 1988, every cell of my body jolted into awareness, every hope and fear buzzing with new energy. The thrill I got from being in his proximity electrified me at first but ultimately proved too much; *he* proved too much, then and now, a level of intensity I could never sustain. How silly of me to try to kiss him, to have risked severing our bond, for what? I see now that my fixation with Shwe has little to do with him. It's about figuring out who I was when our lives last intersected, and who I am now.

The night manager reemerges empty-handed. "I'm sorry. I am unable to locate the store of batteries. I am afraid you will have to wait until morning."

Back in the room, I crawl in bed beside Jason. Listening to the soft cadence of his breath, I recall the last extended vacation we took together—a week in the eternal city of Rome late last year.

We spent our days walking through the cobblestoned streets of *Campo de' Fiori*, gorging on fresh buffalo mozzarella and tomatoes sweeter than candy, and making love more often than I thought possible. Our last night in Rome, we went to the restaurant *L'Archeologia* along the old Appian Way. As we sat surrounded by stone archways and ancient marble sculptures, the rich, earthy aroma of Roman cuisine wafting through the air, Jason placed a small jewelry box on the table.

"Etta Hammond Montgomery, will you marry me?"

Yes, of course. Jason made me feel safe and calm and beautiful and loved. I admired the way he approached life, riding the highs and lows with a gentle, forward momentum. I felt stronger and steadier with him by my side, ready to embrace the future, if not the past. I had no doubt that I wanted to spend my life with him. But as we toasted our engagement with flutes of chilled Prosecco, something about his proposal niggled at the edge of my happiness. I'd heard the many nicknames he'd endured as a child, yet somehow, I'd neglected to tell him the Burmese name listed on my birth certificate alongside my English name.

On that fairy-tale evening in Rome, I brushed the lapse off as little more than an inconvenience—no one called me Aye Tha Kyaw anymore—but as I watch him sleeping now, I see the wider implications of my omission. This is my fault, I know. I'm the one who persistently downplayed the importance of my family's heritage, offering only the broad strokes of an immigrant dynamic, too predictable to be meaningful—but I can't help wondering why he didn't seem to notice, or care, why he didn't push harder.

Maybe Parker's right about our relationship being too easy for him. But then why come all this way? Can it be that this time apart has changed him as well? I remember our first encounter in the computer lab, me frenzied with distress, Jason cheerful and calm, his voice transporting me from panic to laughter in a matter of minutes. Yes, we have work to do, but I'm not ready to give up on our relationship yet. If that means going back to Boston, that's what I'll do. I resolve to tell him everything, to stop keeping secrets, no matter how inconsequential I may think they are.

Chilled from the air conditioning, I turn off the light and curl up next to Jason's warm body, sliding my hand over his chest, down the length of his torso. He rolls over, his eyes still closed as he draws me toward him, exploring the curves of my body in long, lazy strokes. Breathless with yearning, I press closer, determined to eliminate the space between us, to bring us back to the way we were. He responds sleepily, neither resisting nor succumbing to my urgency, slowing us both down, drawing out my pleasure until I feel safe enough to let go.

ELEVEN

The sprawling, outdoor market offers every imaginable ware from velvet slippers and silk *longyi* to everyday household goods, a riot of color and ingenuity that jolts my senses into overdrive. With our flight to Yangon not until the afternoon, Jason and I spend our final morning in Mandalay shopping for souvenirs to take to our friends back home. As we wade through displays of precious gems and *kalaga* tapestries, the weight of my decision to leave Myanmar presses down on me.

How unexpected these weeks have been, how vivid and bright, as if set afire by tiny pinpricks of light and electricity. The pull of Ko Martin's work. The resilience of the burn victims. The tentative courtship between Daw Tin Tin and U Zaw Min. There's so much more to learn and discover, about the new Myanmar and about myself. All those unfinished conversations with Parker and Khaing Zar. The long, meandering drives with Shwe.

"Let's get my parents a puppet," suggests Jason as we pass a colorful display of *yoke thé* hanging along the fringe of a souvenir stall.

"Very good gift," says the vendor. "Foreigner like Myanmar puppet."

I pick up one of the ubiquitous Minister marionettes to examine the workmanship. "They're not authentic. Look. The facial features are too simplistic, and there aren't enough strings." A swell of shaky indignation spills over me.

"I doubt they'll notice," says Jason. He picks up a Palace Ogre in his left hand and a Jungle Ogre in his right, both green-skinned and elaborately dressed, their exaggerated teeth and eyes as mesmerizing as they are jarring. "Which one do you think they'd like better?"

I shrug, shaking off his dismissal.

The vendor considers me thoughtfully, then turns to the back of his stall and begins rummaging through a stack of plastic milk crates.

"Perhaps you like this one, *Siyama.*" He holds up an old horse marionette, and I gasp.

Timeworn but exquisitely crafted, the horse is painted white with a fawn-colored mane and tail that look like real hair. Saddle, halter and hoof coverings are made from thick red cotton embroidered with gold ribbon and sequins, their edges trimmed with tiny silver bells that jingle when they move.

We had a similar one when I was a child, I realize. *Myin.* I must have been eight the first time I saw it perform. I was sitting cross-legged on the living room floor. Parker, still in diapers, bounced up and down in my lap. The puppeteer moved behind the waist-high, black velvet curtain. U Soe Htet. I can picture him perfectly now, his twinkly eyes, jet black hair and wide grin. How odd that three months ago I couldn't recall his face, had forgotten, even, that he existed.

"*Myin*, the first living being on earth." He swooped the white horse marionette through the air with a theatrical flourish.

I nodded, not because I agreed or even understood, but because I couldn't think what to say in response to this strange Burmese man talking and laughing with my grandmother. I was old enough to notice the light in their eyes when they looked at each other, even if I didn't quite appreciate the depth of their attachment.

The horse marionette entered the stage, slowly at first then with increasing speed, leaping across the platform, all four hooves touching down to the beat of the drum. As the tempo quickened, the horse turned to face the audience, swaying its head and stamping its hooves in a crescendo of drumming and emotion. Tiny bells jingled with each step, the wail of the reed pipe swirling in my head until the rhythm changed again, and the horse marionette fell, rolling back and forth on the floor of the stage. The birth of creation: *Myin* descending to the earth before returning to the heavens.

As I run my fingers over the embroidery of this new memory, I realize that Jason is watching me, a pensiveness to his expression.

"How much?" he asks the vendor.

But I already know that I'll pay any amount to bring this marionette back to U Soe Htet, that Myin belongs under his care, together with Minthamee, Yatheik and Nat Pyet. I think back to the broken marionette pieces in Ahpwa's closet, the latest casualties of *America the Beautiful*, of my family's steady spiral into disrepair. U Soe Htet never showed surprise at their condition, never asked how or why they came to be in such a state. Picturing his full-bodied chuckle, that manner he has of evading questions with charm, I realize that he knew all along, not just about *America the Beautiful* but about everything: Ahpwa's brother, Lwin Moe, *tada phyu*. Unlike Ahpwa, he'd found his way through his suffering and came out the other side. He knew that the only way for me to do the same was to return to the Golden Land.

Jason pays the vendor. No more secrets, I promised myself. But does a memory constitute a secret? And if so, does that mean that all my memories now belong to him, that I forsake exclusive ownership of them? I love Jason. I love his thoughtfulness and compassion, the way he nudges me forward without throwing me off balance, reassuring me when I doubt myself. But sometimes a memory is too fragile to let go, like an injured sparrow I must cradle in my hands to prevent further harm.

TWELVE

Back in Yangon, the humidity is so thick, I can't seem to get enough air. Mandalay was hot too, but it was a dry heat, not as sticky or oppressive as Yangon. I wonder vaguely if this is why I became so bogged down in memory and regret.

"Hey, how was it?" Parker asks as we enter the apartment. She's sitting on the sofa with a standing fan positioned directly in front of her, the unstapled edges of her grant proposal blowing up each time the fan rotates past.

"Fantastic!" says Jason. "Want to see photos?" He takes out his camera and sits down next to her.

Resisting an impulse to keep the two apart, I retreat to Parker's room to collect my belongings. Sheila's delayed her return again, so Jason and I can stay our final two nights in my old room. Parker's bedroom is unexpectedly tidy, the bed and floor free of clothing. The little statue of Yatheik sits on the dresser just as I left it, but Ahpwa's urn has been moved to the bedside table.

I pick up the carving and turn it over, noting the intricate details of the robe, feet, and face. He must've begun carving it soon after we met, knowing even before I did, that I would make this journey. Yatheik, the hermit who inhabits the forest, guiding those who have lost their way.

A peal of laughter rings out from the living room. I place the statue on the bedside table next to Ahpwa's ashes and sit down on the bed to think. Parker doesn't understand to keep the two together because she doesn't know about U Soe Htet. Or does she? I try to recall her exact words when she first told me she was bringing Ahpwa's ashes to Myanmar.

The bathroom door opens and closes.

I peek my head into the living room.

"You know, Jason's not as stiff as I thought," says Parker.

I roll my eyes and smile. "Hey, can I ask you something?"

She sets her pen on the table, and I sit down across from her.

"What exactly did Ahpwa say that made you bring her ashes back here? Was it just a general longing for Burma, or something more specific?"

"Both, I guess. She talked about Burma a lot those last few months. About family. It was almost like she knew..." A shadow passes across Parker's face. "But yeah, there was something specific. Some guy she kept going on and on about, some Myanmar dude."

I put my head in my hands in frustration. "Was his name U Soe Htet?"

"Yeah, that's him. How—"

"So, you came here to find him."

"Yeah, I thought—"

"So that they could be together again."

"Wait, what's going on, Etta?"

"But you couldn't find him."

"No. I looked really hard, asked everyone I could think of. Not even Shwe could find him. But I don't understand. Do you know him?"

"Parker, do you know how old Ahpwa was when she married our grandfather and moved to the U.S.?"

"I dunno, like 25?"

"Nineteen. Do you think she had such a serious affair before then that she would still be talking about him from her deathbed?"

"It's possible, Etta. I mean look at you—"

I shoot her a look of warning, and she scowls back at me.

"U Soe Htet lives in a retirement home in Westwood, Massachusetts."

She opens her eyes wide, understanding spreading slowly across her face.

"So, this." I make a big, raging circle in the air, "Has all been a wild goose chase. You. Me. Jason. We came all this way for nothing. To find a man who lives ten miles from home." I don't know why I'm so annoyed.

"That's not true, Etta, and you know it." She glares back at me. "We absolutely needed to come here. Even if it was for a different reason than we thought. Especially you."

Parker watches me with an expression of frustration and concern. I think back to everything that's happened since I returned to Yangon—seeing Parker and Shwe at the airport, visiting with San San and my cousins, meeting Ko Martin, Yangon General Hospital, Shwe's taxi, and more bowls of *mohinga* than I can count. She's right: I needed to come here. I needed to create a new store of memories to replace the old. Even the trip to Mandalay with Jason. Especially the trip to Mandalay with Jason.

"I'm sorry," I say. "I'm glad I came. You know that, right?"

Her eyes soften. "It's going to be weird not having you around."

"I'll miss you too, Bird."

I may have failed in my mission to bring Parker home, but in the process, I've discovered the sister I didn't know I'd lost, a smart, determined woman I love more fiercely than ever.

Jason emerges from the bathroom with the pink, flowered towel from Citymart wrapped around his waist, his long, naked torso still glistening from the shower. I remember last night in the hotel and flush. As he goes into the bedroom to dress, it occurs to me that this may be the last opportunity I have to speak with Parker alone.

"Have you seen Shwe?" I ask.

"Yeah, I saw him yesterday."

"And?"

"I told him you were leaving."

"And?"

"He's fine. Working really hard on some story."

I remember the blog post about the Rohingya and shudder. "No drinking?"

"Not that I know of."

"That's a relief," I say. But is that really what I feel? I don't want Shwe to suffer. And I'd especially hate to be the cause of his suffering. But is he not even the tiniest bit disappointed that our time together—our daily escapades around the city, exploring the dark alleys and secret passageways of our shared past—has come to an end?

Jason reappears dressed in a blue polo shirt and olive khakis still creased from his suitcase. He looks smart, put together. For a fleeting moment, I wonder what he'd look like in a *longyi*.

"So, I'll bring Ahpwa's ashes back to Boston with me," I say to Parker.

She nods, and Jason and I begin discussing our sightseeing plans for the remainder of our time. He must see the Shwedagon, of course. Maybe the lying-down Buddha, too. Bogyoke market and downtown. I wonder what he'll make of the crowded, chaotic streets, the tiny, alley-shaped shops stuffed full of Chinese imports and second-hand sundries, the smells, at once inviting and repellent, seductive and forbidding. The idea of leaving gnaws at my gut, a hollowness spreading slowly outward. At least this time, I'll be able to say goodbye.

"So, what do you think?" I say to Jason, after listing all the options.

Parker has turned back to her proposal, but I can tell by the way she angles her head toward us that she's listening to our conversation, appraising not only what I say, but how I say it, studying my intonation and body language for any sign of doubt about returning to Boston with Jason.

"I'm fine with anything," he says. And then, as an afterthought, "Why don't you invite your cousin? What was his name? Shay?"

"Second cousin," I respond automatically. "And it's Shwe." Does he suspect something? No, I tell myself, this is just Jason being Jason. Family's always been important to him. From the very beginning, he's wanted to get to know my family, and from the very beginning, I sidestepped his requests, pretending not to understand what he was asking. I should be pleased that he cares so much about family. But Jason and Shwe together? My stomach tenses. Their personalities are too dissimilar, their approach to life too contradictory, each bringing out a different side of me.

"Sure," I say in a measured tone. "We could invite Khaing Zar, too. And Parker, you should definitely come."

"I really need to finalize this grant..." she begins, then stops and looks at me, a mixture of compassion and amusement in her blue eyes, "but okay."

THIRTEEN

Khaing Zar is first to arrive. Gracious as always, she slips into conversation with Jason, sharing her own travel experiences as she prises out his impressions of her country. I can see from the openness of his expression that he's fully engaged, going out of his way to show his best side, to prove to my family that he's worthy of me. So far, so good. But Khaing Zar isn't the one I'm worried about. Shwe's the wild card, so erratic and unpredictable. So unlike Jason. Parker says he's coming, but he could just as easily not show up.

I swing between dreading his arrival and burning to see him. But when he saunters in a few minutes later, cleanly shaven and smartly dressed in a white button-down shirt and crisp, red and blue *longyi*, it's curiosity I feel more than anything. He seems different to me, his face fuller and more resolute, hair finally growing in after his stint at the monastery. Some distant part of me wants to grab his hand and run out the door, go back to that place of wonder and discovery that his taxi had become, but the feeling is short-lived and detached, more muscle memory than true longing.

What I really want is to know that he's okay, that we're okay. But what does that mean? What constitutes okay, and what is it that I want to be okay? I hold my breath as he acknowledges me with the briefest of glances before zeroing in on Jason.

"Hey, man. Sorry we didn't get a chance to talk the other day. How's it going?" Shwe claps his hand on Jason's back, an exchange that seems to me at odds with both of their personalities.

I exhale slowly as they settle into an easy exchange, Jason drawn in by Shwe's casual intensity, that ability of his to focus so singularly yet nonchalantly on someone that it becomes impossible not to open up to him. I've watched him work this magic on countless others, from the owner of the button shop to the burn victims at the hospital, not to mention every new passenger who entered his taxi, every teashop attendant who served us *mohinga*. This I know about Shwe. What I didn't anticipate, what never would've occurred to me, is his pointed interest in Jason. I try to catch his eye, but he remains focused on Jason.

The conversation turns to our outing, and I clear my throat. "Maybe we should hire a tour guide so Shwe doesn't have to drive."

He shakes his head. "I know the city better than any tour guide."

"I know that," I begin.

But he's already turned away from me, already resumed his new liaison with Jason. I open my mouth to clarify, then realize that I've been dismissed, our connection severed. So much for all those hours driving around together, shining new light on the shadows of our past. By choosing Jason, I've given up access to Shwe.

A pall of heat and car exhaust greets us on the street. As we pile into Shwe's taxi, I assume the backseat, Jason's long legs rightfully earning him the front, left passenger seat that, for a period, felt like home. Pressed between Parker and Khaing Zar, I tune my ears to the front, where Jason and Shwe glide seamlessly from one topic to the next: Relations with China. The game of *chinlone*. The National League for Democracy.

"I heard your government released 14,000 political prisoners a few weeks back. Seems like a good sign," says Jason.

I hold my breath in anticipation of Shwe's response, worried he might explode at the suggestion that the latest military government is his in any way.

But Shwe doesn't flinch. "Not unless petty theft and prostitution have become political crimes."

Jason turns to him in surprise. "You mean they weren't political prisoners?"

"A handful, at most."

I can tell by the way Jason cocks his head to the side that he's turning over this new perspective, reflecting on its implications. "So why do it? What's the point?"

"Public relations," says Shwe. "They want the international community to think the country's opening up, so they release a bunch of petty criminals and call them political prisoners."

Listening from the backseat, I feel increasingly disconnected, as if I'm eavesdropping on strangers. I thought I knew them both well enough to predict the course of their conversation, imagined I might even need to intervene now and then, serve as a kind of referee, helping to navigate their different outlooks on life. But Jason's doing just fine on his own. And Shwe seems less and less likely to listen to anything I might offer. Not only is my interference unnecessary, it's irrelevant.

Jason's face stills with awe as we enter Chauk Htat Gyi Pagoda. At 65 meters long and six meters high, the golden-robed, Reclining Buddha is considered one of the most impressive in Southeast Asia.

"I know, right?" says Parker. "Doesn't matter how many times I come here. I'm always amazed how big it is."

"Even me," says Khaing Zar.

I look up at the metal rods and aluminum siding that shelter the Buddha. "What I don't get is why such an elegant statue is housed in such an inelegant structure."

"It's a Buddhist thing," says Khaing Zar, laughing.

"Something the West can't seem to appreciate," adds Shwe, not laughing.

He doesn't look in my direction, but his words sting. I'm not Burmese enough. This is what I hear him saying. I recall our recent visit to the Shwedagon with new understanding—how insistent he was that we visit the pagoda that day, how intent on my performing the Garuda ritual. I assumed what he wanted was closure, execution of the fortuneteller's unfulfilled prophecy so that we could both move on. Now I see it as a trial of sorts, a test of devotion that I failed not once, but twice.

I approach the Buddha's head, propped up by a shiny white elbow. With its porcelain white skin, ruby red lips, and black-lined eyes, the statue is more feminine than masculine by Western standards. Some depictions of Buddha portray him as clean-shaven with curly hair and a lion-shaped body, others as emaciated and bearded with his hair in a topknot. Our images come from a complex web of ancient texts, sculpture, and artistic impression. The reality is that no one really knows what Siddhartha Gautama, the original buddha, looked like. No one can legitimately claim that the other is wrong.

Maybe being part Burmese is enough for me, maybe even just right. If *America the Beautiful* taught me anything, it's that being Burmese is not a box to be opened or closed; culture is not hard and fixed but a function of the breath that passes through me day in and day out, an amalgam of everything I touch and experience, past, present, and future. Who I am, which parts of myself I choose to embrace and which to let go, is up to me, not Shwe or Ahpwa or Jason.

My grandmother was willing to forsake her heritage in order to contain the past. She locked away her secrets in dark closets and padlocked trunks, choosing to sever her bond with U Soe Htet rather than endure the shame of her brother's depravity. I want to believe she made peace with Burma before she died, that she forgave herself. But maybe that's asking too much. Maybe the most she could do was recognize her regret, put a name to it in the hope that future generations would not make the same mistake. That was the purpose of the key, unlocking her chest of secrets her real bequest to me.

I reencounter the rest of the group near the Buddha's feet. Parker and Shwe stand on a small viewing platform at the top of a set of freestanding metal steps, while Khaing Zar and Jason examine the Buddha's footprint from the ground. I sidle up to Jason, tuck my hand in his.

"These engravings correspond to the 108 auspicious characteristics of Buddha," Khaing Zar tells him.

"The 108 *lakshanas*," I say, remembering the day Ahpwa taught them to me, back when she wanted me to know everything there was to know about Burma.

"That's right," says Khaing Zar, "we call them the *lakshanas* of Buddha."

"You know all this?" Jason turns to me, a gleam of admiration in his eyes.

I lean against his arm, grateful that he's here to see this part of me, and reassured that I made the right decision to return with him to Boston.

Khaing Zar suggests lunch at Monsoon, a pan-Asian restaurant downtown that serves local Myanmar dishes alongside those of Cambodia, Laos, Thailand, and Vietnam.

"So that Jason can taste some of our most famous dishes," she says in a playful tone. "But don't worry, Jason. They also have Western food."

He laughs, and I can't help envying Khaing Zar's goodness. She seems to hover just off the ground, fully present yet unaffected by the tension that pulls at the rest of us.

My mood lightens as we enter the restaurant. I haven't eaten Myanmar food since Jason arrived and am looking forward to a bowl of spicy Shan noodles. I think back to all those heady bowls of *mohinga* and sour leaf soup, how they comforted me and sustained me over the past month. Reverting to corn flakes won't be easy. But perhaps I can learn to make *mohinga*, slip some fish paste and dried banana stem through U.S. customs.

Jason studies the menu. He may not be an adventurous eater by nature, but he's a good sport, willing to try almost anything under the right circumstances. Khaing Zar cajoles him into ordering tea leaf salad alongside his club sandwich. When the salad arrives, he rubs his hands together in a show of enthusiasm. I can't believe he'll like the bitter, pickled tea leaves, but maybe I'm wrong, maybe I don't know him as well as I thought.

He takes a forkful and instantly screws up his face. Everyone laughs, and the tension drains from my shoulders, not because I'm right, but because he fits in anyway. Having Jason here is so much easier than I imagined, so much more nourishing.

The Shan noodles are excellent, some of the best I've had since coming to Myanmar, the aromatic broth and rice noodles filling my belly with contentment. Shwe ordered the same, I notice. He, too, laughed when Jason tasted the pickled tea leaves, but I can see from the faraway look in his eyes that he's somewhere else, plotting some new scheme to uncover the truth. I just hope he's careful, that he doesn't cause trouble for himself or anyone else in the process.

We funnel back into the taxi. Shwe drives north along Pyay Road, and I wonder vaguely where he'll take us next. My limbs grow heavy in the afternoon heat. I lay my head back against the torn headrest and close my eyes, picturing the sunlit living room of our apartment back in Boston, the various artwork we've collected over the years, a watercolor of the Colosseum from our trip to Rome, the abstract painting we bought at the gallery on Newbury Street, memories of happiness and belonging, of love and security. I imagine unpacking my suitcase, running out to buy bread and milk, a bunch of flowers from the corner store. Something temperate rather than tropical. Hydrangea maybe, or tulips. Soon, I tell myself.

Shwe turns off the ignition.

I open my eyes with a jolt, a spike of adrenaline pulling me into alertness as I see where we are, where he's taken us.

The copse of trees, the slope of grass, the beautiful, deathly lake.

Jason, Khaing Zar and Parker start up the lake's embankment.

I grab Shwe's arm. "What are you doing? Why'd you bring us here?"

His eyes bore into me, his expression firm but not unkind. "Why'd you come back, Aye?"

I begin to tremble, every cell of my body seized by an urge to flee. I look toward the street, where cars speed by without a care, people going about their day as if nothing ever happened here. I feel suddenly as if my whole life has been reduced to this one moment, that whatever I do right now has the potential to alter its course forever. I take a step, then another.

"Come." Shwe's voice pulls me back. "You can do this." He tilts his head in the opposite direction, toward the water.

Thunder rumbles in the distance. The long-awaited rains coming at last. I look up at the sky, still blue for the moment. A young couple walks along the pathway, pausing to buy popsicles from a hand-pushed cart topped with a yellow and red umbrella. At the top of the embankment, stand Parker, Khaing Zar, and Jason, their faces twisted in confusion as they try to work out what's going on, why we're not joining them. On the other side of the pathway is the lake. Here are all the people I love most in the world. Why do I feel so alone?

Once upon a time, my world revolved around Shwe. He was the one I turned to when I needed solace, the memory of our time together carrying me through the madness with Ahpwa, my parents' divorce, my father's heart attack. Then I met Jason, who offered an easy tenderness, a sense of peace and wellbeing, the possibility of another path. But I couldn't share with him what I couldn't see myself. I couldn't go forward without first going back.

I turn and follow Shwe, tiptoeing around picnic blankets and flower beds until we reach the copse of trees.

The rush of the cars fades into the distance. The only sound now the echo of my memories.

"I'm scared," I say.

"I know." He places his hands on my shoulders, turns me toward the water.

Food stands and umbrellas line the shore of the lake, families and friends enjoying a reprieve from the oppressive heat of the city. The surface of the water is still. No steel helmets glinting in the sun. No students screaming in terror. No blood spilling over the flowers. Shwe is here by my side, Jason, Parker, and Khaing Zar close by. I take a deep breath and let the memories flow through me.

The tenderness of that first kiss.

The sense of belonging as we sang and chanted in unison with the students.

The sudden hush.

A whisper of fear curls around me, a figure rising from the lake. The woman in red. The one who welcomed us into the march. So close now I can trace the brushstrokes of her *thanaka,* hear the tremor in her voice as she tells us to run, taste the minerals in the water as it enters my airway.

Pushing, burning, throbbing. The pressure in my lungs so fierce, I feel as if my ribcage might crack.

Until all at once, my chest seizes, and I gasp for air, big convulsive breaths that rip through my torso, turning me inside out, exhuming all my hopes and fears, exposing every last vulnerability to the heavens.

I sink to the ground and weep.

For the woman in red whose future was trampled by injustice and brutality.

For U Soe Htet, who lost the woman he loved to the futility of regret.

For Ahpwa and Mother and Father and Parker, whose lives would never be the same after that day.

And for myself, the thirteen-year-old girl who put her dreams on hold, afraid to live her life lest the horrors of the past repeat themselves.

Shwe rubs my back. "It's okay. You're okay. That's right, breathe."

I raise my head slowly, noting what has changed and what remains the same, comparing the tidy purple plants and neatly clipped grass with the tangled memories of that terrible day. All those innocent students killed, all the families who lost their children, many without knowing what had occurred, only that their son or daughter didn't come home for dinner that evening, or the next evening, or the one after that. My family didn't lose any loved ones that day. But the damage crept through us like a cancer, extending deeper and wider as time passed.

I understand now why Shwe brought me here today, what he's been trying to make me understand ever since I gave him the letters. Memories are like bricks, each one building on the last, lending shape and meaning to our existence. The secret to living a full life, an authentic life, is to allow each brick to sustain the weight of the others.

I look up at the yawning purple clouds, ready to burst at any moment. They're all here now: Jason, Parker, Khaing Zar, and Shwe. I stand and hug Parker and Khaing Zar, then turn, uncertainly, to Jason. He opens his arms and I nestle into his chest.

Thunder cracks. Palm crowns bending backwards in the wind.

"What now?" asks Parker.

"The Shwedagon is beautiful in the rain," says Khaing Zar.

As the five of us rush toward the street, big, round raindrops begin to fall, hitting my face with the promise of the monsoon.

The storm is brief but intense, a sudden apparition that throws the city into a state of confusion, flash floods causing temporary chaos on the streets as pedestrians and vehicles swerve unexpectedly to escape rivers of water. Sheltering in the back of Shwe's taxi, its windows washed clean by sheets of rain, I watch two young women huddled together under a single, broken umbrella as they run through the rain, their faces glistening with joy.

Author's Note

The Golden Land is inspired by the six years I lived in Yangon, Myanmar. Writing it was a labor of love for my host country, undertaken in a spirit of respect and solidarity— my humble attempt to communicate to the outside world the fascinating, cautionary history of Myanmar and the remarkable resilience and ingenuity of the Myanmar people. I write for the same reason I read, which is to better understand the world around me, what makes us unique, what brings us together, and what we can learn from each other when we take the time to listen. To me, fiction is the ultimate act of empathy, a quality too often lacking in today's world. By placing ourselves in the footsteps of others, we can begin to craft a world that is not only kinder but also more just, liberated from the restraints of imperialism and autocracy.

The characters and plot of *The Golden Land* are products of my imagination, but the historical events that shape the novel are real. Despite a long and rich history that dates back millennia, Myanmar has been plagued by violence and oppression over the last two centuries. In the 1800s, the British launched a series of Anglo-Burmese Wars culminating in the 1885 exile and dethronement of King Thibaw and Queen Supayalat that is referenced in *The Golden Land*. After a brief occupation by the Japanese during World War II, Burma began to negotiate self-determination from the British, only to suffer a devastating blow when transitional leader Aung San and several members of his cabinet were assassinated on the eve of independence. In 1962, the elected government was ousted in a military coup d'état that marked the beginning of over a half century of military dictatorship.

Though poorly documented, the White Bridge massacre that haunts Etta in *The Golden Land* is also based on a true event. In March 1988, thousands of students took to the streets of Rangoon to protest the many injustices of the authoritarian military regime. Upon reaching Inya Lake, the unarmed students were blockaded by riot police. An unknown number of students were either drowned or beaten to death. Dozens more died from suffocation while being transported to the notorious Insein Prison in an overcrowded police van.

In 2010, the military junta began to slowly ease its grip over the country, releasing political prisoners, relaxing censorship laws, and promising democratic elections. My family and I were fortunate to be living in Yangon in 2015 when Daw Aung San Suu Kyi's National League for Democracy (NLD) won in a landslide election, ushering in a period of optimism and rebirth. For the first time in 50 years, people were free to follow their dreams: expressing themselves openly in print and online, starting new business enterprises, and reengaging once again with the outside world.

Despite these advances, the military never fully relinquished control. With 25% of parliament reserved for the military and a 75% parliamentary majority required to effect any meaningful change, Aung San Suu Kyi's government enjoyed little real power. State violence against ethnic populations in the border regions continued unabated. A 2017 military crackdown in the northern state of Rakhine forced nearly one million Rohingya refugees to flee into neighboring Bangladesh.

A second landslide victory for the NLD in November 2020 confirmed the Myanmar people's continued demand for freedom and democracy. Three months later, the military launched another coup d'etat, annulling the results of the election and arresting duly elected government officials. Mass protests ensued, and martial law was declared, with thousands of protesters being killed, tortured, and detained without trial. Despite little support from the rest of the world, the people of Myanmar continue to fight for the future they deserve, whether through nonviolent protest, armed opposition, or quiet acts of disobedience.

My hope is that *The Golden Land* will help raise awareness about the current situation in Myanmar and inspire those even more intimate with the country than I am to share their own stories. For more information on how to support the people of Myanmar in their quest for justice, please see my website.

Acknowledgements

A great many people, both inside and outside Myanmar, have contributed in some shape or form to the development of *The Golden Land*. Any inaccuracies or other missteps in the portrayal of Myanmar and its people, however, are entirely my own. My profound thanks to:

The people of Myanmar, who welcomed my family into their country with graciousness and tolerance, and the many individuals in Yangon, who took the time to speak to me about their experiences as citizens, journalists, and political prisoners during the previous military regime.

Mu Mu Winn for her invaluable advice on Myanmar culture, from hairstyles to methods of extracting coconut milk, and much, much more. Kyi Kyi May for her enthusiasm and her advice on umbrellas, rivers, and shortwave relay stations. Cyril Chin for sharing his own story with me and for helping to shape a near final draft with his keen insight.

The members of my Myanmar bookclub—Nwe Nwe, Mu Mu, Aye Aye, Kyi Kyi, Louise, Jackie, Marjolein, and Freya—for six wonderful years of inspiration, discussion, and friendship. Special thanks to Nwe Nwe for bringing us together and for her amazing cooking, which inspired many of the dishes in *The Golden Land*.

The real Khaing Zar, my Myanmar language teacher, for her patience and humor. The little Myanmar I managed to retain is thanks to her. *Jezu tin badeh*.

Ma Thida for exposing me to a diverse range of emerging Myanmar writers and for offering me the unique opportunity to edit the prize-winning poems and short stories of PEN Myanmar's 2014 Peace Writing Contest.

The dedicated and talented team of artisans and puppeteers at Htwe Oo Myanmar for introducing me to the mesmerizing world of Myanmar marionettes.

The many wonderful teachers, administrators, and fellow Board members at the International School Yangon for giving my children a world class education while I was busy scribbling away on what would become *The Golden Land*.

The Myanmar office of the World Food Programme, especially Nan Soe, U Ngwe, and the IT team, for supporting and guiding our family in more ways than I can count. Lu Lu and San San for their cheerful and tireless assistance during our stay in Yangon.

Amitav Ghosh's *The Glass Palace: A Novel* and Sudha Shah's *The King in Exile: The Fall of the Royal Family in Burma* for introducing me to and educating me about the fascinating and controversial history of King Thibaw and Queen Supayalat. Karen Connelly's *The Lizard Cage* and *Burmese Lessons*, Charmaine Craig's *Miss Burma*, Aung San Suu Kyi's *Freedom from Fear and Other Writings*, Emma Larkin's *Finding George Orwell in Burma*,

Daniel Mason's *The Piano Tuner*, Thant Myint-U's *The River of Lost Footsteps*, George Orwell's *Burmese Days*, *Animal Farm* and *1984*, Jan-Philipp Sendker's *The Art of Hearing Heartbeats* and *A Well-Tempered Heart*, Ma Thanegi's *Nor Iron Bars a Cage* and *Myanmar Marionettes*, Ma Thida's *The Road Map* and *Prisoner of Conscience: My Steps Through Insein*, Mu Mu Winn's *A Gentle Kind of Poverty*, and many other wonderful books that helped shape my understanding of the country.

The Lesley University MFA program, Cambridge Common Writers, and the MFA posse for ongoing inspiration, fellowship, and community. The amazing Lesley MFA mentors from all genres, who taught me so much about the art and craft of writing. Michael Lowenthal for his invaluable lessons on momentum and emotional logic and for holding my hand through the shock of publication; Kyoko Mori for her sharp editorial eye and unwavering enthusiasm for this project; Doug Bauer for his wise literary counsel and for his willingness to start in the middle; and Hester Kaplan for her speedy and clear-eyed eleventh-hour insights. Fellow alum Mundy McLaughlin for reading and critiquing more iterations of *The Golden Land* than everyone else combined, and for her ongoing friendship and support.

Nancy Aronie of the Chilmark Writing Workshop for providing a safe place to begin my writing career over twenty years ago. The Martha's Vineyard Institute of Creative Writing for recognizing the opening chapters of *The Golden Land* with an Author Fellowship for me to attend its inspirational Summer Writers' Conference.

Supriya Bhatnagar and the Association of Writers and Writing Programs (AWP) for hosting the 2021 Award Series.

Sabina Murray for selecting *The Golden Land* for the 2021 AWP Prize for the Novel and for offering precious, post-prize feedback on the manuscript.

Kim Kolbe at New Issues Poetry & Prose for shepherding my words into book form, and for patiently responding to my many novice questions about the publication process. The Design Center for the stunning cover design.

Julia Borcherts and the team at Kaye Publicity for their enthusiasm and encouragement pre-publication and for making the prospect of book promotion a little less daunting.

Many friends, family members, and colleagues around the globe who have nourished me and my writing with their love, kindness, and generosity.

My mother, Sondra Shick, for sharing her love of reading, and for her continued love and support of me and my writing life. My father, Blair Shick, and my brother Jeff Shick, neither of whom lived to see the publication of this book but whose love and support continue to sustain me from beyond the grave.

My husband, Dom Scalpelli, and our daughters, Rebecca and Amanda Scalpelli, for their boundless love, support, and understanding. You are everything to me.

Photo: Maria Thibodeau

Elizabeth Shick lived in Yangon, Myanmar from 2013 to 2019. Longtime American expatriate and international development consultant, she has also lived and worked in Angola, Malawi, Mozambique, Tanzania, The Gambia, and Italy. Liz currently resides in Dhaka, Bangladesh and West Tisbury, Massachusetts. She holds a Master of Fine Arts from Lesley University and a Master of International Affairs from Columbia University. *The Golden Land* is her debut novel.